Sima's Undergarments
for Women

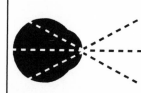

This Large Print Book carries the
Seal of Approval of N.A.V.H.

SIMA'S UNDERGARMENTS FOR WOMEN

ILANA STANGER-ROSS

WHEELER PUBLISHING
A part of Gale, Cengage Learning

GALE
CENGAGE Learning

Detroit • New York • San Francisco • New Haven, Conn • Waterville, Maine • London

GALE
CENGAGE Learning™

LIBRARY OF CONGRESS CATALOGING-IN-PUBLICATION DATA

Stanger-Ross, Ilana.
  Sima's undergarments for women / by Ilana Stanger-Ross. —
Large print ed.
    p. cm.
  ISBN-13: 978-1-59722-958-6 (hardcover : alk. paper)
  ISBN-10: 1-59722-958-X (hardcover : alk. paper)
  1. Jewish women—Fiction. 2. Orthodox Judaism—Fiction.
3. Female friendship—Fiction. 4. Lingerie industry—Fiction.
5. Man-woman relationships—Fiction. 6. Brooklyn (New York,
N.Y.)—Fiction. 7. Large type books. I. Title.
PS3619.T3652S56 2009
813'.6—dc22   2009000088

Published in 2009 by arrangement with The Overlook Press, Peter
Mayer Publishers, Inc.

for my parents

■ ■ ■ ■

AUGUST

■ ■ ■ ■

1

Sima surprised herself by blushing at the round perfection of the young woman's breasts. For thirty-five years, after all, breasts had been her business: she knew the slight curve of the preteen breast, its nipple rigid when unveiled in the cool air of her basement shop; the aching breasts of pregnant women, skin shiny and striped from stretch; the parchment breasts of the elderly, liver-spotted, soft with down; she knew breasts with pink nipples, olive nipples, brown nipples; nipples pushed in and pulled out, tiny as dimes, large as the ringed stain of a coffee cup; she knew heavy breasts on thin women and thin breasts on heavy women; breasts 28-A, 52-K, and breasts with a cup size between them. She even and of course knew the knotted red scar of the breast that was no longer there, the twisting keloid marker of what science had stolen away.

But this young Israeli in tight jeans and platform sandals, slightly worn, revealing fuchsia toenails — in all those years Sima had never seen breasts so beautiful as hers.

Sima thrilled to the swirl of the nipple, the soft shell of the skin. She remembered eighth-grade geometry: planting the sharp point of the compass on a friend's notebook and, with the stubbed yellow pencil carefully belted in, tracing perfect circles of friendship. This girl's breasts, Sima was sure, would be 360 degrees by the pencil's lead trace.

"I brought you a few to try," Sima said, approaching the dressing room. The girl stood in the center, the curtain — orange cloth, grayed at the edges — pulled to one side. It was a large space, big enough for five women at a time to preen, choose: a bench on one side with hooks above, a rectangle of carpet (slightly frayed, lavender wool unraveling) below, a wide mirror angled against the back wall. Sima dangled three bras, each a shade of beige, before her. "See which you like."

The girl eyed the bras suspiciously, held one against herself — thick, with a high, wide cut — so that her breasts pushed through the satin, frowned at her reflection in the mirror. "Do you have anything sexy?"

10

she asked.

Sima forced herself to carry on the usual conversation. "You like lacy? Demi?" She saw herself in the mirror behind the girl, gray hair pulled into a tight bun, rounded body all in black. The old witch in the fairytale, Sima thought, selling apples to a young beauty.

"Doesn't matter, just so long as my boyfriend will like it. Not that he'd notice — men just like to take them off, no?"

Sima smiled. Years in the basement bra shop had taught her the ease of a conversation teasing men. With knowing looks and careful shakes of the head her customers commiserated with one another, complained about them: their stupidity, their cheapness, their emotional distance; their inability to remember birthdays and anniversaries, the location of their own kitchen appliances, the day to pick their suits up from the drycleaner.

"My Lev," Sima said, "doesn't even know how to tell one bra from another. You think he pays attention? I've had this business for three decades, and we've been married, what, forty-six years? Ten dollars he couldn't even tell you what underwire does."

The girl laughed, revealing a smile made more beautiful, Sima thought, by the slight

11

gap between her two front teeth. "Forty-six years is a long time. Mazel tov."

Sima shrugged. "People act like being married a long time is some big accomplishment. Let me tell you, it's the easiest thing in the world. We married young, and that was that." She made a brisk motion with her hand, as if smoothing the covers over a bed. "Now," Sima said, reaching for the bras she'd brought the girl, "What did you say your name was?"

"Timna."

"Timna, I'll bring you something special, yeah? To make his jaw drop."

Sima closed the dressing-room curtain and walked behind the counter. Three shelves stretched ten feet across, each shelf filled with boxes, each box filled with bras. Sima never spent a cent on advertising and never had to — though the dressing room rarely filled to capacity, she kept busy enough that her legs ached each evening from too many trips up and down the stepladder, each in pursuit of the perfect fit. Sima's regular customers, and almost all her customers became regulars, would enter the store already pulling off their coats, unbuttoning their starched blouses. "Something for my cousin's wedding, to keep my tummy in and these" (a quick shove to the large breasts) "up while I dance."

"For my daughter, for her bas mitzvah. Can you believe? Seems just yesterday I used to rest her stroller behind the counter."

"Something simple. Cotton."

"Something lacy. Black."

"Something with underwire."

"Without underwire."

"On sale?"

Sima's wasn't the only hidden business in the neighborhood: Farrah sold purses and shoes, Shoshana designed stationery and invitations, Gussie carried wigs and head scarves, Bernie and Ida Neuman's basement was filled with suits for boys. A secret downtown hidden beneath the red and orange brick two-story homes of Boro Park, Brooklyn.

Those who didn't know Sima stood awkwardly for only a moment. In a glance she could see their size, the back and the cup combined. "Thirty-six-D" she'd say, and, pointing to the dressing-room curtain, "Over there." In vain the women protested, "But I'm a thirty-four. I've always been —" "You've always been wearing the wrong size," Sima told them, and when on her advice they slipped back on their shirts to evaluate the shape a new bra gave, they inevitably agreed. "Isn't that something?"

the women said, smiling at the high curve in the mirror, "After all these years."

"How long have you been in Brooklyn, Timna?" Sima called when she'd found what she wanted, let the box lids fall to the floor in her eagerness.

"Only one week. I'm staying with some cousins while I wait for my boyfriend to finish the army, and then we're driving to San Francisco."

"A beautiful city," Sima told her, though it had been decades since she'd been there. As she hopped off the stepladder she felt her ankle curl beneath her: a spot of pain and then gone. She paused a moment, regained her composure. She couldn't help but be excited to fit this girl, she told herself; if she thrilled to imagine the smooth lay of her bras on Timna's skin, it was no more unnatural than a dentist admiring a flawless arch of pearl-white teeth.

Sima handed Timna two bras, the kind she thought of as most wild — crimson lace on one, the other, black, cut low and wide for maximum cleavage. She pulled the curtain closed while Timna tried on the crimson, waited until she heard the usual sounds — a step backwards, a turn to the side — that signaled readiness.

"Everything okay?" Sima asked.

14

Timna opened the curtain. "What do you think?"

Sima took her in. Timna looked like the women on the covers of drugstore romances: cream-smooth skin arched over full curves, the lace covering just enough to promise removal. Sima felt something like a sigh inside, swallowed it down.

"Lucky for me," she told Timna, forcing herself to do what she always did — spread a hand against the cup to check the shape, smooth the fabric — "this bra looks like it was made for you. My seamstress isn't in today and I hate sewing, so here I was praying — let it fit just right."

"And it does?"

"Like a glove. Just a little adjustment —" she tightened the strap on Timna's left shoulder, her fingers almost trembling to touch a dark brown beauty mark perfectly placed on the soft slope between neck and shoulder — "and voilà. Try it with your T-shirt," Sima told her, stepping back, "and you'll see how nice it fits." She looked away as Timna slipped on her shirt, the act of dressing somehow even more intimate than that of undressing. "Of course," Sima told her, as Timna pivoted lightly before the mirror, admiring, "the crimson is a little dark for that lavender shirt, but with a dark sweater or dress, or —" Sima paused — "to really impress this boyfriend, on its own —"

Sima colored: it was a joke she'd normally never dare, and certainly not with a new customer. She swallowed, desperate for something to say — Israel, she thought, ask something about Israel — but Timna laughed, said, "Absolutely," and Sima grinned wide like she'd guessed the right answer: what was behind which door.

Timna closed her eyes, clasped her hands together, and reached into a stretch. Sima watched as she raised her arms above her head and breathed in deep, her whole body supple and soft as a child's. She gazed at Timna: her eyelids the palest shade of purple, her lips parted slightly, bright with gloss, her neck soft white, arched toward the ceiling, and her breasts — Sima couldn't resist glancing at Timna's breasts, the full round of them waiting perfect beneath the lavender tee, the crimson bra.

Timna opened her eyes.

Sima looked quickly away but knew, by the catch in Timna's breath, that she'd been caught.

"So try the black," Sima said, speaking quickly as she curled her hands into fists, her nails pressing half-moon wrinkles into the soft of her palm, "hopefully it'll fit just as well. You're staying somewhere nearby?"

"A few blocks away." Timna's voice was flat; Sima couldn't read it.

"That's good," Sima told her, "because if it needs adjustments you just leave it here, pick it up in a day or two." She drew the curtain closed between them; spoke quickly to hide her shame — how could she have looked, how could she have been caught? So many years, she thought, so very many years, and never before an unwanted glance. She kept talking, hoping to distract. "She might actually be moving — my seamstress. If you ask me, it sounds just terrible: one of these depressed towns in the middle of nowhere in upstate New York, with nothing but jails and gas stations for miles, but she has this idea that the country is better than the city, so —"

"Oh, I could always do the sewing myself," Timna said. "I've never altered a bra, but I make my own clothes sometimes —"

"Yeah?" Sima touched her collarbone, relieved Timna was speaking to her, hadn't run out of the shop in horror, disgusted by the lecherous old woman in the basement. "If you make your own clothes, you could handle this, for sure." She glanced at the empty seamstress's table — the sewing machine unattended atop the old wooden school desk, a white scarf abandoned on the back of an olive chair. "We just do basic stuff — take in the sides, shorten or lengthen straps —"

The doorbell rang as two teenagers entered the shop, Hadassah's daughter with a friend Sima didn't recognize. Sima waved to them, grateful for the interruption. She spoke loudly so Timna would overhear, "What can I get you? What do you need?" eager to prove herself the devoted saleslady, serious about fit.

"My mom said you carry yoga clothes now," Hadassah's daughter said, and Sima nodded yes, of course, and helped them pick out a few outfits, although she knew it was only a matter of time before one or the other asked, as if the thought had just occurred to her, to try on a bra-and-panty set, or silk pajamas, or a Japanese kimono slit deep. In the end they'd only buy the yoga outfit — where would they hide such fancy lingerie, and what trouble if it was found — but Sima didn't mind the dress-up, knowing they were literally trying on what they took to be the future, not suspecting what Sima knew: real women, tired and busy and recalling with longing their own lost teenage bodies, usually bought to contain rather than expose.

Hadassah's daughter and her friend followed Sima to the dressing room, each carrying a tank top with matching pants. Timna opened the curtain as they approached.

"I think I like it even better than the last," she told Sima, placing her hands on her hips before the mirror. "What do you think?"

"Look at that," Sima said, shaking her head, "again like it was made for you." She allowed herself a quick glance before stepping aside so the teenagers could enter, noticing how they looked at Timna and turned away, Timna both embodying and making unattainable their own ideas of womanhood. Sima checked the fit and had Timna once again slip on her T-shirt; both satisfied, Timna dressed and followed Sima to the counter while the girls changed. "Sixty one and sixty three," Sima told her, entering the numbers on an old cash register, "with a ten percent discount is one eleven sixty —"

Timna bit her lower lip. "I swear, I could go broke on bras."

"Well, we all have our weaknesses."

Timna smiled, pulled a credit card and a jar of lip gloss out of her purse. "Want some?" she asked, as she smoothed the gloss along her lips with her pinky finger. "It's mango-flavored."

Sima dipped her finger into the jar as Timna had, dotted the gloss lightly on her lips and smacked them together, evaluating the strange taste. "Nice," Sima told her, aware of a spice around her mouth, a slight heat that lingered even as she waved good-bye, watched Timna disappear up the steps.

"I had an interesting customer today," Sima told Lev as she poured skim milk into their coffee mugs, watched with dismay the pale gray effect. "A young Israeli woman."

Lev nodded, but did not look up from the paper.

"She was —" Sima hesitated. She rarely told Lev about her work — he could never keep anyone's name straight, anyway, and didn't care about the daily gossip: who said what about whom, and why. But she kept thinking about Timna, the dazzling disorientation of her beauty, the crimson bra and quick smile. She wanted to both remember and justify its effect. "She put on this bra," Sima told him, picking up the coffee mugs, "and it fit so perfectly that it was like —"

Sima paused, suddenly shy to finish the sentence, describe another woman's body to her husband. She felt the heat from the mugs course beneath her skin as she recalled how she'd lost herself looking at Timna, the shame of it.

"Like what?"

Sima shrugged, sat down at the table. "Nothing really," she said, "just she was in her early twenties, fresh out of the army, and living here with some distant cousins."

Lev looked at her a moment, and Sima tensed: he'd ask her why she'd brought the girl up, and what would she say: because she was beautiful, almost truly breathtaking? But Lev just turned back to the paper, lowered his head.

Of course he wouldn't ask, Sima thought, of course.

"Isn't it funny," she said, "there's Irene's daughter living in Israel, and now this one here. It makes Irene crazy, I know, and I'm sure this girl's mother must be worried sick; New York City of all places, and she's practically alone."

Sima watched how Lev hunched over the paper: his body soft and fallen like her own. "Imagine," she asked him, "what it would be to have a child so far away?"

Lev took a sip of coffee, frowned. "Skim milk?"

Sima gave an exaggerated sigh. "Of course skim milk, Lev. It tastes the same, and remember what we read, how —"

"I remember, I remember." Lev waved his

hand dismissively.

Sima watched him a moment before slowly rising, her hands on the table pushing down as she straightened, steadying herself for the step away.

Sima was eighteen when she met Lev; he was twenty. "What's wrong with Lev?" her mother had asked, arms crossed, leaning against the yellow kitchen counter. "He seems perfectly nice to me."

Sima, sulking, admitted she couldn't find fault with him. "But that's just because I don't know him," she said.

"Why not get to know him then?" her mother asked, giving Sima that sad look she used when they went shopping and Sima had once again gone up a size. Sima listened while her mother reminded her it was time to think of growing up, her friend Connie was going steady and she wouldn't want to be left behind and, "You have no idea what it's like, Sima, to be in this world alone."

Sima thought to say that maybe she did, growing up in the shadow of her older brothers — her mother's true loves, she called them to Connie — but instead she quietly nodded, allowed the gold-flecked linoleum floor to blur beneath her gaze.

She sat next to Lev the next time he came

over with Art and Connie. He told her a few jokes, made her smile. She liked the way he looked at her, softly complimented her earrings — nothing, she told him, fake rubies she'd won at a carnival with Connie when they were thirteen. And while she wished she were back there, on the Ferris wheel holding hands and shrieking, giggling, coasting through the black night above the bright lit-up booths with the buttered smell of popcorn in the air and the excitement of the crowd below and money in their pockets; while she turned to Connie to remind her and saw her arms wrapped around Art's neck and whispering; while she felt inside the downward swoop of the Ferris wheel as it descended, too quickly, toward the dark parking lot pavement, she found herself saying yes, she was free next Saturday night, yes, she'd like to see a movie with him.

He whispered to her in the dark of the theater, his breath warm against her skin, made her laugh so that an older couple sitting behind them said, "Sshhh!" and Sima, thrilled to be taking part in such a display, leaned her cheek against his shoulder and thought how nice it fit.

After the movie he walked her home, hands held warm together as they strolled down quiet streets. They pointed out the houses they liked best — one with a wide porch, another with a slim, ivy-draped balcony — and Sima thought how it could always be that way: looking into their future as easy as looking through the windows of other people's houses, gold squares of light in a dark night.

Sima walked along 13th Avenue, Boro Park's main commercial boulevard, on her way to meet Connie for lunch. Friday afternoon and the sidewalks and streets were packed with pre-Shabbos shoppers, a chaos of double-parked cars, blocked hydrants, beeping horns.

In the sidewalk-crush beside a peddler (psalm-inscribed key chains and pictures of Jerusalem arranged along a folding table), Sima had to step aside to let a brigade of strollers pass. Nearly all the women wore tailored suits (light shirt, black skirt cut just below the knee, nude stockings, low heels), their makeup neatly applied, their wigs (brown or auburn, less often blond, but all of them perfectly straight) cut in clean lines around their face. The women pushed strollers: single, double, triple; the older children trailing behind or rushing ahead ("Menachem, stop at the corner!") or, if old enough, pushing an extra stroller themselves.

Passing Netanya Grocery, Sima stopped to say hello to its owner. Eddie wore jeans, a worn T-shirt, and a knit *kippah;* a gold *magen davod,* Star of David, hung from a chain around his neck. "What can I get for you?" he asked. He mentioned the melon, the pamelos — special from Israel. "On my way home," Sima promised, stepping aside as Eddie bent down to greet a curly-headed three-year-old clinging to her mother's leg.

A cluster of yeshiva girls stood gossiping on the corner, backpacks slung over button-down shirts, dark tights under pleated skirts. Sima knew the yeshiva by the uniform: *Bais Rivkah* a white blouse, blue sweater-vest, and tartan blue skirt; *Bais Tzipporah* a powder-blue shirt worn with a navy skirt. Across the street, a few teenage boys averted their eyes and looked, averted their eyes and looked again. They dressed exactly like their fathers: black suits, white shirts, black hats and shoes, curled payot dangling beside their ears. The only exception was their lack of beards; they grew stubble on sweaty upper lips, rubbed at patches of thin hair on their cheeks. Sima knew what they couldn't quite believe — the beard would come.

And with it the wife, the children.

Sima passed the girls, nodding hello to one of them — Sarah Gold's daughter, though Sima couldn't remember her name.

As she crossed the street, a man rushed past her — close, but careful not to touch. Sima watched him as he walked away, talking loudly into his cell phone in Yiddish. Although she couldn't walk 13th without running into someone she knew, aside from the store owners, those someones were almost always women. Men were an anomaly in her shop; she wouldn't recognize the husbands of some of her most loyal customers. And though Sima could identify each Hasidic sect by subtle differences in the men's clothing — this hat, that coat, this stocking — she was herself, as a nonobservant Jewish woman, an outsider.

Boro Park had always been her home, and her store was a neighborhood fixture. But no one gathered at her table for Shabbat dinner, no one caught her up on the gossip outside synagogue on Saturday. Lev talked sometimes of moving — Florida, like everyone else. But she knew she'd never survive there: the highways, the shopping malls, the streets that curled one into another, stealthy cul-de-sacs that entrapped.

She liked the numbered grid, ugly as it was. She liked even the noise, the traffic, the rudeness; for every shopkeeper who smiled hello there'd be another who shouted into a cell phone, gesticulating angrily.

Boro Park was a community.

Sima could glance in some of the passing baby carriages, see through the baby's sleeping face and into the grandmother's just like that — the generations known to her. Together they moved through the days, weeks, seasons: the rush and then rest of each Shabbat; the joy of each holiday. By late August the shop windows were displaying their best for the High Holidays: dark velvet for the girls; wool suits for their mothers. A few weeks later and you could buy from parked trucks *lulav* and *etrog* — palm frond, willow, and myrtle woven together, citron on the side — while families erected their own *sukkot,* makeshift outdoor huts, in the alleys and on the balconies in honor of the harvest holiday. Simchat Torah brought dancing in the street; Hanukah doughnuts in the bakeries. For Purim, costumes crowded the children's stores and every school prepared its own carnival. In the days before Passover small piles of bread product burned in the streets, the fires carefully tended by shop owners who shooed away the eager school children.

Even for Sima, who participated in so little

of it, the holidays brought excitement and comfort. In Boro Park there was order to the passing of time.

It helped.

Sima stopped at the butcher, bought chicken breast and brisket. Sharif, a young Turkish man whom the locals nicknamed Sheriff, rang up her purchases while she dropped a quarter into each of the counter donation boxes: the local ambulance service, kosher food packages for Israeli soldiers, and money for infertility treatments: "I will greatly multiply your seed as the stars of the heavens" the last box read.

Outside the Dairy Delicious, Sima ran into Tova Braunschweiger, an occasional customer. They kissed hello, Sima asked after her grandchildren, Tova promised to stop by soon. After an exchange of "Good Shabbos," Sima stepped into the restaurant. She saw Connie wave to her from one of the sought-after corner booths; the woman sitting opposite Connie turned too, smiled hello. Sima smiled back, trying to remember if she'd met the woman before. She was disappointed that Connie had brought someone; Sima always felt a little possessive of Connie, who had so many friends.

"Meet Suzanne," Connie said, as Sima approached, "Art's new secretary." Art was a partner in a local family law firm; a terrible business for Boro Park, he'd joke, where hardly anybody divorced. "I'm showing her around, your shop is next."

Suzanne (divorced, two teenagers, Bay Ridge born and raised, Connie casually dropping each detail in between debating and then placing a food order while Suzanne filled in the sketch: a "good for nothing" husband, twins, the house a wedding gift from her parents) would be pretty if she didn't try so hard: makeup like a teenager herself, Sima thought, and the dangling diamond cross only drawing attention to poorly supported cleavage.

Their food arrived as a Hasidic family sat down at the table next to them. Suzanne looked over and then back to Connie. "Tell me," she asked, her voice just above a whisper, "is it true they do it through a sheet?"

Connie rolled her eyes. "This is the number one thing people ask," she said, unwrapping the straw for her Diet Coke. "Honest, we go on vacation to wherever — Hawaii, Bermuda — and if I get talking about where we're from, what it's like, everyone wants to know this."

"Well?"

"Ask Sima, she knows all their secrets."

Suzanne looked at her with wide eyes, waiting.

"Right. All their secrets. And by the light of the moon we prick our fingers and mingle our blood."

"Really?"

Sima stared at her. "What 'really'? I'm joking. I have no idea what they do and don't do, though I'd be pretty surprised if it involved holes in sheets. One thing I can tell you, though, whatever they do, it works." She motioned with her chin toward the crowd of strollers at the front door.

Suzanne looked, laughed. "So many kids. God. How do the women stay so polished? When Mark and Mel were little, I was a wreck; it was all I could do to shower."

"Me, with Howie and Nate," Connie said, "two boys —"

Sima pasted on a smile and stabbed at her salad, waited for the meal to end and the crush to carry her home, where she wouldn't light the candles, wouldn't make a special meal, no challah, no wine, just her and Lev and quiet before goodnight.

2

Timna returned the next week. "Was there a problem?" Sima asked, remembering the stare, but Timna said no, just her cousin had put an old bra in the dryer and the underwire had bent. "Luckily," she told Sima, "I knew where to come."

"Well then," Sima said, "let's see what we can get you."

Sima went straight for the most intriguing lingerie this time, choosing a deep green bra with leaf-embroidered straps and an ivory tulle demi-cup popular with brides. They both cost more than Timna could probably afford, but Sima had already resolved to bring down the price. It was worth it to see such gorgeous bras on the right body, and the green wasn't something she'd have an easy time selling otherwise; she'd bought it on a whim, unable to resist it when she saw it in the catalog.

As she approached the dressing room, the

doorbell chimed again. Sima pressed the bras into Timna's hand and turned to see Sylvie Rosenthal walk in, asking for slips.

"I'm going on a cruise to the Caribbean," Sylvie said while Sima drew aside hangers on a clothing rack, searching for a size 5. "For one of the ship dining rooms, you need to dress for dinner. Poor Herbie, I haven't even told him yet that we're going to need to buy him two new suits."

"Two? What, are you going to eat there every night?"

"Absolutely. You think I'm going to give up a chance to dress for dinner? I've always wanted to do that. It's like something out of an old movie."

"If only life really was like in the old movies," Sima said, handing her two beige slips, "an orchestra playing, and everyone so beautiful."

Timna pulled aside the curtain as they neared the dressing room, modeling the green bra. "Why were you hiding this one last time?" she asked Sima, teasing. "It's the prettiest thing I've ever seen."

Sima looked at the lay of the green silk against her skin, a lizard asleep on desert sand — dangerous, alluring. She shook her head, admiring. "You're right. It couldn't look better."

"Is that gorgeous," Sylvie said, kicking off her heels as Sima, stepping inside the dressing room, closed the curtain behind the three of them. "I'd try it myself, but I think it'd give my husband a heart attack."

Sima watched the two women change: Sylvie grown thin with age, the outline of bone visible beneath pale-veined skin; Timna all soft curves as she buckled the ivory bra across her breasts, slid her shoulders through the straps.

"Finally one that's not quite perfect," Sima told Timna as she stood back to evaluate, "just a touch too big. Here, turn around." While Timna faced the mirror, Sima moved behind her and pulled at each side of the bra. "See how much better?" she asked, drawing two pins through the tulle to mark the alteration. "Now you're ready for the wedding."

"Right. And the green bra I wear on the honeymoon."

Sima grinned; turning to Sylvie, she angled her head to check the hem. "And you, unless you're going to be wearing a train, that slip has got to be shortened."

"So, what else is new?" Sylvie took off the slip and gave it to Sima. "Where's the Russian?" she asked, pulling on her skirt as Sima opened the curtain, the ivory bra and beige slip draped over one arm like a waiter, "You never do alterations yourself."

"Her husband took a job upstate," Sima told her. "I'm looking for another."

"Are you hiring?" Timna asked, pulling on her navy T-shirt that, Sima noticed, did not quite cover the curve of her belly. "Because I really can sew. My grandmother was a seamstress, and she taught me —"

Sima looked at Timna, surprised. She thought to dismiss the suggestion — what would someone like Timna want with her shop, all day in a basement with middle-aged women — but didn't want to seem rude.

"Oooh, hire her," Sylvie said. "You'll get a seamstress and a model in one."

Sima forced a smile. "Let me ring up Sylvie, and then we'll talk."

Sylvie paid in cash and, kissing Sima, promised to return the next day for the slip. Timna waved goodbye to her like a beauty queen.

"So," Sima asked, leaning over the counter, "tell me, how did you find my shop anyway?" She'd been wondering about it all week, fantasizing that she'd made it into an Israeli tour book of New York City.

Timna touched her necklace — a thin gold chain — twisted it lightly. "Actually, I was just walking down the street and I saw some women leaving with bags —"

"What? Last week?"

Timna nodded. "So I asked, was there a shop inside the house, and they said yes. I'm looking for work, and I'd already stopped in a bunch of clothing stores on that main avenue —"

"Thirteenth —"

"But no one was hiring." Timna paused a moment, looked down at the counter and then up at Sima, smiling. "The truth is, I came back today to see what happened with your seamstress. I haven't had much luck so far — I don't exactly have a work visa, which complicates things — and you'd mentioned she might be leaving —"

Sima leaned back from the counter, too impressed by Timna's resourcefulness to be disappointed about the tour book. So many of her customers complained about their children, "They're so lazy, they don't know what it is to work," while here, she told Timna, was a young woman literally walking the streets for a job. Timna shrugged off the praise, explained that she didn't know her cousins, didn't want to take advantage, and Sima warmed further to that dismissal — she believed in brushing off a compliment.

Sima asked how it was she didn't have an accent, and watched as Timna, her hands thrust casually into her back pockets, explained her flawless English: a year in Australia when she was nine — something about her father's business that Sima didn't quite catch: importing, electronics — then later shedding that accent for an American one mastered through movies, television, music. She marveled at how simple Timna made it sound: language like clothing you could try on and take off, choosing the best fit.

"Any more questions?" Timna asked, her head angled toward her shoulder, teasing.

Sima glanced at the counter, avoiding Timna's wide smile. She worried whether her customers would be put off by Timna's beauty; her store was a space they could trust, one where the only evaluation they underwent was how well something fit — the body the given, the clothing forced to work for it. And then there was Timna to think about: she was young and energetic; she'd die of boredom.

"There are so many Israelis moving to New York all the time," Sima told her, "there are cafés, bars — you could probably get a job where you'd have a chance to meet more young people, no?"

Timna paused, a slight frown as she withdrew her hands from her pockets, brought them together before her. Sima listened to her assurances — she'd waitressed before and didn't want to do it again; she was interested in fashion, planned to study design, and looked forward to the opportunity that this job might afford her — and though she suspected the last line was well rehearsed, Sima was pleased despite herself to hear Timna's enthusiasm: she'd never had a seamstress express such interest before.

"How long are you here for?" Sima asked.

"Nine months, until —"

"Until your boyfriend gets out of the army, that's right." Sima looked down at the counter, scratched at an imaginary stain. "The hours here are ten to six, Sunday through Thursday. The pay is only ten dollars an hour, but then it's off the books."

Timna nodded. "That sounds great."

Sima looked up, forced herself to resist one final time the pull of Timna's tentative smile. "To be honest," she told Timna, so that she might always be able to say I warned her, "I don't know if this is what you're looking for. It's not high fashion here; my biggest sellers are support bras, and the alterations we do are basic —

there's only so much you can do to a bra. As you can see," Sima said, gesturing weakly across the shop floor, "it's function rather than fancy."

Timna turned, and Sima followed her gaze. The store was crowded with furniture: a cluttered wooden sewing table; a few fold-up chairs for sitting; two oval metal racks thick with slips, nightgowns, and bathrobes. Along one wood-paneled wall hung a few faded posters sent free by lingerie companies — a manicured hand unhooking a nursing bra; a bouquet of lilacs fanned against a white silk camisole — along the other long shelves stacked high with boxes stretched above the counter, marked in a code only Sima understood. A dusty ray of light from the shop's sole window shone on the sea-green linoleum floor, illuminated curved indentations long since gone to gray.

Timna looked at Sima, smiled. "I just, I'd so much prefer working in a neighborhood shop like this to working with beer and French fries."

Sima hesitated a moment, but her urge to please Timna won. "Welcome aboard," she said.

Timna clasped her hands like a child.

■ ■ ■ ■

Sima looked out the living room window as Timna approached, ten minutes early for her first day of work. She'd hardly slept for worry — what would they talk about, what might she say — eventually convincing herself that Timna wouldn't come at all, a conviction that alternately relieved and annoyed her.

Yet there she was.

Sima watched as Timna reached over the short metal fence to open the latch, stepped onto the cement path that ran down the center of their struggling lawn, and closed the gate carefully behind her. Sima rapped on the window — the only one that had been renovated, divided into five tan-toned sections — and signaled to Timna, who looked up, waved, that she'd be right out.

"I got keys for you," Sima said as she locked the front door of her red brick house, "Follow me so you know how to work them."

Timna shaded her eyes from the sun as Sima descended the five cement steps to the walk, followed it around to where another three steps, running alongside the basement window, led to the shop.

"It's not much of a security system," Sima said, motioning toward the old wood door and the black-buttoned bell, above which "Sima's Undergarments for Women" was written in blue cursive on white paper, the words cramped into two short lines and covered by a few layers of shipping tape, "but so far I haven't had any trouble, even with the door unlocked half the day, thank God." She touched a glass mezuzah that hung in the door frame, and, bringing her fingers to her lips, turned to Timna. "You can't be too careful, right?"

"I guess not."

"The truth is," Sima said, lowering her voice, "I normally never remember the mezuzah is there. But a lot of my customers, maybe eighty, ninety percent, are observant, so I have it for them. This neighborhood, since I grew up here, such changes." Seeing Timna glance down — strappy sandals this morning, and the fuchsia beginning to chip from one toe — she hurried to keep her interest. "So, okay," she said, handing Timna the key, "try the door so we know if it works."

Timna practiced with the key twice, opened the door successfully both times.

"Perfect. And if for some reason I'm not here when you come in," Sima said as they entered, "you can just call up." She pointed toward the back of the shop, where a green-carpeted staircase ascended from the corner beside the dressing room. "That leads to my kitchen, and that's where I usually am." Sima paused. "My husband, too."

"When do I get to meet him?"

"Lev? Oh God, I try to keep him out of the bra shop. But he'll appear sooner or later. He's retired from teaching two years, so he tends to lurk about."

"And the rest of your family?" Timna asked. "Do your children and grandchildren help out sometimes?"

"Children?" Sima asked, as if the idea had never occurred to her. "No, we don't have any. Listen, for the first few days it'd be great if you could follow me around a little, learn how everything works. Things here aren't exactly immediately understandable," Sima motioned toward the box-stocked shelves, "but as long as you remember the cardinal rule —"

"The customer is always right?"

"Almost. The rule is that the customer is almost never right, but we try not to let them know it. No, really," she said, seeing Timna smile, "I have to sell what works; I just can't stand to let someone leave with a badly fitting bra or panty. I swear, sometimes I'll want to go up to some woman in the streets, shake her, and say, 'What are you wearing, don't you know your breasts shouldn't be on your belly?' " Timna raised one eyebrow and Sima, catching her glance, smiled. "Don't worry — I've never done it. Yet."

Timna sat down at the sewing table, opened the drawer and began arranging spools of thread, needles. She kept her head down as she worked, running the sewing machine across a few old fabric samples while Sima pretended preoccupation with her accounting book. As Sima cursed the quiet of the shop — she never cared with the Russians, never worried so much what they might think of her — Dottie Katz entered. Though Sima knew Dottie's size as well as her own, she made sure to evaluate her customer's shape openly — her hand on her own hip, eyes sweeping down — wanting to remind Timna that it was her job to stare, her eye as cool as any surgeon's.

"Can we use you as a model?" Sima asked. "I want to show Timna how to properly fit a bra."

"I knew it was only a matter of time before I was discovered as a model," Dottie laughed. Following Sima's directions, she bent forward as she inserted her arms through the bra straps and tucked her breasts into the cups. After fastening the back hooks, she straightened while Sima adjusted the shoulder straps.

"Everyone looks at the cups," Sima explained, "but the band matters more." She ran through the check with Timna: the bra should close on the middle hook; the band shouldn't rise up the back or cut into the sides; the cup seam should cross the nipple; the fabric shouldn't pucker or pull; the bridge between the cups should lie flat against the chest; the straps should lift, but not pull, the breasts.

"Wow," Dottie said. "I had no idea how complicated this was."

Sima smiled. She handed Dottie a new bra, nodded at Timna to take the lead.

"Bend forward," Timna said.

Dottie followed orders once more, though she teased that Sima had never taken such care before.

"You closed on the middle hook, excellent," Timna said, running a finger under the band as Sima had done, "not too big and not too small." Sima watched Timna touch Dottie. Most of her assistants were nervous at first, tentative, but Timna didn't hesitate to pull along the edge of a cup, nudging it into place.

"That's it," Sima said, after Dottie left with four bra-and-panty sets, having come in for one, "you're a hit."

"Did you see how she really wanted the silk one, but was shy to admit it?"

"It's true, and you guessed it."

"I just saw her looking at something, and followed her glance." Timna grinned. "And you thought I'd prefer working in some bar to this? A secret lingerie shop, hidden underground — Sima, this place is the stuff of legends."

"Right. The legend of the sagging body, maybe," Sima said, but inside she thrilled to Timna's enthusiasm, her whole life suddenly redeemed, special as seen through Timna's bright eyes.

3

"So here's the mother insisting on God knows what, a chastity belt or something for under the dress, and I go running all around for corsets and onesies and the whole megillah."

Timna leaned against the counter, listening.

"But the daughter doesn't like anything. I mean I'm going crazy. And she and her mom are screaming at each other like you wouldn't believe and the mother's threatening to call off the wedding if that girl doesn't just buy some underwear already — they had the dress-fitting the next day."

"And her mom was paying and everything?"

"She was willing to spend whatever it cost. But the girl doesn't like anything. Finally, the mother goes out to feed the meter and the daughter grabs my arm. 'She doesn't know,' she tells me. 'Know what?' I ask, and even as I say it I'm realizing, this girl is pregnant. Turns out she's gonna be four months on her wedding. Of course she can't wear those tight things, they'd be no good for the baby. So I run over and find this elastic-front onesie just a size too big for her, and by the time her mother returns, the Russian is already shortening the straps to make it fit up top."

"Did it work?"

"For the wedding, sure. She sent me flowers. Of course, one month later she had some explaining to do. But she played innocent, and she got to have her day."

Sima heard a cough, looked up to see Lev watching from the staircase. "You scared me," she said, though he hadn't. "Don't sneak up like that."

"Sorry."

"Timna," Sima said, noticing that Lev's drawstring pants were baggy and stained, his shirt untucked, "this is my husband, Lev."

"I'm so glad to meet you," Timna told him. She smiled, flipped her hair over one shoulder.

Lev smiled back.

Sima watched them watch each other, a little nervous for what Timna might think: Lev wasn't much for entertaining, always ruined a joke. But he made the right small talk — how do you like New York, what have you seen so far — and she answered with her usual enthusiasm, praising Central Park, Times Square. Sima was relieved at first, but, as the conversation progressed — Timna answering his questions about her hometown, a suburb of Tel Aviv — she found herself growing impatient; it wasn't right for Lev to come downstairs and take up Timna's time with his questions. She kept her eyes on the window, waiting for the first customer to arrive, and ordered Lev upstairs as soon as legs appeared on the steps outside.

Lev retreated as a group of new mothers entered the shop, giddy with the excitement of shopping together, with their babies in strollers and their husbands at work. Sima brought them silk nightgowns and bathrobes to try — "believe me, now is the time for a little treat, you've earned it"; watched, impressed, as Timna complimented each baby, cooing even over the ugly one so that his mother beamed.

After the women left, Sima smiled at Timna. "He was completely bald," she said, "and you managed to convince his mother that he had the most beautiful curls you'd ever seen."

47

"The potential for the most beautiful curls," Timna said. "And he did have one, just above his ear."

"Right. Maybe if you looked at him with a magnifying glass you could see it."

Timna laughed. "I had to say something."

"You're a natural," Sima told her, pleased at their shared secret, "just an absolute natural."

"And she's gorgeous," Sima told Connie, "I'm telling you, a body like I've never seen — a real knockout."

Connie turned to Art, laid a hand on his arm. "Think I'd let a knockout into our house?"

Smiling, he shook his head no.

She looked at Sima, raised an eyebrow. "You trust Lev that much?"

"Lev? I'm not worried. Lev, you gonna make a pass at Timna?"

Lev reddened; did not respond.

Art leaned across the table, his face flush and the corners of his mouth purple from wine. "Start flirting with her, Lev," he said, whispering loud enough for the next table to hear. "I'm telling you, women love this jealousy thing."

Sima frowned, turned back to Connie. "Anyway, Timna says that in Israel —"

"The thing you have to understand," Art said, pointing his fork at Lev, "is that women like to be teased. Take Sima here. She acts so in control, yeah? A real businesswoman. But I bet that at the end of the day —"

"Art. That's enough." Connie reached for his arm, brought it back to her side. "When he's drunk," she said, turning to Lev, "he's a real monster. Aren't you, Art?"

Arthur growled happily in response, kissed Connie's cheek. Connie grinned; Sima brushed some crumbs off her lap while Lev, smiling politely, bent over his steak, slowly shifting his knife through the thick meat.

That evening Lev lay in bed while Sima washed her hose in the sink. "You know I love Connie," she told him, watching the suds gather as she kneaded the material, "but she can be so self-centered. I mean, there she goes on and on about Nate's new lab job again. Enough already about Nate. If you ask me, he's a weird kid. Calling her every night — what forty-four-year-old calls his mother every night?"

"So anyway," she said, when Lev didn't respond, "Timna did the funniest thing today. You know that bin where I keep old lingerie? You know, the clear plastic one? Well, I hadn't been through it in who knows how long, so I asked Timna to take a look, see if there was anything worth anything. Anyway. She goes crazy. Starts trying on the stuff, my God, she put on this fur-trimmed nightie, I swear she looked like a movie star. Then Edna comes in. She almost died laughing when she saw Timna all dressed up. I had to stop Edna from trying on the stuff herself — can you imagine?"

She rinsed out the hose, moving them back and forth under the tap.

"So I said to Timna, 'You should be an actress. What are you doing selling bras in a Brooklyn basement? Hollywood needs you.' So you know what she says?"

Sima paused to bunch the pantyhose into a ball, squeezed them dry.

"She says, 'But in Hollywood I couldn't have so much fun as here.' Huh? Isn't that sweet? I never thought of myself as such fun before."

She hung the hose on a white plastic shower caddy and switched off the bathroom light; slowly made her way to the bed.

"You know, Sima," Lev said, after they'd lain quietly a few minutes, "if you're not careful, soon you'll be talking about Timna more than Connie talks about Nate."

"What do you mean?" Sima propped herself up on her elbow.

50

"You complain that Connie's always on about her son, but here you are on about Timna and she's not even your daughter."

She lay back down, turned away from Lev.

"What, I offended you?"

"Don't talk to me."

"Suit yourself."

Sima sighed, rolled so she was facing him. "You know, here I finally found someone to give me a little pleasure, and you can't stand it. You're so jealous, you have to put me down."

Lev was quiet a moment. "Someone to give you some pleasure, huh? I guess I'm not that for you."

"No. I guess you're not."

"What am I then?"

There was a need in his voice that surprised Sima, scared her too — she didn't know how to answer. She watched the lights from the street outside move in patterns across the curtain, cars rushing through the night, escaping. "Lev," she said, when she felt that she must say something, "I only mean that with Timna —"

"She lights up a room."

"Yes."

"You used to light up rooms, Sima."

"You must be joking. I never looked like that."

"It's not how she looks, only. It's an energy."

"Don't talk to me about energy, Lev. If you walk a block it's a major trek." She paused a moment. "Did you take your pills?"

When Lev didn't answer, Sima got out of bed, slowly made her way to the bathroom. She brought back cholesterol medication and a glass of water, waited while Lev accepted both.

Once again Sima lay awake, listening to the sound of his breathing and waiting for something to give way inside herself, make her free.

The night before her wedding Sima had locked herself in the bathroom, stood naked in front of the mirror, cringed. She had been a tall, skinny girl, until tenth grade still looked like a child, and then in a matter of weeks grew breasts and hips. Her skin could hardly keep up with the changes, which left red stretch marks like cat scratches. When she married, the lines, which would eventually turn white, still pointed with pink highlights to what was most secret.

They spent their first night at his cousin's house. Sima turned off the lights, drew down the shades so the room was dark. In bed she lifted her nightgown above her head, dropped it to the floor beside her, and slid quickly under the covers. Her stomach was thick with cake and her head still dizzy from wine and dancing; when he kissed her, his mouth was smoky from the celebratory cigar and his hands, running through her hair, pulled too tightly. He bent his head under the covers to kiss her breasts, and she, glad for the blanket hiding her body from him, watched from above the movement of his tented head. When he entered her, she felt a sharp burning, a pain that was shameful, punishing.

And could his cousins hear? She stayed silent, felt the echo of each scuff of the bed.

When Lev was done, Sima leaned over the side of the bed, vomited into the folds of her nightgown.

It took Lev a minute before he leaned toward her, lightly placed a hand on her back.

Sima had an impulse to bury her head beneath the covers, wait for her mother to come and clean up the vomit as when she was a child hot with fever, and though she could almost hear her mother's complaints — such a mess, she'd say, the things I have to do — still that predictable disappointment seemed far more comforting than

Lev's nervous hand on her back. But down in her stomach a deep sadness reminded her that her mother would not come, that childhood was over, and that she would be a mother herself soon.

Sima took a deep breath, managed a weak apology, and, gathering up her nightgown, crept downstairs in her bathrobe. In the kitchen she placed the gown in a plastic bag, buried the plastic bag deep in the garbage. Under a single, quiet stream of water she washed her arm: coffee grinds, the stick of egg yolk, the wet slap of carrot peelings.

When she returned to the bedroom, Lev was asleep. Or pretending. Without speaking, she got back into bed.

4

Sima touched the back of her neck, felt the dampness there. The clock radio that morning, before she shut it silent, had promised ninety-six degrees. Even with two standing fans — one angled at her, the other at Timna — some loose strands that had escaped her bun were pressed to the side of her face, tipped with sweat. She exhaled deeply, fanned her blouse against her body. "I don't know how you take it, Timna," she said, "I can't even imagine how hot Israel must be right now."

"Think cool thoughts."

"Cool thoughts? I've exhausted all my cool thoughts. Give me one of yours."

Timna paused, drummed her fingers on the sewing table. "All right," she said, "I'll tell you my favorite." She sat up straight, clasped her hands before her like a model student readying for a recitation. "So, Alon's father owns a small supermarket," she began.

Sima looked at Timna. She was curious about Alon, Timna's boyfriend, entranced by his power to still a brightness like Timna, keep her steady despite the ocean between them.

"The summer we graduated Alon worked in the store most days, helping out. His dad wanted him to learn the business, but Alon liked stacking boxes, unloading trucks —"

"We could use him here."

Timna smiled. "Guys before the army — they're so scared, you know, so they try to get big. Lift this, lift that. Like he insisted his dad order these baby palm trees and he spent days digging holes and laying irrigation hose —"

Sima slumped forward in mock-collapse. "You're not making me any cooler."

"I'm getting there. Anyway, that summer I worked nights at the restaurant. My days were free, so I'd go to the supermarket to see Alon. We planted flowers, and —"

"Timna!"

Timna laughed. "All right, all right. So, one day we discover the freezer."

"That's more like it."

"We were stacking some boxes there, and it was such a relief from the heat that we just stayed. And then we started going in

56

there whenever possible, taking quick breaks to cool down before going back outside."

"Don't tell me you got locked in there."

"Sima, you always assume the worst."

"No, just you hear stories." Though she protested, she wondered how Timna had so quickly picked up on that — Connie was always telling her the same thing.

"Anyway, after a few days I decided to bring clothing for the freezer, so we could hang out there longer. I brought us sweat-pants and sweatshirts and we kept them beside the freezer door. We'd go for a break and get all dressed up and then we'd be able to stay cool, but warm, for a longer time."

"My God, is that smart." Sima imagined Timna and Alon in the crisp darkness, their bodies wrapped in wool like children: hats, mittens, scarves.

"Once we had the right clothes, we made a real space for ourselves. We took two boxes of frozen peas and made them chairs, and a huge box of frozen pita became a table. And then the walls — you know how freezer walls are all iced and wet and stuff? So as a joke we used to leave messages for each other on the walls: Alon loves Timna, that sort of thing." Timna traced a heart through the stale air of the shop. "By the time Alon left for the army, it'd really become our home. We had these pink tea candles we stole from aisle two, and we'd light them all around the freezer —"

"So you start with helping, and end with stealing."

Timna laughed. "Alon's dad didn't mind. Once it was only a few weeks to army he just wanted us to enjoy ourselves, have fun." She ran a hand along the spine of the sewing machine. "It's funny, but whenever I got tense in the army, whenever I couldn't sleep or wanted to cry or whatever, I would think of that freezer. Just sitting there in our sweatpants with the candles burning, drinking tea or coffee at our makeshift table while outside it was boiling hot in the shade. I never felt more safe than I did there."

"It's like a poem," Sima said, though she was struck as much by the thought that Timna, too, had hard times, cried, as by the beauty of the image: the young couple, the dark freezer, the pink candles.

"You think? I had one friend, she said when I was with Alon it was like the two of us were playing house."

"But that's nice, no?"

Timna shook her head. "She meant it to hurt. And we both knew it was sort of silly, hiding in the freezer. But the thing is, it's something, isn't it, to have a place like

58

that?" She looked at Sima. "This shop. That's it for you."

Sima nodded, startled to suddenly recognize such an obvious truth. "Yes. I guess it is."

"When you find that, you keep it, you know? No matter what other people say."

"But you're so far away now —"

"But it's not the freezer; it's Alon. So every time I speak with him, I get the space back. And," she said, smiling, "like all the stupid love songs say, even when we're not together I keep him with me."

"Of course," Sima said, "that's true," though she knew the shop mattered only to her, stood for no special love in her life.

Sima and Lev went on their honeymoon two months after they'd been married, when the novelty of sharing a bed with a man hadn't yet faded — his breath in the night belonging to her, his body there each morning reaching out, making her laugh as he gathered her close (and though she'd protest she had to brush her teeth, get dressed, yet she cherished all the same the warmth as he hugged her good morning and she thought, I am wanted) — but the fear mostly had. They drove to Boston on a hot May weekend, a city neither had been to before. From

Brooklyn to Queens to Westchester to the Hudson Valley, her thighs sticky against the car seat but the breeze blowing her hair, and green pasture on the side of the road just like it should be: dotted with clover, the occasional horse behind a wood fence.

They pulled over for lunch. She spread a blanket in the green shade beneath an old tree, unpacked the food: tuna sandwiches she'd made the night before, two apples, juice in plaid thermoses, and sugar cookies Connie had baked for their trip, carefully wrapped in wax paper. After they ate, Lev leaned back, his hands linked under his head. Sima kicked off her mules, placed her own head on his chest. He stroked her hair and she listened to his breath and together they looked up at the green leaves canopied above them.

"I could stay here forever," Sima said, but a few minutes later they were standing to straighten and smooth clothing, pat down hair. The rest of the drive they listened to the radio and sang along when they knew the words: *save the last dance for me, Georgia on my mind.* "You're tone-deaf," Lev told her, and so she sang even louder.

When they arrived at the hotel, Sima brought her hand to her mouth to hide her wide smile. White lawn chairs fanned out around a circular blue pool; a white-jacketed waiter paced behind a pink stucco bar. "Where did you find this place?" she asked, slowly removing her sunglasses as she stepped outside. "It's like Tahiti or something."

Lev smiled. "I have my ways." He threw the car keys up in one hand, caught them with the other.

The room was bright and clean. Sima moved through it, calling out to Lev as she admired each luxury: the crisp white sheets, the cut-glass cups, the olive drapes that, pulled back and secured through brass hooks on either side of the window, gave way to a view of the magical courtyard below. After finishing her inspection — a color television, larger than any she'd ever seen, within a wooden cabinet — Sima suggested they change for swimming. But Lev closed the curtains and collapsed on the bed.

"Come on," she said, the energy of a new place, of vacation, coursing through her.

"Come here, instead." He smiled up at her, patted the bed beside him.

She was disappointed, yet pleased to be wanted. She watched him watch her as she undressed, his hands behind his head and his shoes kicked off. She unbuttoned her

Capri pants — sliding them slowly down her legs, with pointed toes kicking them away — lasso-swung her blouse onto the orange tweed chair across the room. She stood before him in her underwear a full moment (it took something, that moment, but she forced it for him) before crawling into bed beside him, drawing the covers up and over their bodies.

They slept after, a heavy, late-day sleep, then woke and showered and dressed for dinner and Sima thought, so this is what vacation is. She wore her hair in a French roll like Connie had showed her, and when she paused at the top of the outdoor staircase to fix her sandal strap, Lev kissed the back of her neck before taking her hand, leading her slowly down the steps.

They had time before them, everything was time before them, Lev's eyes sharp on the road and both hands on the wheel and the trip-tik open on her lap with the restaurant she'd chosen a few weeks ago circled, and just because she could, she told him, "I love you," because for now at least there were no children to roll their eyes in the back seat, and just because he could, he placed a hand on her thigh, squeezed.

Sima leaned back, closed her eyes content.

"I don't ever want to go home," Sima told

him as they lay in bed on their last evening, having woken together from another late afternoon nap. She thought of the town they'd walked through that day — tiger lilies pressed against the white fences of Victorian homes — and then the gray-brown of Brooklyn, the heat, the garbage. "I want to stay here, like this."

Lev rolled toward her, smiled. "Okay," he said.

They allowed themselves to dream a little, how they might keep driving, until Sima, excited, got the road map from her purse and unfolded it on the bed between them. She traced the shore highway through the pink state of Maine, pausing a moment at the black border line before continuing into the beige of Canada: New Brunswick, Nova Scotia.

Early the next morning they left their hotel room and began the drive home.

"I brought pictures," Timna said, turning to Sima as Idy and Chanie exited the shop, a slight argument, the whispers of sisters, between them.

"Oh? Let me see." Sima stood up from behind the cash register and dragged a chair over to Timna's table.

Timna opened her purse — new, Sima

noticed, feeling a small thrill that her payments allowed Timna such a purchase — and took out a small album, placing it on the table between them. On the cover was a red rose, a few dewdrops on each petal; "Memories" was scrawled underneath the flower in a pink, lipsticked font.

Sima leaned forward as Timna opened the album, looked at the photos: a young girl, blond hair drawn back in a ponytail, held a baby.

"Me and my sister, Liat," Timna said, smiling. "Wasn't she a gorgeous baby?"

Sima nodded. "My God — you and the baby both." She lifted up the album, considered. "You look just like yourself, Timna. How old are you here?"

"Twelve. Liat's eight now."

The girl in the picture was holding the baby with both hands, one leg thrust out for balance. She was laughing; the baby looked to the side, her mouth a wide O of pleasure.

"Your parents waited a long time between you two, huh?"

Timna turned the page. "Actually, they're divorced. My dad remarried; Liat's my half sister. Here," she said, pointing at the picture on the left side of the page, "is my dad, Liat, my stepmom, and me and there

—" she pointed at the opposite page — "is my mom and me."

Sima bent over the photographs, focusing on the new family first. Timna's dad had her broad, confident smile; he looked like the kind of man who advertised watches in magazines — tall, muscular, silver-haired. His wife was much younger — fifteen, twenty years, Sima guessed — with long blond hair like Timna's. Sima thought but did not say that they could have been sisters.

The four of them stood in a row, arms behind each other's backs, a slice of beige ruins and the blue of the ocean behind them. "That's in Caesarea," Timna said, "right before I left for the army."

Timna's hair was longer in the photograph, a few strands streaked a faded red against her face. She wore jean shorts cropped inches above her knees and her legs were long, a little too thin — still the legs of a girl.

Timna rotated the album for the next shot. Timna's mother was in a kitchen, leaning against brown metal cabinets. She was a thin woman, well-dressed, Sima thought, in dark jeans and a red cashmere sweater, but her face had a pinched quality to it: she lacked Timna's open expression, smooth skin; she looked not just older but closed.

The kitchen was a mess. The countertop was cluttered with bowls; a small hill of flour spilled onto the floor, dusting the yellow tile white. Timna sat at the kitchen table, which was crowded with newspapers and magazines. It must have been morning: she was dressed in her army uniform, but she was barefoot; she was eating cereal, the spoon half-raised to her lips. She did not look at the camera.

"We were making pancakes," Timna said.

"But you're eating cereal."

Timna smiled. "Very observant."

Sima blushed, realizing she'd been staring at the picture. She glanced at Timna — an excuse already forming: something about an interest in Israeli kitchens, were they the same as here — but Timna was looking at the photo, a perfect crease between her brows.

"She was trying to impress some guy," Timna said, "and I just wanted to get back to the base on time." She shook her head. "I was annoyed, actually. But it's a good picture, I think. It captures something, doesn't it?"

Sima nodded, though she wasn't sure whether that something was worth capturing. "Who took it?"

"Her boyfriend." Timna looked up at

Sima, shrugged. "I never pay much attention to her boyfriends. They're not bad guys or anything, just she dated one for a few years when I was fourteen and it was hard for me when they broke up."

"Oh," Sima said. She'd heard of women who did things like that. "And how old were you at the divorce?"

"Ten and a half. But he was having an affair — he was never home anyway."

Sima nodded. Such a pity, she thought, looking once more at the chaotic kitchen, so sad for Timna — and yet a relief to discover Timna's family so flawed.

Timna turned the page. "These are me and my high school friends," Timna told her, and for the next few pages Sima looked at images of girls with dark red lips and long black hair as they toasted bottles of beer on the beach or ate burgers on sunset patios, palm tree shadows behind them. Sima nodded as Timna moved through the album, a slight envy growing with each image — how popular Timna was, how easy her life seemed.

"And Alon?" Sima asked, looking at a photo of Timna on a girlfriend's lap, giggling.

"Here." Timna carefully flipped the page, and Sima saw that Alon's photos had been

looked at so often that the album had grown
worn at the center; Timna had to hold both
sides to keep it from coming apart.

Sima looked first at his neck, his body. He
wore a white, long-sleeved cotton shirt and
blue jeans; his chest was broad, his shoulders round but thick, substantial. Around
his neck — a slight Adam's apple, some
stubble — was a thin gold chain. The neck
was long and sensual; it didn't match the
thick shoulders and was better for that.

Alon was handsome, but not beautiful like
Timna. He lacked Timna's glow, it seemed
to Sima as she lifted the album and held it
closer for inspection. He had green eyes and
slightly hollow cheeks and he was grinning,
Sima saw, in that crooked way men do when
they're overwhelmed with happiness but still
trying to look tough. In the next picture
Sima knew the cause of his joy: he held
Timna, both arms wrapped round her body,
as she stretched out a hand to capture them.
The picture was blurry, but Sima could see
they were leaning into each other and laughing in that easy way that signaled love.

The photographs that followed were almost all of Alon and Timna, taken by one
or the other: Alon emerging from a tent, the
morning sky white with heat above him;
Timna, wearing long braids like a child, dip-

ping her hands into a river; Alon in shorts and a T-shirt, kicking a soccer ball in a city park; Timna gorgeous in a tight green dress, her eyes rimmed with black liner and her hair swept back like an old-time Hollywood star.

It seemed to Sima that there was so much joy in the pictures, so much love: in one Timna held Alon's chin between her hands, kissed his cheek — and the grin on his face, the brightness in his eyes made Sima want to close her own.

"He loves you very much," Sima said.

"I miss him so much," Timna told her. "I look at you and Lev, and I can't wait to be that way — old, having spent a lifetime together."

Sima did not respond.

Timna turned the page. "I just hope we make it through this year," she said as she traced the edge of Alon's body on the beach blanket, asleep. "He's the best thing in my life."

"Of course you will," Sima told her, closing the album. "When you're in love, it lasts."

After Timna had left, her photo album tucked back in her purse, Sima stayed in the shop. She wasn't ready yet for the slow, creaking walk upstairs: her hand heavy on the banister, her ankles swollen after a day on her feet. And the tasks that would follow, the well-worn path from the moment she pulled open the plastic accordion door at the top of the stairs until rolling on to her side, gathering the blanket in her hands. She'd prepare dinner: salad with low-fat dressing followed by chicken breast, or a white fish, or pasta. They'd eat quietly. Sometimes she'd have a story — and more and more it would be about Timna — but often she listened to the sound of their forks on the porcelain, the way the angle altered the noise from tinny to coarse, depending.

When they were done, Lev would carry the dishes to the sink and return to the table, sponge in hand, to wipe the yellow placemats clean. Sima would rinse the plates, load the dishwasher, brush crumbs from the counter into her open hand with a wet paper towel. She'd sweep while he went upstairs, making sure to get the broom under the cabinets — that open space she always meant to block in but never did — before banging the dustpan against the side of the garbage can, putting it away with the broom in the pantry, turning off the light.

It'd be eight months still until Alon would get released. Such a long time. Maybe she could do something to speed it up — pay for a plane ticket, host a visit. She indulged a moment in the fantasy, imagined saying, it's my pleasure, while she watched Timna beam with gratitude. It'd be rushed, sure, the two of them on a whirlwind tour of New York: Timna's cheeks red with winter outside Rockefeller Center, the Fifth Avenue taxi cabs squealing to a stop as she'd raise a hand, just so, for the ride while Alon, impressed with the ease with which Timna negotiated the city, would hold the door open, gaze at her a moment through the window glass.

But as the two of them leaned back, their heads resting on the green upholstery of the cab, Sima saw herself outside unable to hear the destination they gave the cabbie. And what would she do, she reasoned, while the two of them, running with joined hands, forced the pigeons to scatter from the fountain beside the Met? She'd be alone in the basement, just some old woman wasting her money on a love she would never share. Of course he couldn't leave the country while in the army, and even if her plane ticket could buy a visit, it wasn't her gift to give.

Sima walked toward the staircase, turned off the light. She placed her hand on the banister, paused. After Timna had taken that first picture of the two of them together, she would have wrapped her arms around Alon, they would have kissed. He would spread both his hands on her back; feel the bone beneath, the fragility. Their mouths would be warm and open to each other and slowly she'd lean back, exposing the smooth of her throat that his lips, eager, would press against, circle, until, with a moan, her legs bending beneath her and the camera dropping gently down, Timna would pull Alon onto the grass, feel his body against her own, wanting.

Sima closed her eyes, wishing to give in to their bodies. She touched her stomach, fingers trembling, for just a moment before, blinking hard, she forced her hand to the banister, pulled herself up the stairs and into her life.

■ ■ ■ ■

SEPTEMBER

■ ■ ■ ■

5

"You'll come, then?" Sima asked, midway up the ladder. She concentrated on looking through the boxes — Mrs. Adams wanted something black, without too much trim — not wanting to see Timna's face in case she looked flustered, desperate for an excuse.

"Of course, I'd love to." Timna glanced at the drawn dressing-room curtain, creased her brow a moment. "Will you bring down one of the wireless bras too? Ellen might find them more comfortable."

Sima had just lowered one foot but now raised it again, opened another box. "Because I thought your cousins might mind, so if it's any trouble —"

"No. They only do the first night of Rosh Hashanah, so there's nothing I'm missing anyway."

The doorbell chimed, and Sima turned to see a middle-aged woman with enormous breasts enter the shop, encumbered by shopping bags. "Rochelle," Sima called, for once amused rather than annoyed to note that though she'd been fitting Rochelle for years, still she always showed up hanging out of some demi-cup. And though Rochelle established herself in the dressing room for over an hour, trying on everything in her size while complaining of various medical ailments, Sima did not try to hurry her, even found herself laughing at the e-mailed jokes Rochelle produced from a canvas bag.

Timna was coming for Rosh Hashanah.

Sima had not felt so excited for the new year's holiday since, as a young child, she would sit on the counter to peer into the soup pot, try to count the carrots and potatoes, chicken necks and celery stalks, that bobbed in the yellow broth. The holiday then had truly signaled new beginnings; the bowls of nuts and raisins, the honey in its glass dish, and the round braided challah all gathered up with a fresh school year, the leather smell of new shoes and shirts still crisp to the touch.

Those early holidays had been followed by others less hopeful — the worry of her first years of marriage; how she'd hurried to the shops, waved her hands for attention at the butcher, grocer, baker and, rushing home with plastic bags cutting red lines into the skin of both hands, filled her kitchen with food. All four burners crowded and the inside of the oven too, and in the sink more dishes to be done and butter, melting, staining the edge of a clipped recipe. But then the tentative pride when, the food shifted into her new Corning Ware — the blue flower on each side not yet faded, the white ceramic still bright — and rounded on top with a wooden spoon like the magazine said, she served it carefully to guests gathered round her table, watched as they ate.

"Is it all right?" she'd ask. "More salt? I think maybe the brisket is a touch too dry —"

But her guests dismissed her worries, and every year she was pleased to see that though she'd doubled, sometimes tripled, each recipe, the leftovers would last for little more than one dinner for her and Lev.

Their parents were guests at the first few holidays, when Sima's father was still alive and Lev's not yet living in Florida. One year her two older brothers visited, and then she and Lev took trips to see them in Dallas and Los Angeles, but they'd always been too much older than her. For several years they'd had friends — someone from Lev's school, a few of the women she'd known —

but at some point they'd just stopped inviting, settled for being guests at someone else's celebration.

But now Timna was coming, and Connie and Art had said sure, they'd be there, and her old Cousin Millie and Lev's Uncle Abe. Sima reduced the hours of the shop the week before the holiday, and her hands stiffened from cutting vegetables, and she shifted her feet standing in line at the butcher — willing to fight like any of the women, proud of their families and wanting only the best cuts.

Sima raised the lid of the soup pot and, breathing deep, felt the fragrant steam seep through her, the rolling boil carry her back to an earlier time when there was excitement in the changing of seasons, when the sweetness of honey signaled hope.

Timna had brought yellow daisies and Connie red roses and Sima placed each in crystal vases at either end of the table, just slightly blocking Art and Millie, Connie and Abe, but leaving Timna, at the center, beautifully framed. Sima felt flushed with the evening. Though Lev teased, as he sat down, that she'd cooked for an army, and for a moment she felt ridiculous — pressed her nail into her hand to try to check her eagerness and hoped that, with the table so covered in food, it did not look bizarre, desperate — Timna had said, "To me it looks wonderful — I can't wait to try it all," and Sima had opened her hand under the table and smiled.

Connie talked about Nate over matzoh ball soup. "You know," she said, looking at Timna, her eyes moving up and down, inspecting, "he also loves to travel. But it's so difficult, being a scientist, to find the time. He was in school forever, not that he didn't do it as quickly as you can, but there was college and then the doctorate and now he's ten years with this lab and hardly a vacation."

While Connie bragged — "You know what it means, Timna, epidemiology?" — Sima looked on, nervous. She hadn't anticipated this: Connie capturing Timna for Nate, making Timna her own. Sima had no way to compete, no smart, appealing man she could set as her own bait.

"He studies diseases," Art explained. "To find a cure." He draped an arm around Connie and ran his hand along her shoulder.

Sima noticed the gesture: a thoughtless, casual touch, yet one entirely absent from her own marriage.

"And it doesn't put him at risk?" Sima asked, knowing it was something Connie worried about though Nate had assured her, no. "How can it be?" Connie had lamented more than once, "that handling viruses all day is safe? It doesn't take a Ph.D. to realize you could end up sick." Sima always attempted to reassure her: "In this day and age everything gets sterilized," "In this day and age they know enough not to expose anyone to anything harmful." Of course, she knew nothing about what happened in this day and age, or in any day or any age, in laboratories — and the truth was that the word itself, *laboratory,* seemed sinister to her; she half-expected to hear Nate only worked at night, or when it was stormy.

Connie glanced at Sima, raised an eyebrow. Sima shrugged. She knew it was wrong to feed off Connie's own fears, but she could almost hear Alon clapping at her quick jab, smiling to see the image of Nate — Harvard degree in one hand, microscope in another — falling backwards toward the floor.

"It's not exactly a high-risk job," Connie said. "Your boyfriend is in what," Connie asked, turning to Timna, "the army?"

Sima cringed. Of all the unfair —

"Yes," Timna said, "thank God, only eight

months to go." She looked down at her fingers, eight outstretched and two folded down, smiled. Sima looked too. Eight fingers above the table cloth, each one a month she'd have Timna; Sima imagined the calendar images of the seasons on each nail, the gold of early autumn turning to falling leaves, pumpkins, holly and red berries, skaters on a frozen river beside a painted Dutch village, and then birds, yellow flowers pushing through dark soil — spring.

The punching-bag image of Nate still grinned up from the floor; Sima could fight all she wanted, but she'd still lose Timna in the end.

Sima watched Timna cut the slices of gravied meat and stab the spiced carrots with her fork. Her mouth opened and closed, her lips moved with the chewing, she smiled slightly. Sima observed her closely, proud each time Timna lowered her fork to the plate for more. When Timna put down her wineglass some residue remained, a dappled redness along the glass rim, the press of her lower lip opening to a kiss.

"Did you see how Timna jumped to take some brisket home?" Sima bragged to Lev, loading the dinner plates in the dishwasher.

"I didn't have to offer twice."

"What was she supposed to say?" he asked, placing four wineglasses beside the sink. "You pay her, after all."

Sima frowned. "Thanks."

"What? I'm just saying."

Sima added detergent to the dishwasher and closed the door. "You didn't like the food?"

"I liked it, I liked it. Just the brisket was a little dry."

"There was gravy."

Lev shrugged.

Sima turned around. Behind her hot water rushed into the dishwasher, the sound humming through the room and filling her too. "It's a lot of work, you know," she said. "I was in the kitchen practically all week, not that you so much as volunteered to help —"

"You said how good it was to be cooking again —"

"Yeah, for a day or so. But after that you really could have helped out too. Not that watching baseball on TV all the time isn't important, I'm sure, but —"

Lev closed his eyes, rubbed them with his hand. "Forget it, Sima. Forget I said anything. I'll help clean up tomorrow, but for now I'm going to lie down."

Sima watched him leave. She took out the Saran Wrap and began covering the leftovers — one lunch and half a dinner — while the hum of the television drifted in from the bedroom: the steady plod of the anchorman followed by a few dramatic notes signaling a commercial break. She tried, while she rinsed the serving spoons, to picture again how Timna had leaned in, pressed her finger to the hot wax that had dripped onto the old silver tray just as, Sima had remembered at the time, she had done as a child at holiday dinners. But the image was no longer clear; it was nothing, just an idle movement, nothing she should be repeating in her mind as she cleaned the kitchen, alone, all the guests gone and Lev too. Probably Timna was out now with friends, laughing about her dinner with the old people. The brisket really had been drier than usual; there was cork in the wine. Sima turned off the tap, suddenly heavy with sleep, and went to watch the news in the bedroom.

6

Sima stood at the top of the stairs on a Sunday morning, looking down into the bra shop. Everything was clean and organized, ready for the week ahead: even the counter had been polished with wood oil the previous Friday. Never mind it wasn't real wood; she liked all the same the clean, sharp smell of the oil.

Descending the steps, Sima walked over to what she'd begun to think of as Timna's sewing table. She picked up a pale blue cardigan folded on Timna's chair and brought it toward her face, losing herself in the sharp smell of inexpensive perfume. A creak upstairs brought her back; she dropped the cardigan onto the chair and walked quickly away.

"Tell me," Sima asked when Timna arrived a half hour later, a cup of coffee in one hand and a Hebrew newspaper in the other, "what will you most want to show

Alon when he gets here?"

She'd thought the question out the night before.

Timna sat down at the sewing table, casually tossing the cardigan Sima had doted on over the back of her chair. "I'm not sure," she said. "By the time he comes, I'll know this city so much better. I'm just a tourist now —"

"You work here, you have a job." She didn't want Timna to think of herself as a tourist — it was all more permanent than that.

Timna smiled. "I guess so." She removed the lid of her coffee cup, took a long sip. "It's funny you ask though," she said, wrapping both hands around the cup, "because the truth is wherever I am I think about being there with Alon. I have imaginary conversations in my head where I'm showing him things or we're commenting together — a woman will go by walking a dog or something, and suddenly I'm talking with Alon about that." She paused, ran a finger around the rim of the cup. "Does that sound crazy?"

"Not crazy at all," Sima said, remembering vaguely that she'd once dreamed up conversations with Lev.

"But then sometimes it only makes me

feel more alone. Yesterday I walked over the Brooklyn Bridge, and it was just a beautiful, perfect morning. The sky was bright blue and the bridge was filled with families and people jogging." Timna lifted the cardigan from the back of her chair, folded it in her lap. "It was the sort of day, you know, when everybody seems to smile at you?"

Sima nodded, though she wasn't sure — would she have remembered to smile on the bridge? Of course, she thought, she wouldn't have been there.

"But then, to stand there looking into the water and feeling part of such a perfect day, and to feel so much — joy, just joy for the day and the place and the time in my life, you know? But to have no one to share it with, no one beside me who I could turn to and point and say, 'Look.' " Timna placed the folded sweater on the counter, smoothed it with her hand. "It's hard, that silence. It made it all less real somehow, because there was no one there to understand."

"Yes," Sima said, "Yes, I know what you mean." And it seemed to her that she did, as she imagined Timna on the Brooklyn Bridge, looking into the river between the woven ropes, though she wasn't sure, after all, if she'd walked across the bridge even once in the last three decades, and then again how long it'd been since she tried to share what was inside, parted her lips to say, "Look."

They were just shy of their first wedding anniversary when Lev took her hand, observing her so intently as she put down the grocery bags that she ceased her description of the traffic, waited, the beginnings of fear clawing her stomach, for what he might say. Was it Connie, did she have the baby, did something go wrong? She didn't ask aloud; thinking it alone reassured her — it was the unimagined, the unanticipated, that could hurt you. And then Lev's mouth quivered slightly, turned just a bit toward a smile, and Sima moved to release her hand, unpack the groceries — there was nothing to fear, after all, he was just teasing, and right off she'd assumed it was bad news —

"Sima," Lev told her, gripping her hand, "Your mother is dead."

She pulled away, put the milk in the refrigerator. It should not go bad. And then the eggs too, and the lettuce, and as she moved about the kitchen, emptying the bags, asked, "What? When? But we just saw her last Friday. Everything was fine."

"Your father called this morning," Lev told her, standing still as she moved around him. "She died in her sleep. Probably a stroke, they say. She didn't feel a thing."

So her mother was dead then, and she hadn't told anyone she was planning anything of the sort. Why wouldn't her mother have told her? Did her father know? Her brothers? She was always treated as a child, never informed, "Why didn't I know this was going to happen?"

"Sima, what are you saying? No one knew. She died in her sleep. Really, it's the best thing you can imagine for her."

Sima couldn't say no, she'd wished for her a long illness. A slow-gasping death filled with intimate moments between the two of them — her mother finally turning to her, focusing on her, telling her about all the years that had come before, the story of her life that Sima had never known, never felt part of. And she'd care for her and they'd be close, finally, and it wouldn't just be her brothers, the original family, she tacked on only at the end when her mother was over forty and her youngest brother ten and no one, an aunt once told her, was expecting you, that's for sure. A long illness was needed to narrow the space between them. Sima had been counting on it; as the daughter it was her role. And now she'd disappointed again.

"Do my brothers know?"

"Your father was waiting to call them, just for the time difference, though I guess by now it's seven in Los Angeles so probably —"

Sima nodded. She'd call them too in a moment. They'd weep to her, they'd moan. How proud her mother would be to hear their cries.

Why wasn't she crying? She seemed to think it at the same time as Lev; she saw him look at her suspiciously — hadn't he seen tears in her eyes from magazine articles, the evening news? She closed the refrigerator door, lowered her head, concentrated. "My mother's dead," she thought. Nothing happened. She gathered her hand into a fist, pressed her nail into her palm, clenched her eyes shut. Feel something. A little wetness gathered in the corner of her eyes. Lifting her head, she made sure Lev saw the tears' slow descent.

Her brothers flew in with their wives and children. They spoke at the funeral, choked on their words, reminded the audience how she'd been the best of mothers, the most devoted, the most loving.

Sima leaned her head against Lev's shoulder. It wasn't loss she felt, but envy — she envied them even their grief.

Outside the funeral chapel she stood beside her father, one hand under his elbow, steadying. "She's taken care of me since I was twenty," her father said, staring at his wedding band like a young bride taken by the shine of it. Sima shushed him, promised, while she smiled at the old relatives who reached for her, thanking them for coming with the quiet voice of the bereaved, to care for him, cook for him.

"And to think," an elderly cousin said, pausing to cradle Sima's head between her hands, "that you should be so tested during your first year of marriage. Oh, your mother would be so sad to know."

Sima nodded, remembered overhearing her mother on her wedding day —

"I'm the one discovered Lev" — while she and Lev stood hand in hand beside the dance floor like the imitation bride and groom atop the wedding cake.

After the guests left that evening, Sima settled her father at the kitchen table while she opened drawers and overturned sofa pillows, searching for her mother's treasures. Her father wrung his hands, agitated, as he lamented that he'd never thought to ask where she hid her jewelry — the cheap gold, imitation diamond trinkets he'd bought her during their decades together. Sima found them finally in a tallis bag at the back of her mother's closet, hidden behind a pair of violet heels.

Curled against the costume jewelry was a worn envelope containing two thousand dollars cash.

"I knew she put away what she could, now and then," her father said, "but I never knew she'd saved much." He lifted the bills, his hands as gentle as if it were his wife's own weight he held, and, cradling them, looked at Sima. "You take the money," he told her.

Sima had never seen so much money in one place, could not believe that her mother, who saved the twine from bakery boxes for reuse, had accumulated it. She shook her head no. "We have to give Mac and Lou some."

"No, no, your mother wouldn't want that. She always told me, my boys are wonderful, but Sima's my joy, my comfort. She always said, 'A mother needs a daughter.' She was so proud of you, said you had such a head on your shoulders." Her father took her hand, placed the money in her palm. "This money belonged to her; she'd want it to be yours."

Sima closed her hand around the soft bills.

Sima could sense Lev's relief when she

clung to him, cried on his shoulder. He stroked her back, her head, murmured that it would be okay. This was something, she couldn't help thinking, as, wiping her face with the back of her palm, she looked at Lev, saw the tears in his own eyes; this was something: to weep on her husband's shoulder for the mother she lost. Her mother was right; it was good to have someone. She loved him; he loved her. Everything was right.

They celebrated their first anniversary with champagne and dinner out. She mentioned, as they tipped their glasses together, how it'd been her mother who insisted on the champagne toast at their wedding, said it was worth the extra money. "How sad," Sima said, "that not even a year later —"

"Let's try to put that to the side," Lev told her, patting her hand. "Let's focus on good things."

As Sima watched Lev take an awkward gulp, she recognized suddenly that her mother's death had in a strange way been a good thing — had made her feel loved. She thought to explain this to Lev, began to speak, "The thing is," and then, suddenly cold, stopped. Her father could be lying. He depended on her now — she brought him food every day, had him over a few times a week — he had his own reasons to give her that money. And what would it hurt, his wife dead, to assure his daughter of the love he knew she longed for?

Lev looked at her. "What were you about to say?"

Sima paused while the waiter placed two bowls of mushroom soup before them, asked if everything was all right. She nodded, her face pale. "Lev," Sima said, her voice almost a whisper, though the waiter was at another table now, offering specials, "Do you think my father was right?"

Lev stirred his soup with his spoon; reached for a roll. "Right about what? The money?"

"No. Well, yes. What he said about the money, about her and me."

Lev blew gently on his raised spoon.

Sima explained to him, her voice halting, this new fear; a rawness inside as she sewed shut the last month, the only time in her life she'd felt wanted by her mother.

Her cheeks were hot with the shame of it, but Lev gave an easy smile. "Of course she loved you Sima," he said, reaching for the salt, "you're her child, after all; it's only natural." He sprinkled his soup with salt, bent his head to taste.

Sima stared at him, willing him to look

up. She wanted to shake him, remind him it was her mother, dead, and without saying goodbye and never having told Sima she loved her, never having said she was proud.

Lev did not notice her gaze; Sima closed her eyes, pressed them clear. "I guess you're right," she said instead, ripping open a roll, dipping it into her bowl.

"So at school," Lev told her, "Mr. Cheswiks said —"

She nodded as he spoke, smiled at the right moments, thinking, while not listening to anything he said, what an easy role it was to play after all.

7

Sima watched Timna unbutton her blouse. The delivery man had stopped in that morning, his eyes, Sima noticed as she signed the receipt slip, on Timna's body as she bent over one of the boxes, pulled at the thick tape with both hands like a child eager for gifts. They'd had to wait for the lunch crowd to clear before Timna could try on the new merchandise — a tradition Sima would never have allowed with anyone else. "How can you recommend what you haven't worn?" Timna had asked. "When I was a waitress I tried every dish in the house." At two o'clock Sima locked the wood door, sat down, and nodded for Timna to begin.

Timna undressed behind the curtain, but pulled it aside to model the wares. "Ta da!" she cried, stepping out in a peach bra-panty combo. After performing an exaggerated catwalk circle, she evaluated the fit: the bra, she told Sima, made her a little too pointy, no? "But the underwear," she traced a finger along the elastic rim, "fits nice."

Sima kept her hands on the arm rests, her legs crossed demurely. It was beautiful, the young body before her. Like art, she reminded herself, though she knew that the heat on the back of her neck — she reached back, fixed her bun — was from want rather than appreciation. If only she'd known, she thought to herself as Timna retreated to the dressing room, to love her body when she was young. Why hadn't someone told her? How had Timna known?

"You're very lucky, you know that?"

Timna pulled aside the curtain. She'd changed into a blue satin nightgown with ribbon shoulder straps.

"Why? You're giving me this nightgown?"

Sima smiled. "No. But you're young," she paused, "and beautiful, and you have such confidence."

Timna smoothed the satin across her belly, pouted at her reflection in the mirror. "I don't feel so young. I'm twenty-one, and I haven't even been to university yet."

"What's the rush? When Lev and I married, we were so sheltered, we knew nothing. Here you are traveling the world — when I was married, I'd never been farther than the Catskills."

"It's not too late for you," Timna said, turning before the mirror. "Lev's retired, and your business does well. You can close for a month, go anywhere you want."

"Maybe someday. We'll see."

Timna looked at her but did not respond, returned to the dressing room to change.

"So speaking of travel," Sima said, speaking to the closed curtain, "Have you explored the city more? Before you see the world, you have to see some of New York's neighborhoods. Talk about foreign —"

Timna mock-sashayed out of the dressing room, modeling a purple silk bathrobe tied loose around the waist. Sima admired her while Timna described a trip down the west side of Manhattan — jogging with a friend along the water, sunning in the grass at Battery Park City, drinking cocktails in Tribeca. "It's really amazing down there," Timna said as she untied the bathrobe, went to change, "so beautiful."

"Oh? I've hardly been since they did that area up," Sima told her, though the truth was she'd never been at all. "So what friend is this? Someone your cousin knows?"

Timna answered through the curtain — a guy she'd met at a café, Israeli, some friends in common back home. She walked out of the dressing room in her own faded blue jeans and a fitted black short-sleeved sweater; sat at the seamstress table, half-suppressed a yawn.

"And this guy, what's his story?"

Timna smiled. "His name is Shai, and he's been here two years already, working security for a Jewish organization." Timna opened her purse and took out lip gloss, dotted it across her lips. "It was just like you said, Sima: I went to a café in the East Village and suddenly I was surrounded by Israelis."

"Terrific," Sima told her, though she couldn't help but wish it had taken Timna just a little longer to make friends. She walked over to the UPS box, open before the dressing-room curtain, picked it up. "And Alon," she asked, pausing, "how is he doing?"

"Oh, he keeps changing the travel plans. Now he says he wants to go to Yellowstone, see a bear. I want to see Hollywood, and he's talking bears."

Sima smiled. She knew Timna loved this: the easy frustration with Alon, the chiding. Most women did at first, when they strived to know everything about their beloved, delighting in his bright-edged outline even as they sighed over differences, faults, think-

98

ing that, after all, the weaknesses just pointed to the ways they were needed, like a new mother who, complaining that the baby screams every time she gives it to someone else, thrills nonetheless to those cries that signal her worth.

But of course it all changed, the small faults that teased the love growing into gaps, missing pieces that left you one day looking at a face, searching for what you'd loved and finding it empty.

"Let's get back to the good part of the trip," Sima said, lifting the package onto the counter. "I can't even handle how many places you're going; I picture you two like the heroes of an old film, riding off into the sunset."

"You want to come along?"

"Very funny. Just what Lev and I need, four months on three continents —"

"Six months."

"Six months." Sima removed the inventory list from its plastic pocket. "So first you travel the world. Then you earn big money in Tel Aviv's best bra shop, go to university for fashion —"

"Sounds good." Timna gathered her hair into a ponytail, walked over to the dressing-room mirror.

"And then after university," Sima said,

pleased with how well she knew her, not even two months together and Timna's future an easy road open before them both, "you'll get married and have children —"

"Sima, don't be so quick to marry me off. After university I'll just be starting a real career for the first time. I'll need five, ten years to work my way up —"

"But children?" Sima asked, taking hold of a lilac nightgown. Timna had to have babies: that soft stomach, those full breasts. "Aren't they on the timeline?"

"Children? With children I can't go to Asia, Australia. When I'm in my late thirties," she said, checking her face in the mirror, "maybe then —"

"Your late thirties?" Sima placed the nightgown on the counter. "No, it's too long to wait, Timna. Women aren't like men, you need to start early."

Timna pulled some strands of hair loose, arranged them to frame her face. "So why didn't you have children, Sima? Lev didn't want?"

Sima felt a stillness inside, a blank feeling like her own breath stopping on its smooth backwards-forwards path and instead gathering inside her stomach, stirring for rebellion like a tornado turning slowly on those empty, windswept pieces of America she'd only seen in movies. "We tried. I couldn't — we tried and tried but I couldn't have any."

Timna turned away from the mirror, attempted a smile. "Well, but the trying is the best part, no?"

Sima looked down, studied her own hands: the strange sketch of blue veins, the large curl of her knuckles, the pale, pink-rimmed pull of her skin. "Sure," she told Timna, seeing already the liver spots that would colonize, the transformation of her skin from oil-flesh to whisper-parchment — the bone becoming sharper beneath, readying — "the best part."

During the early years of their marriage, Sima and Lev lived in a cramped one-bedroom apartment. "We'll move," they would say, "when the time is right." In the darkness of their bedroom he'd reach for her and she'd gather him close: her arms around his body, his heat against her skin, his lips just touching her ear as his breath quickened along with her own, both their bodies damp with sweat and their mouths open, their wedding night left long behind as they learned to stroke each other awake and then again to fall together into sleep. And their savings grew, and there were small houses they could buy in the right area, but though his body thickened above her, the children never came.

Each month there was the terrible excitement of hope. She'd try not to think about the possibility, put it out of her mind until she knew for sure, but inevitably she'd press her breasts in the shower, thinking maybe there was some tenderness, or pause when she was hungry or tired to wonder if the sensation wasn't stronger than usual, if there wasn't something else behind it. She sat with her legs crossed, a hope to keep something inside from leaving, and with each trip to the bathroom searched for, and dreaded to find, the blood that would signal the end to that month's hope, that month's child.

Always the moment came, the blood escaping her body an affront like the slap that her mother had given her when, mumbling, Sima first admitted her period. "May that be the most pain you feel in childbirth," her mother had said afterwards, while Sima, cheek-stinging, turned her face away in shame. She was thirteen, no longer a child and indeed older than all her friends had been, the only one among them who could not whisper proudly and, with cupped hands, pass a sanitary napkin beneath the bathroom door. And yet, and still, she'd wanted to bury herself under the covers, hide until the bleeding went away.

At twenty-two Sima sat on the toilet, saw the brown stain on her underwear, taunting. She slapped herself once. Twice. Tried for three but doubled over instead, and wept into her own body.

8

"She's never been fitted for a bra before," Connie said, pushing Suzanne toward Sima. "Come on, Sima, do that trick — tell her what her size is."

"You make me sound like some kind of circus freak," Sima waved Suzanne forward. "Come, we'll see what we can do for you."

While Timna and Sima brought them bras, Connie and Suzanne laughed about Art. "Admit it," Connie said, "you've never heard a man sneeze so loud. Tell me it doesn't drive you crazy. Once he set off a car alarm, I'm not kidding."

Suzanne giggled. "I can believe it."

Sima ignored the conversation, watched instead as Suzanne ran her hands over lace cups.

"Fits well, see?" Sima tugged at the straps, adjusting them.

"I can't believe I've been wearing the wrong size all this time."

Connie nodded. "That's what everyone says. What did I tell you? She could be on *Oprah.*"

"If only I had someone to show it off to," Suzanne said, slipping a black camisole Timna had brought her over the bra. "You guys should provide that, too. One-stop shopping."

Timna snapped her fingers. "I think I've found my calling."

"With you recruiting I could retire in style," Sima said, gathering Suzanne's purchases (three bra-and-panty sets, in addition to what she'd wear out) into a pile. "Assuming you don't get deported first."

"See how she threatens me with deportation?"

"How else am I supposed to keep good help?"

Sima turned to Suzanne. "Anyway, you don't buy for a man. You buy for yourself. Trust me."

"Oh, now you really sound like Oprah." Suzanne buttoned her blouse. "I think I'd still choose having someone to see a movie with over self-empowerment, but whatever."

"Did you notice how much they look alike?" Timna asked after they'd left.

Sima nodded. Suzanne was ten or fifteen years younger, but they were both of average height and weight, and with the same auburn hair blown straight to the shoulders. "They must use the same bottle of hair dye."

"I guess that's how Art likes them."

"Timna!" Sima said, but she laughed despite herself.

The end of another week. Timna waved goodbye, pulled the door shut behind her; Sima turned away, folded a camisole above the counter. Where did Timna go, she wondered, smoothing the burgundy silk, what was her home like, the evenings she spent there? It frustrated Sima that Timna consumed her whole world when she was just a piece of Timna's. The working week: the hours to get through.

She imagined for a moment Timna moving along her block, what she might see. The end of September and gold light sifting through the streets; if Boro Park had a chance at beauty, this was it. Sima walked to the store entrance, opened the door, looked up the stairs to the sky above. It might not be enough for Timna, raised as she was under a deep gold sun, but Sima hoped it was.

Returning to the counter, she absently picked up her date book. Scrawled on the inside cover was Timna's home address, just a five-minute walk away.

A whisper of a question: Why not?

The excuse was easy. She could use the walk, and it was practically on the way to the hardware store, and she'd been meaning to buy energy-saving lightbulbs, and didn't she deserve to see Timna's house, after all this time?

She locked the store door and climbed the back staircase to the kitchen, calling, "Lev!" even as she moved through the living room to the front door.

"Sima?"

She could hear the television volume lowering.

"I'm going out to the hardware store," she yelled, pulling on a khaki overcoat. "You want anything?"

"What?"

"Never mind, I'm going out, is all."

She didn't bother waiting for a response.

Up two long blocks and over three short ones and then rounding a corner, her body tense, looking for Timna's house. A block like any other: houses crammed together, postage-stamp lawns too small for even the most enterprising children to play on, their sun-faded plastic toys confined instead to the cramped balconies above. It always amazed Sima that in a neighborhood filled with children there was not a single park or public playground, though each commercial block boasted at least one ride: the orange kangaroo or pink horse bucking not quite enough to truly thrill even the youngest child, but still they clamored for quarters, clenched their hands around the worn leather reins as they rode to the tinny beat of all-time Top-40 Jewish hits — "Hava Negilah"; "Moshiach, Moshiach, Moshiach."

Halfway down the block she forced herself to slow down. It'd be worse, she decided, if she were caught hurrying past; strolling, she could pretend she was out for a reason. Though Timna was nowhere in sight — she checked, half-turning every few feet — Sima practiced a surprised smile, ready to say, "Oh, is this your block, I just needed some lightbulbs from the hardware store on Sixteenth —"

She almost missed the house. A disappointment: an entirely ordinary brick home. The cement steps could use a new coat of gray paint, but the living room curtains hung clean and pink in the wide front window. Semidetached, a narrow alley separated the house from its neighbor on one side. Stepping forward, Sima peered down the thin passageway.

She was looking for something magic. If not in the façade of the home, then in a glimpse of garden out back: bluebells, beanstalks. Instead she saw only two olive garbage cans beside a chain fence. Above her, a thin piece of wire connected the house to its neighbor, part of the figurative gate, *eruv,* that enclosed Boro Park: thin plastic string wound from telephone pole to street sign, the neighborhood itself drawing its arms around the residents, allowing the women and men to push strollers and carry keys on Shabbat. Volunteers patrolled Boro Park's *eruv* each week, alert to even the smallest breach that would render the entire border (which stretched to Flatbush, taking advantage of walls and train tracks along the way) unkosher.

A car slowed down, and Sima tensed, forced herself to keep walking. She passed a new red-gloss brick building — curved marble steps, cascading miniature hedges, French windows — that stood beside a crumbling two-story stucco a shade of smoker's gray. In Boro Park such juxtapositions were common: everyone walked to synagogue, and so everyone lived crowded together, wealthy and poor alike.

Now that it was over, and for nothing, Sima felt ashamed. She decided to skip the hardware store — she'd waited this long to get the lightbulbs, she could wait a little longer. On the way to Timna's she'd amused herself wondering over what Timna would notice: would she have smiled at the knot of children on the stoop, waiting for their mother to carry down the triple-stroller? Did she give a few coins to the old woman on the corner, "Saving money for Aliyah to Israel" scrawled in black marker on a cardboard sign? But as she turned down her block, she realized that Timna might take any number of routes home. Pointless to wonder what she'd notice, what she'd look at, and all of it anyway so pathetic: a cluster of pale children, a beggar; so little to offer, and her own life, the least.

"I'm back," she called out as she bent to unlace her shoes in the entranceway.

"Oh?" Lev said, coming through the kitchen. "I didn't notice you were gone."

■ ■ ■ ■

OCTOBER

■ ■ ■ ■

9

Sima watched Timna rummage through her desk drawer, searching for hooks to match a bra Ida Horn had dropped off earlier. She took out four extensions in different shades of off-white — one tinted yellow, another blush — lined them up to check the color. "Hold it up to the light," Sima told her, putting aside the catalog she'd been leafing through, "That's the only way to tell."

Timna did as Sima suggested. "What do you think?" she asked, pressing one and then another against the bra, a double-D cup in plain stretch-nylon, "I think the darkest one, no?"

Sima nodded. "Seems that way."

Timna lowered the bra, put the other extensions back in her desk drawer. "So I wanted to ask you if I could have next Sunday off," she told Sima as she cut off the original hooks, two of them bent beyond repair. "We're thinking of going to Philadelphia."

"Who with," Sima asked, "your cousins?"

"Oh no, not them." Timna positioned the bra under the sewing machine, lined up the new extension with the edge of the bra strap. "I'd go with those Israelis I told you about, Shai and our friend Nurit. The ones I met at that café." She bent her head over the sewing machine, guided the fabric under the needle. "Assuming it's okay with you."

Sima let the question hang just a moment before acquiescing. "You have a way to get there?"

"We have a car. Shai has a brother who lives in New Jersey, and he's lending us his."

"So it's all worked out."

Timna nodded, removing the bra from the sewing machine. The new hooks blended perfectly, Sima saw: if you didn't know, you wouldn't have been able to tell.

"Well then," Sima told her, "it sounds like a plan." She bent over the catalog, feigning preoccupation. After a few minutes she allowed herself to glance at Timna — she was leafing through a fashion magazine, seemingly unfazed by what Sima took to be an awkward silence.

"So," Sima asked her, "have you and Alon traveled together a lot?" It was a lame question, she knew, but Timna could never resist talking about Alon.

Timna bent her head slightly to the side, considering. "We went camping a few times," she told Sima, "but we were in high school and then the army, so it's not like we had much time, and it's not like Israel's some big country to explore." She closed the magazine, smiled. "But did I ever tell you about the time Alon and I almost sailed to Jordan?"

Sima leaned forward in anticipation. She loved the brightness in Timna's eyes when she spoke about Alon, the way she smiled wide, sometimes shyly tucked her head to hide the grin. "Such romance in my shop," Sima had told Connie, "it gives me a reason to get up in the morning."

Connie had frowned. "You've only been working together two months — what got you up before?"

Sima didn't answer, could only think: I have no idea, no idea at all.

"We were on our senior class trip to Eilat," Timna began, "so you can imagine the scene — typical high school stuff. A lot of eighteen-year-olds lying in the sun, trying to get someone else to go buy soda and beer."

Sima nodded, as if she'd ever experienced

115

anything of the sort.

"Anyway, a bunch of us went for a walk and found this sailboat attached to a yacht. So we start talking about how nice it would be to rent the boat and go for a ride, but of course no one knows whose boat it is. Well, at the end of the beach is this tiny, dark bar, and so we go in and ask the bartender if he knows anything about the boat. And he — it was like a movie, he just pointed his hand toward the back and there was the owner, sitting there eating lunch."

"Is that a coincidence." Sima shook her head in wonder; it was just the sort of luck she ascribed to Timna — the water always warm, the chariot always ready.

"We asked him about the boat, and at first he says no way, he won't rent it, but then he sees we're just some kids looking to enjoy our last few weeks together before the army so he says, fine. So we pay him and get the boat and we're so excited — sailing along the coast and waving to everyone on the beach, and of course getting further and further away from shore." Timna ran her hands through her hair; Sima watched it cascade perfectly back to place. "Now, the thing about the Gulf of Eilat is that you have Egypt right below Israel, sharing the same shore. And then opposite Israel is Jordan, and right below Jordan is Saudi Arabia. And they're all so close — you can see each country on a clear day. So there we were, sailing back and forth, right and left across the sea," Timna moved her hand in a zigzag before her, "and we keep getting close to Egypt and then Jordan, Egypt and then Jordan. Finally we decide why not, let's sail to Aqaba. So we turn the boat around and start heading straight toward it. Pretty soon we can see the city right before us, and we're getting closer and closer —"

Sima saw the boat cutting through the sea, Timna leaning against the sun-warmed ledge with her hair in the wind.

"And suddenly, just as we're sure we're going to make it to shore, these Israeli military boats appear out of nowhere. There are all these soldiers, and they're shouting," Timna deepened her voice, curled her fingers around her mouth like a megaphone, " 'Turn back, reverse course!' "

Sima leaned back, impressed. "Did you get in trouble?"

Timna shrugged. "Looking back, I can't believe we were ever that stupid, that young. The way things are now, and having been a soldier —" she paused, ran a hand across the curved back of the sewing machine. "Sometimes I still can't believe that Alon's

117

an officer, that he outranks all those soldiers who seemed so old and serious at the time." She placed her hands in her lap, looked at Sima. "I still haven't forgiven him for that, for becoming an officer."

"I thought you were proud?"

"No. I mean, I'm happy for him because it's what he wanted, but I worry about him all the time, and I can't stand to think what he does." She paused. "Ever since he was a kid, he idolized those soldiers. Most of the boys do, and the girls too I guess. But you grow out of it. Once you put that uniform on and see yourself in the mirror looking just like all the heroes of your youth, you realize then it's not real. Because you know you're scared and young and unprepared and insecure, and you know then that all those soldiers you looked up to all those years were the same."

"But maybe for Alon it was okay?" Sima asked, wanting to defend him. "Maybe to him it felt right, felt real?"

Timna opened her hands, a gesture of not knowing. "He thinks he can do more good from within than without, but he's wrong. No matter how much you try, once you've got the gun —" She leaned back in her chair, closed her eyes and rubbed the back of her neck. "Anyway," she said, looking at

Sima, "Where was I?"

"On the boat," Sima told her, eager to return Timna to a story of love. "About to be arrested."

"Right. Well, we weren't arrested. They treated us like a bunch of criminals and we had to talk them out of filing a report, but in the end we got them to let us go."

Sima raised her eyebrows, teasing. "And how did you do that?"

"My friend and I were in bikinis. It wasn't hard."

"You really are something," Sima said, proud. "You know that?"

"Well, it was better than lying on the beach. Our teachers were furious though — we weren't allowed to go to the dinner that night. They made us stay back at the hotel."

"Something tells me you didn't mind."

Timna grinned. "Anyway. That's the story of my almost-escapade to Jordan. Not much of a travel adventure in the end." She looked up, smiled. "Shai and Nurit and I have all sorts of plans, though — Philly this weekend, then Washington, D.C., for Thanksgiving, and then over that winter break you mentioned Boston —"

Sima watched Timna a moment before turning away, aware of how foolish her feelings of pride had been. Timna was not hers to be proud of: the excitement of Timna's life was as inaccessible to Sima as the most well-guarded foreign shore, silent boats skimming through darkened seas, silhouette men speaking a language she could not understand. She opened a drawer beneath the counter and placed the catalog inside, forced it shut.

Just after their third wedding anniversary, Sima took the subway into Manhattan to see the doctor. Among the other passengers were secretaries on their way to work. She found herself imagining their lives, envying the dull gleam of their mahogany desks and the steady click of their polished nails on the typewriter; the easy condescension to their bosses — solid, red-faced men — the "Good morning, Mr. Thomas" and "Good afternoon, Mr. Thomas" and the jostling subway ride home with the grocery list clenched in one hand, the leather of the subway strap in another.

And yet, she realized, looking down, she too was a young woman in a navy skirt, a cream blouse, a wool jacket. Maybe all the women on the train were young wives without babies, maybe all the women on the train had thrown their underwear in the garbage, furious at another month lost.

Sima opened her purse, checked the doctor's address for the fourth time that morning. Just looking at it relaxed her, the slow curve of the letters spelling Park Avenue. It wouldn't be just her problem anymore, it would be Park Avenue's problem, and with all the marbled height of those buildings supporting her, surely something as insignificant as her own body could be made to work for a baby.

Sima blinked as the train emerged from the tunnel-dark, arched across the Manhattan Bridge. She breathed in deep; the space between the cables casting patterns across the floor: shadow and light, shadow and light. She had never been so far on her own, thrust not just out of Brooklyn but up in the sky, the East River blue beneath her. Remembering her father's stories of swimming in the river, she looked expectantly toward the train doors: as if she might see a diving board, as if she might see her father, pink with the thin muscles of youth, scissoring through the gray air, body braced to meet the water.

Nothing: just the steel girders, one after the other after. One, two, three, she counted, one, two, three.

It wasn't until after the train slipped back beneath the sidewalk that Sima realized someone was watching her. She became aware of a concentrated presence across the aisle, looked away from the window and toward the source of this stillness.

The man smiled.

He wore a hat pulled low to one side; Sima thought, but couldn't be sure, that he winked at her. Her cheeks warmed as she registered his gaze, lowered her own eyes to her hands.

Well? the man's look seemed to ask when she dared another quick glance.

Well nothing, Sima answered silently, concentrating on the crooked edge of her thumbnail.

The receptionists wore white uniforms, their hair smoothed back underneath their caps; when they passed her forms to complete Sima could smell the soft scent of baby powder on their hands. She answered their questions quickly: her name, her address, her husband's occupation. She didn't realize she was nervous until, hearing her name called, she was suddenly overcome with hunger, fought the urge to vomit.

The doctor looked like the doctors on the soaps, his light brown hair perfectly peppered with gray and his mustache trim above his lips. He leaned forward across his desk, shook her hand warmly. "What can we do for you, Mrs. Goldner?" he asked, glancing at her file.

"I've been trying to get pregnant for almost two years," Sima said, a sense of failure as she spoke — unnatural woman, to need a doctor's help — "and nothing has happened."

"Quite common, absolutely," the doctor assured her, leaning back casually, balancing on his chair. He asked her a series of questions, and she answered clearly, trusting. She'd been married three years, never used the pill or an IUD, always had normal periods. She forced herself to answer even the most personal questions, blushing to tell him two to three times a week on average, though for the last four months she'd asked Lev to wait, taking her temperature each morning in the hope of, averting his gaze, "timing it right."

He nodded as she spoke, made her feel as if such troubles, to her a source of secret shame, were the most natural thing in the world. She was shy to show him her temperature charts — fumbling in her bag for the graph-paper pad, apologizing for the shaky lines sketched in the half-light of winter mornings — but he complimented them, pleased that they showed a regular pattern of ovulation.

Sima smiled, proud that she'd done her homework and without even being asked. She imagined announcing her pregnancy to him, how he'd grin, shake her hand, tell her that under those circumstances he didn't mind losing a patient —

The doctor leaned forward, hands clasped on the dark wood desk. "I should warn you, Sima, that the tests we'll need to perform can be," he paused, half-smiled, "somewhat uncomfortable."

Sima crossed her legs, folded her hands neatly in her lap. "I'll do whatever it takes," she said, taken by her own determination.

The doctor grinned, surprising Sima with the yellow of his teeth. "And your husband," he asked, "have you spoken with him about this? We do try to see couples together these days."

Sima assured the doctor that Lev knew she was there, but that it wasn't easy for him, a teacher, to get time off in the middle of the day. She didn't tell him about the argument they'd had a few nights before, when she realized he wasn't planning on coming with her.

"Find out how it works," he'd said, as he sat down at the kitchen table, anticipating dinner, "and then we can figure out a schedule that makes sense. But I can't just miss class for no reason —"

"No reason?" Sima asked, thinking of her body, her heart, her longings all centered, more and more, on a wish for a child so strong it almost physically ached. She'd canceled plans with Connie that week, stayed at home feigning sickness just to avoid the tightness she felt inside when she watched Connie cradle her baby, coo as her lips grazed his skin.

"The doctor's going to tell you not to worry," Lev told her.

"No?" Sima said, standing to check on the chicken. "Then why haven't I gotten pregnant in two years?"

"But it's only four months with that chart thing. Listen, Sima," he told her, as she opened the oven door, "If you want to see a doctor, I think that's fine, no reason not to. But it's not like you're being rushed to the emergency room or something. It's not like I need to miss work for this."

Sima lowered her head to the oven heat. "Okay," she said, too furious to protest further — he should understand, she shouldn't have to explain — "I'll go alone then." She'd prodded the chicken with a fork to check whether the juices ran clear, noted grimly the thin stream of blood that trickled forth.

The doctor nodded at her explanation of Lev's absence, his face unreadable. "Well then," he told her, "we'll begin with some blood tests and a basic pelvic exam and then take it from there." He outlined a course of action: a sperm sample from Lev and a series of "investigations" for her: a cervical mucus exam, an endometrial biopsy, a Rubin's gas insufflation test possibly followed by a hysterosalpingography. He said the strange words quickly, ticking each off on his fingers as if he were listing recipe ingrediants.

Sima nodded, did not ask questions. She was grateful for his attention, for the office of white coats and the smell of baby powder in the air, felt if she followed carefully the dotted line — one test after another, scheduled in time with her cycle — she'd receive her reward in the end. She gave her blood willingly, almost eager to bare the white of her arm to the nurse, and she did not cringe when the cold metal of the speculum pressed against her flesh — the doctor stepping between her legs as his hand disappeared inside her — reminded herself it was, like everything else, just a test.

10

"Sorry I'm late," Timna said, pulling off her jean jacket as she entered the shop. "We got back from Philly in the middle of the night, and I could barely get up this morning."

"Oh?" Sima asked, glancing at her watch as if she hadn't noticed the time, though she'd checked it repeatedly since coming downstairs twenty minutes before. "You want coffee? There's some upstairs."

"That'd be great, thanks." Timna raised her arms in a stretch; Sima looked quickly away. "And how was your weekend?" Timna asked. "Did you get that thing done — the leaves in the gutter?"

Sima nodded, embarrassed that she'd mentioned such a mundane chore to Timna. How pathetic she must sound, getting Lev to clean the gutters a major weekend event. Yet she had needed to hound him, and it was necessary: the old tree beside their house lost its foliage early; by the first week of October the roof gutter would be crowded with leaves that, left unchecked, would freeze and threaten collapse come winter.

She'd begun reminding Lev two weeks before, and the morning of the big event hurried him through his coffee. Lev protested, pointed out that since it was the only major task of the day, there was no need to rush. Sima didn't admit that she was afraid for him to have too much caffeine before he climbed up the ladder; instead said only that she knew him, and if he didn't do it first thing —

"It's Shabbos, Sima. Relax."

Sima took his coffee cup from the table, spilled it into the sink.

"Sima!"

She shrugged. "I'll make you more later. Come on, let's get to work."

In the first few years of their marriage they'd observed Shabbat: the proud walk to synagogue in their nicest clothing, Sima's heels pinching just enough that she would reach for Lev's hand, hold it close the final block before they separated inside the cool lobby beside the gold-leafed memorial Tree of Life. The women would hurry through one door and the men through another and the children choosing between as she nodded to Lev goodbye, found a seat in the women's section, and leaned in for "Did you see" and "Have you heard," pinning straight the lace circle on her head as she widened her eyes, and no, standing up, sitting down, she hadn't seen, she hadn't heard. Eventually she'd follow a few of the women out to the lobby so the children could play while they talked, every now and then pausing to call shush as they exchanged their news, the women waiting for the service to end and Sima waiting for the day when her child would join them.

After services there would be a long lunch with friends: the afternoon sun playing on the table, the sleepy fullness of too much bread and wine. They'd return home to the pleasure of an afternoon nap, the luxury of turning to touch each other in the middle of the day, and with the coming of evening a new sense of freedom.

Saturday nights had their own rituals back then, as special, it seemed to Sima, as the lighting of the candles, the blessing over the bread and wine. "What should I wear?" Sima would ask, emerging from the bathroom in evening makeup: black mascara instead of the usual brown, red lips rather than pink. Lev would turn off the television while he considered, finally venturing a guess to make Sima laugh — "The purple? The blue?" — both of them knowing he never noticed what she wore, rarely remembered to compliment an outfit.

"Well," she'd say, turning to him after she'd dressed, "how about this, is this okay?"

"Yeah," Lev would tell her, smiling, "that one's all right."

They'd hold hands as they walked out the door, on their way to a restaurant or a movie or, a few times a year, a show, the city all lights and waiting for them. And when at the end of the evening he reached for the keys in the small tiled square of their apartment building lobby, held the door open for her to enter, he'd ask, "Did you have a nice time?" and she'd turn to him, her young husband, and say yes.

But things changed. Her own children never racing through the synagogue lobby, forcing the women to call shush and an old man, entering late, to frown; her own business crowding the week, Friday and Saturday her only days off and too many chores, too many errands, to allow time to walk hand in hand to synagogue, linger over a long lunch with friends, indulge in an afternoon nap. So they stopped. As the years passed and the neighborhood became Hasidic, most of their friends moved to different areas: Marine Park, Flatbush, Canarsie. Sima and Lev stayed; her business was in Boro Park, and in the end that was all, she often thought, she had.

Sima watched nervously from the living room window as Lev leaned over the gutter. He was too old for this work, she thought, as she watched the wind blow the soft whiteness of his hair; they should have called a professional. When he seemed to be moving too quickly to maintain his balance, she yelled, "Lev, watch it!" nodding to herself to mark his progress as he moved along the roofline, her lips set thin.

Thank God, she thought when he finished, promising herself next year to find someone through the Yellow Pages, no need to go through such anxiety. But she thanked Lev for just a moment before noticing the dirt on his shoes, and what was he thinking wearing them inside?

"Mud everywhere," Sima told Timna, though really there'd been just a few scuffs on the floor, nothing her sock couldn't smooth over.

"Oh. That's too bad."

Sima nodded, struggled for what else to say. She wanted to make Timna laugh. "I mean, if I don't keep an eye on Lev there's no telling what he'll do." She looked at

Timna, lowered her voice. "Did I ever tell you the kitchen magnet story?"

Timna shook her head no.

"Oh, I have to — hold on, your coffee. Lev!" Sima called, moving toward the staircase. "Lev!"

"What?" The response came muffled through the door.

"Will you bring Timna some coffee? Coffee! No milk, one sugar!" She turned back to Timna, waved away her thanks. "It's no trouble, he's doing nothing all day anyway. So, this is hilarious, we had these magnets, I don't even know where we got them. They looked like cookies, glazed and with sprinkles." Sima made an O shape with her thumb and forefinger. "Well. There they were on the fridge I don't know how long, two years maybe. I mean, just there on the fridge where Lev could look at them every day."

Timna nodded, placed her hands on the back of her chair.

"One day, who knows why these things happen, one of the cookie magnets falls on the floor. First I know of it is I hear a scream from the kitchen. I come running in —"

"And Lev had eaten the magnet?"

"Well, he bit into it," Sima said, disappointed that Timna had stolen the punch line. "Almost chipped his tooth. He was lucky, actually, because it costs a lot to get a chip filled and insurance doesn't pay. But can you imagine? To just see a cookie lying on the floor and, never mind it's a magnet, pick it up and eat it?"

Lev came down the steps with coffee for Timna, the cup cradled carefully in two hands and held away from his body to prevent spilling.

"Thank you," Timna said, taking the mug, "You have no idea how badly I needed this."

Lev shifted, opened his mouth to speak. "Lev," Sima said, dreading whatever ridiculous comment he might make, "customers will be here any minute. You need to get back upstairs." He looked at his watch, nodded, and, lifting his hand in a salute goodbye, left. Timna smiled up after him.

"So," Sima said, waiting until she had Timna's attention, "big weekend." She raised her eyebrows, excited to hear about it — she'd tell Lev the details that evening; it would make for a good story.

Timna nodded. "Especially last night," she said, putting her coffee on the sewing table, taking some hand cream out of a drawer. "Nurit's into music, and there were a bunch of shows in town —" Timna rubbed the cream between her hands, massaging —

133

"and last night the band just kept going. It was after two by the time we left."

"And your cousins don't mind, you coming in so late?" Sima had her doubts about the moral backbone of those cousins; they never came to the shop, seemed to take no interest in Timna's life.

"Oh, I stayed at Shai's so I wouldn't wake them."

Sima stared a moment, actually shocked. "And where does Shai live, with his brother?" She knew she shouldn't pry, but didn't like it: Timna staying out late, sleeping at strangers' houses.

"No, he lives in the East Village. This apartment, Sima, you would love it. Half the walls are brick and there's this huge marble fireplace, and the bathroom is so old that to flush the toilet you need to pull on a chain —"

Sima looked at her, wondered why Timna thought she'd like anything of the sort.

"And his bedroom window overlooks this community garden that's taken care of by a Puerto Rican group. It's the most amazing garden — there are these massive squash, just huge, and benches where you can sit, and this big statue of a frog that kids can climb into." She took a sip of coffee. "It's like an oasis, right in the middle of the city."

Sima looked at Timna. "That's quite a view to have from a bedroom." She thought of Alon, sent a silent message to him: *you better come soon.* "No wonder you're late, the train must have taken an hour —"

"I borrowed his car. We have to take it back to New Jersey this evening, anyway."

Sima was about to ask, he lends you his car?, but the doorbell chimed as someone entered the shop. "Mrs. Gilman," Sima said, kissing the elderly woman who came inside, glad to escape Timna's terrible story, each detail worse than the last, "I've been thinking about you." Mrs. Gilman's hands shook lightly in Sima's clasp. "I just got a shipment," Sima said, gesturing vaguely toward the shelves of boxes, "they call them arthritis bras. Front-close Velcro. I tried it myself, it never opened."

"Velcro?" Mrs. Gilman's mouth wavered at the edges, a slight turn downward.

"You won't have to fumble with hooks or snaps; I'm telling you, you'll love it. Timna?" Sima was relieved to see she'd put down the coffee, gone to get the bras. "Okay, Timna will help you. I just need to run to the bathroom."

Sima ran the water in the sink while she looked at herself in the mirror, shaking her head at the grim, set face that looked back

135

at her. It's not your life, she told herself, it's not your business; let her lose Alon if she chooses, he's not yours to keep.

She turned off the tap, unconvinced.

While Sima waited for her next doctor's appointment — hoping he would solve the mystery, fit the final puzzle piece in place — she dreamed of babies. On good mornings she couldn't remember her dreams, but on bad mornings she could, and though the nightmares were terrible, the dreams of love were worse.

At the supermarket the babies grew thin with hunger and slipped through the metal grating of the shopping carts to disappear in the fluorescent aisles. When she opened her mouth to ask the stockers if they had seen a child, she found herself asking instead for cans of beans, jars of pickles, so terrified was she to reveal what she'd done.

In the swimming pool she meant to dip the baby beneath the water just once but forgot to lift him up again. Weeds flourished along the bottom of the pool, and though she pulled at the plants with clenched hands so that the ground grew muddy between the slick tiles, still she could not find him. Or her own apartment was the scene of her crime — she put the baby in the bag just for a minute, for holding, but he fell so quietly beneath the plastic and when had he stopped breathing, exactly, and was it too late?

In those dreams she searched frantically for missing babies or crouched over the silent bodies of dead ones. They were so fragile, so easily killed, and she was the one forever lost and the regret like a casing around her soul: if only, if only, if only, her empty mouth condemned forevermore to call each day for a child who would never come.

She woke up from those dreams moist with sweat, her teeth clenched and her body curled. But in the shower she rinsed away the shadows and, thank God, she'd tell herself, it was all just a nightmare.

But then there were the other dreams.

It was always a boy. She held him and sang to him and rocked him to sleep. She bathed him, and his skin was warm and soft and there was light in the room; she lay beside him in bed and brought the covers above them, the two of them giggling under the soft weight of their secret world. She played with him in the green outside: blew rainbow bubbles, flew fish kites, bent her head toward the grass to trace the path of beetles, and as she showed him each piece of magic

— look, she would say, look — he leaned into her, his body loose with trust, and she wrapped her arms around him and breathed in the scent of his hair and inside felt a fullness that she knew was love and kissed her little boy and sighed with pleasure.

But when she woke up, how then to stop the cold air rushing in to the empty space, needling it like a tongue might worry the hollow where a tooth had been? She would bring her fist to her mouth and bite softly against the tears, but for days and days after she'd feel the loss.

11

"So we went first to Greenwich Village and did some shopping —"

"What did you buy?" Sima asked, bending over some open boxes on the counter, refolding the bras within.

"I bought a pair of jeans and an ankle bracelet. See?" Timna raised the edge of her pants, smiled as Sima admired the thin strap of silver that cut perfectly across her ankle. "I wasn't going to get it, but Shai made me. Anyway, then we walked to Central Park and went to the zoo. And then —"

"There's more?"

Timna laughed. "Shai said I was killing him, but I love walking in Manhattan — it's endless. But the zoo was relaxing. Have you been there recently?"

Sima shook her head no. She remembered, but didn't tell Timna, occasional Sundays at the children's zoo with Connie, when Nate and Howie were young. She and Connie

139

would sit on a bench talking while the boys ran between the attractions — the walk-in whale where Howie had once found a rat, the mock-castle's twisting staircase that smelled faintly of urine — every now and then returning to Connie, stepping between her knees as they explained something wonderful with tumbled-over words while Sima waited for the boys to finish, to allow her and Connie some time alone.

"So after the zoo, then what?" Sima asked, thinking as she looked at Timna how many years had passed since then — the old children's zoo had been completely renovated, she'd read somewhere, the whale and the castle, the rats and the urine, gone.

"We walked over to Lincoln Center to look at the fountain —"

"You really never stop, huh?"

"But by then we really were tired, so we just went for a drink somewhere. We sat in the bar three, maybe four hours — I thought the waitress was going to kill us."

Sima imagined Timna laughing in some darkened bar, dizzy with alcohol; replaced the lids on the open boxes before her. "And how does Alon feel about your going out with other men?" she asked, thinking: someone has to. "Does it bother him?"

Timna paused a moment before responding. "He knows to trust me. It's not like I can't have my own friends, my own life."

"Sure," Sima said, pretending distraction as she climbed the stepladder to return each box to its proper place, "It's only —"

"We're just friends. Shai knows about Alon; he understands." Timna spoke lightly, dismissively. "Like you said yourself, Sima, it's important for me to get around the city, meet people my own age."

Sima nodded, though she wasn't sure she still felt that way.

The door chimed. "I'm back!" Suzanne called, stepping inside the shop.

"Of course you are," Timna said. "We're addictive, aren't we?"

Suzanne sighed dramatically. "Well, my little brother's getting married, and his witch of a bride has decided we should all wear these cheap sky-blue bridesmaid dresses. Only when I say cheap, they actually cost a small fortune — they just look like something from a junior high prom."

Sima clucked in sympathy.

"And what makes it even worse — the other bridesmaids are all her twenty-something sorority friends. I have a decade on all of them at least, not to mention two kids, but we'll all be decked out in the same dress. I think she's trying to humiliate me."

141

"Ouch." Timna cringed.

"Exactly." Suzanne exhaled. "At any rate, I figured I could at least get the right lingerie for underneath. I need serious stomach control."

"Not a problem," Timna told her. "But have you tried speaking to your brother about it? I'm sure if you explain —"

Sima wagged her finger. "Never, ever contradict the bride. It's never worth it."

"Yeah? Too late for that. I kind of mentioned the dresses looked like something from *The Love Boat,* and my brother hasn't returned my calls in two days." While Timna fit her, Suzanne recounted the story for them both. Her brother, Adam, was ten years younger than she was. She adored him as a child, still had him for dinner two or three times a week. "My kids worship him," she told them. "He's sweet, he's funny, he's amazing. But this bitch got him on the rebound, and Adam's too easily taken advantage of —"

Sima nodded and sighed at the right moments. All the stories sounded the same after so many years, but still they tugged. Suzanne was lonely — anyone could see that.

"Let me bring you one of my sets," Timna said after fitting her for a bodysuit. "They're fantastic, and you need a pick-me-up."

Timna had begun purchasing for the shop a month earlier. Sima had encouraged it — she didn't want Timna to get bored. Now there were boxes filled with bright lace fabrics that she would never have chosen: animal prints; primary colors. She'd been skeptical. "Remember who our customers are," she'd told Timna, gesturing toward a rack of long-sleeved, ankle-length black velour robes — some of them even mock-turtle. But Timna had a knack for pushing boundaries, it seemed. She didn't show the new goods to every customer, but when she did, she sold them.

Sima gave Timna the stepladder, watched as she selected a few items for Suzanne. "These are from the 'Sunset Horizons' collection," Timna called out. "With your auburn hair —" She chose three bra-and-panty sets: peach, gold, and lavender, each with a red-lace trim.

Naming, even noticing, a collection, matching color to hair-dye — Sima had never done either. It felt gimmicky, yet she had to admit it worked.

Suzanne chose the peach bra-and-panty set. "Who knows," she said, as Sima rang up the purchase. "Maybe I'll catch the bouquet, hook up with the band leader, and live happily ever after, right?" She smiled bitterly, her eyes cold and bright.

Sima handed her the shopping bag. "It'll be better once the wedding is over," she said. "I see it all the time."

"Yeah, right. They're moving to Michigan, so I'll never get him back." Suzanne exhaled again. "Oh well, all good things, right?"

"Right," Sima said, thinking how had she missed it, and had Connie and Art noticed — Suzanne was one of the saddest women she knew.

Sima returned to the doctor a month after her first appointment. It was a comfort, almost, to be back, now that everything felt familiar: the waiting room with its yellow tweed sofas squared around a white rug; the ladies magazines she'd leafed through last time, too nervous to read, fanned on a small side table beside a crystal ashtray; the smooth curve of the receptionist's desk where she gave her name, watched as a young woman — dark hair, a quiet smile — checked her off a list. The doctor shook her hand warmly when he came into the waiting room, said, "Good to see you again," like he meant it.

Her blood tests had been normal, and Lev's sperm count too. "Congratulations," she'd told Lev, when they received the report, and he joked about it, pretended he was going to call the sample jar for another date. She laughed, feigned jealousy that he got to have all the fun, but was aware of a deeper envy, hidden: it was over for him; anything the doctor discovered now would be her fault.

"I guess you're off the hook, then," Sima told him, a false brightness in her voice.

"I guess so," he said, still smiling.

He was teasing, she knew, but it hurt like a slap and how wrong for him not to know, not to guess how alone she felt. She moved away to avoid his touch. "I have to check on the laundry," she told him, her voice wavering, "I told Mrs. Rosen that I'd knock when we were through with the dryer —"

"Sima," he called after, "it's not a competition —"

She was crying by the time she reached the stairwell, her feet quick on the tiled floor, her hand loose on the wrought-iron banister as she propelled herself down each flight. She'd worried about Lev's test, already imagined her reaction to the news: how she'd hold him, tell him she loved him, smooth his skin the way he liked — her fingers brushing upwards from his chin to his cheek, caressing — let him know it wasn't his failing, she didn't blame him. "It's not an end," she'd tell him, "but a new beginning." When they felt ready they'd adopt, and one day they'd tell their children, "We chose you, just like we chose each other."

But instead it was Lev who had called after her, his voice thick with the same soft pity she'd already rehearsed. "It's not a competition," he'd told her, and all she could think was: that's easy for you to say. Sima pushed open the heavy basement door, stepped inside the dim room: concrete floor coated with dust, splintered pieces of old wood stacked beside the cinderblock walls. Sima opened the dryer and gathered the warm clothing to her breasts, rocking slowly back and forth. She hated herself for the clarity of her longing: I wish it had been him, I wish it had been him.

"So, Sima," the doctor said as he entered the examining room, her file in one hand, a clipboard in the other, "let's see where we're at today."

Sima lay back, slipping her feet through the stirrups as he glanced at her file.

"You remembered to have intercourse within the last twenty-four hours?"

She nodded yes.

"Good girl," he told her, pushing her

knees apart. "We'll just get a sample of that sperm, then, to see if it's still active inside you —"

Sima turned her head to the side, trying not to hear what he said. The exposure of this most intimate of details, even more than her own body stretched around the speculum, filled her with shame.

The doctor inserted a thin tube inside her body, withdrew something small from deep inside. "There," he said, patting her knee, "we're nearly done, nearly done."

She passed the test.

"The sperm were active and abundant," he told her over the phone, "everything looked fine."

Sima held the receiver against her ear, unsure how to respond. She focused on the grocery list on the wall beside the phone: carrots, cucumber, tomato, thought about walking to the store to buy them, chopping them into neat squares. "Terrific," she told the doctor, "I'm so glad."

"It means your body isn't killing the sperm," he said. He paused for a moment to ask his secretary a question — Sima could make out a few words, something about his brother-in-law, had he called — and Sima thought that at least it would make for an amusing report: guess what, she'd tell Connie, turns out I'm not a sperm murderer.

"Where were we?" he asked. "Oh, right, the next test. So we'll do the endometrial biopsy. Take a sample from the uterine lining, make sure your uterus is able to support a fetus —"

"Oh," Sima said, "okay, that sounds fine," and when Connie called that evening, Sima did not joke about the test results, terrified that despite having passed one test, it was only a matter of time until her body betrayed her on another.

12

"Are you feeling okay?" Sima asked as Timna pitched her empty coffee cup into the garbage. Timna's hair was pulled back into a ponytail, her mascara smudged below her eyes.

"I'm fine."

"Your cousins okay?"

"They're fine. Everyone's excited because Leah, that's their daughter, got a promotion at work."

"That's good."

Timna nodded, pulled an old *Vogue* magazine across the counter.

Sima looked, saw there was a pull to her lips, some sadness scratched there. She opened her mouth to ask why, but paused, unsure she wanted the answer. Still, she stole sidelong glances at Timna, noted the way Timna wrapped her hands in the sleeves of her sweater like a child.

It was distracting, Timna's sadness. Sima

tried to concentrate on her books, and though usually she blamed Timna's stories for taking her attention away from the accounts — before Timna arrived she'd always been organized about bookkeeping, but now she'd take three hours to add a column, putting down her pen to ask a question or giggle over a comment like a teenager on a study date — it was her silence she now found disruptive. She could hear the garbage truck on its uneven path outside, the scream of the brakes and the creak of its metal jaws, the scuff of the garbage cans tossed to the sidewalk, spinning on their edges before settling. Sima lowered her head to her hands, lightly closed her eyes.

It wasn't that Timna was always in a good mood — she was tired sometimes, or had a headache, but Sima had never seen her sad. "Why is that?" she'd asked Lev once. "Why is she never homesick?"

Lev said something about being young, experiencing new things.

"Sure," Sima told him, "but still, to be so far away for so long, and not to miss home. And even Alon — Timna talks about him all the time, and it's obvious she loves him, but she never seems to fight with him or worry about him, fear that he'll meet someone else or that they'll drift apart."

"So she's young and happy," Lev had told her. "So are lots of people. You may not know this, Sima, but there's nothing that strange about being happy."

"Very funny," Sima had said, thinking of course he wouldn't anticipate a young woman's sadness, of course he wouldn't know.

Helene Neuman's daughter Nechama came in for an exercise bra; Sima grabbed a few and followed Nechama, along with her three-year-old son, her two-year-old daughter, and a baby in a carriage, to the dressing room. Nechama's son leaned against her leg as she unbuttoned her blouse, took off her bra. He had long blond curls that would be cut for the first time in a week — Nechama had already started cleaning the house to prepare for visiting relatives who wanted to witness the rite of passage.

"I'll never lose the weight from this baby," Nechama said, sighing at her reflection in the mirror: the heavy breasts full with milk. "With Yossi and Leah it was bad, but this time my whole body aches."

Sima fastened the bra across Nechama's back, tugged at one of the straps. "You need to sleep in a bra is all — your body needs more support."

"My mother used to sleep in a bra. I

151

always swore I never would. And here I am, not even thirty —"

"And with three children. Give it a few months; you know that. A few months from now you'll hardly remember the ache." Sima moved in front of Nechama, looked at the bra. "Too narrow," she said, shaking her head, "I don't like the way the cups pinch like that." She reached for another.

Nechama nodded, unhooked the bra, and held it out for Sima. "You're right, you know," she said as she slipped the other bra over her head, pulled it down over her swollen breasts, "I'll hardly remember the ache, and then I'll be pregnant again in a year." She nodded with her chin toward the baby carriage. "I know they're a blessing. But Sima, I get so tired sometimes."

"This bra is better for you," Sima told Nechama, forcing a finger underneath the thick cotton straps, "See? Almost no give, but it doesn't pinch."

Nechama frowned at her reflection. "It makes me look like I have just one breast."

"That's what an exercise bra does," Sima said, "presses you down so you won't bounce. Flattering it's not, but it does the trick." She held her hand out for the bra; waited while Nechama pulled it off over her head. "Now, I'll get you a sleeping bra,"

Sima told her, "something cotton, without underwire."

As she closed the curtain behind her, she glanced at Timna, who was staring absently out the window. There was nothing to see: the cement wall of the outdoor staircase; a few thin cracks curved unevenly as if drawn by a child's hand.

"Timna, you sure you're okay?" Sima asked, a slight tease in her voice to hide her concern.

Timna shook her head, smiled. "Sorry. Just tired, I guess."

Sima nodded, wanted to ask Timna more — thought Timna would want to say more — but Timna simply turned back toward the sewing table and began cleaning up the remains of that morning's breakfast: a paper bag from a chain doughnut shop, a Styrofoam coffee cup stuffed with damp napkins.

Yossi was leaning over the baby's carriage when Sima reentered the dressing room. Nechama smiled at her son, but when she turned back toward the mirror, the sleep bra on, she took his hand firmly in her own. "When Leah was two weeks," she whispered to Sima, "Yossi started stroking her cheek, soft like that. Then when I went into the other room, he pinched her so hard her skin turned blue." She looked at him, sighed.

"He begged me for a little brother this time," she told Sima as she posed sideways in the mirror, checked the fit, "he thinks I made another girl on purpose, and he's angry with me."

"He'll be all right," Sima told her. "Next week he'll get all the attention at his first haircut, and then he'll be proud to be the only boy." Sima glanced over at Yossi. "Such beautiful curls he has. It's really something, cutting them."

Nechama followed Sima's gaze. "It breaks my heart to think of him without those curls. He won't be my little boy anymore. Even this, even just being here with him in the dressing room — he'll have to start waiting outside."

"It's just a curtain."

"It's more than that."

At the register Nechama pulled out folded bills from the change purse of her wallet, one eye on her son as he slowly pushed the carriage, his whole body leaning into it, back and forth before the counter. Sima gave her the bras in a plastic bag, dark brown with gold diamonds, which Nechama asked Yossi to hold for her. He cradled it carefully, proud of such an adult responsibility.

Timna held the door open and helped Nechama negotiate the carriage up the steps; Sima could hear her outside, complimenting the children, calling goodbye.

Sima didn't hesitate this time.

Something was wrong for Timna to be so sad; she'd follow her just a little bit, to see if anything came up. She rushed up the stairs, calling, "Lev! I'm going out!" even as she slipped on her coat, fumbled for her keys. Just before closing the door she grabbed a paisley scarf from its hook inside the front closet, threw it over her hair, and knotted it under her neck, not quite admitting it was for disguise.

Timna was still within sight.

Sima hurried after her, slowing when she came within twenty feet. Her breath was ragged from rushing; she watched, everything suddenly still, as Timna turned her head to the side, registering the heavy breath behind her.

A cell phone rang. Thank you, Sima silently intoned as Timna paused to unzip her purse, check the number on the phone. "Nurit!" she cried out as she brought the phone to her ear, "What's up?"

Sima moved in pace behind Timna, who spoke rapidly in Hebrew, gesturing with her free hand as they walked up one block and along another, passing the corner where Timna should have turned for her cousin's house.

Where is she going, Sima wondered, thinking an apartment building, an empty lot, and thank goodness she was there to watch over her. She crossed the street when Timna said goodbye, forewarned by the series of "okays" that proceeded it. She felt proud of her sleuthing — such discreet choreography, to know the right moment to cross. But then two Hasidic teenage boys passed Timna too closely — they should have stepped aside for extra space — and while Sima watched, they turned around, one play-punching the other's arm as they grinned after Timna.

Sima looked away, appalled at how low she'd sunk.

Timna turned onto 16th Avenue and stopped into a small convenience store; Sima watched for her from the windowed ATM room of a bank across the street. It was a store Sima had never been to, though like so many others she had: outside the plate-glass windows, plastered with fluorescent signs promising calling cards and a sale on Half-n-Half, a *Daily News*–sponsored blue wooden rack was stacked high with newspapers. A kerchiefed woman sat on the ground beside the stand, held out a paper coffee cup for change.

Timna emerged from the store, a glossy magazine tucked under one arm, just as a bus pulled up. How does she time it so well, Sima thought, watching as Timna paused before the driver to insert and retrieve her metrocard before pushing her way through the crowd.

The bus pulled away, and Timna was gone. Impossible to follow her further, though Sima suspected she'd take the bus to the subway station, and from there into the city. It was getting dark already; it'd be nearly night by the time she arrived. Sima shook her head, too late to protest, and slowly made her way home.

Another month gone, a series of slashes through the daily boxes of her calendar until Sima reached the appointment she'd recorded there, her neat handwriting a direct contrast to the dread she felt: the doctor again, the uterine biopsy. She struggled to stay alert during the early morning subway ride, aware of the men around her, their eyes. There were so many people on the subway, so many strangers, and to be pressed so close — someone else's thigh warm against her own as the train jostled them together — was an intrusion Sima had never before experienced.

At first she kept her lips pressed tight, her eyes on the advertisements, windows, floors — not wanting to smell or see. But then she began to sneak looks, stare: the faded outline of a bull tattooed on the arm of a middle-aged Italian man, one hoof raised, ready to run; the proud shadow of a mustache above the chapped lips of a Puerto Rican teenager, blue-pen scribbles covering his canvas sneakers.

How strange she thought, as she scanned the subway car, that each one here had once been cooed over, doted on: white ribbons carefully tied beneath their soft chins, scallop-trimmed cotton hats centered on wispy-haired scalps. Each had been a baby like the one she coveted, now grown to mediocrity: this one a mole on her chin with the obligatory curl jutting from it; another a pale belly not quite concealed by a gray oil-stained tee. Had this ugliness not always existed? Were the large pores, the gummy smiles, the stink of slick-backed hair — a stripe of grease still glistening on a yellow-nailed finger — really once concealed beneath a newborn's smooth-skinned perfection?

She'd always thought of the subway as

both exciting — the giddy rush of escape as she surged under the city — and terrifying — the people pressed tight together the same she would flee from on a dark street. Up close, though, she saw it was neither. There was no mystery among strangers, just the same imperfections arranged in different ways. She began to smile whenever she caught someone's eye, an innocuous niceday smile, thinking how far she'd come, already, to relax on the subway, a stranger in a strange land.

And then she knew her way to the doctor's office — two long blocks, two short — could casually tell the elevator boy "Twelve," as she checked her reflection in the gilt-edged mirror, not caring if he caught her glance. And the receptionist smiled when she entered the room, asking "And how are you today?" and the doctor shook her hand when he saw her, said, "Ah, there you are."

But then the gown; the cold table; the long wait before a cracked-open door for the doctor to reenter, for it all to begin again.

She closed her eyes not to see the long needle, managed to stay silent but for a slight whimper when they inserted it into her spine. She felt nothing when they rolled her onto her back, spread her ankles and secured them in stirrups, inserted scissors deep inside to cut a tiny piece of tissue, a little flag to wave around the lab.

Sima didn't smile on the subway ride home, instead stared out the windows at the dark tunnel walls, waiting to catch the moment they'd emerge into light.

13

Timna arrived to work rain-wet: her hair pressed to her head and dull with water, her blue jeans and black sweater damp against her body.

"What, they don't make umbrellas in Israel?" Sima asked.

"It doesn't usually rain like this there," Timna replied, almost defensive. She wiped her nose with the back of her hand, flipped her hair toward the ground, and tried to dry it with a few squares of paper towel.

"Enough," Sima told her, smiling, "you're soaking the floor. Come upstairs and we'll get you dry. I must have something that can fit you."

Timna followed Sima up the stairs and into the kitchen, where Lev sat reading the *New York Times.* "There's an interesting article in here about Israeli youth," he began, as soon as Timna entered the room, "it says that —"

"Lev, what are you, blind? This girl is soaked. Come, Timna, go into the bedroom and then give me your clothing. I'll put it all in the dryer."

Timna winked at Lev. "I like hearing about articles," she told Sima, "I've learned more about Israel being here —"

"You're a real peacemaker, huh?" Sima said, shaking her head. "Well, that's not the job of an Israeli." Sima led Timna down a short hall lined with framed pictures: sea-birds, a woods scene somewhere. At the end of the hall she opened a door. "Change here," she said, her hand sweeping across their bedroom. "You can wear my robe — it's on the bathroom door."

Lev looked up when Timna returned to the kitchen in a green terrycloth robe, her hair pushed back behind her ears revealing her long neck. Sima caught Lev's glance and the slight blush that followed, thought, with some satisfaction, that she'd seen Timna in less.

"There won't be customers this morning anyway," Sima said, taken with how beautiful Timna looked dressed even in her old robe, the worn material all soft folds along her body. "I should have just told you not to come," she said, reluctantly turning away as she took Timna's wet clothes to the dryer, "but here you are, so you might as well stay a little. It's supposed to be like this all day — heavy rains and winds."

"It doesn't matter," Timna told her, "if I wasn't here I'd just be moping around my cousins'." She sat down at the table, her feet tucked under her body. Lev brought her coffee, which she sipped as he described the article to her. He spoke quickly, his eyes on the paper; when he raised his head Sima saw his eyes linger just a moment on the soft shadow of cleavage visible at the robe's opening.

How long, Sima wondered, since she'd seen his eyes linger on her body? How much longer since she'd wanted them to?

"Since he retired," Sima told Timna, noticing how the faded green of the robe matched perfectly Timna's olive eyes, "he goes out every morning to get the paper. We used to have a subscription; he canceled it. This is his joy," Sima said, gesturing toward Lev, "a daily trip to the newsstand."

Lev rubbed a coffee stain off the dark wood table. "A walk and the paper," he told Timna, "these are the good things in life."

"He reads it all morning. All morning, right, Lev?"

Lev paused before answering. "Most days."

163

"Most days. And then what?" Sima looked at Lev. "The TV?"

Lev traced a finger absently across the table.

"The TV," Sima said.

Lev looked at her and frowned; Sima shrugged. He turned away to where the rain came down in sideways wind-blown sheets, staining the concrete square of their back-yard a darker shade of gray, filling the uncovered garbage cans with brown water.

They drank coffee and shared the paper while they waited for Timna's clothing. Sima ignored the whine of the dryer, but Lev jumped up immediately, quickly retreating to the den so Timna could dress in the laundry room off the kitchen.

"Do you need a bathrobe?" Sima asked, as Timna stood to change. "You can keep it if you want — it looks a thousand times better on you than it does on me."

Timna looked surprised. "Oh," she said. "Thanks, but I don't usually wear one —"

"Well, maybe you should start. I'm telling you, it looks terrific —"

"That's so generous of you," Timna told her as she entered the laundry room, "But really, I'm okay."

"Are you sure? Because I should get a new one anyway, and the green matches your eyes so well —" It felt suddenly important, to give Timna that little piece of her own life. She could imagine Timna wearing it on a rainy day, curled up beside Alon, or, even better, pregnant, the robe's roominess just right as she'd pull the soft fabric across her belly —

"Thank you," Timna called back, "but I don't think I'd wear it. I mean, it was perfect for this morning, but —"

Sima bit her lip as she imagined the rest of the sentence: perfect for this morning when sitting around with just her and Lev, but not something she'd otherwise be caught dead in. An old robe, faded and stretched and dull — just right for herself, but nothing Timna could possibly want.

"So speaking of rain," Sima said, to change the subject, "A little rain like this shouldn't be such a big deal for you. I picture you in the army, running through the mud, water streaming down your face —"

"Right, like Rambo. In the army I taught Hebrew to Russian immigrants — I wasn't exactly wearing face paint and crouching in the bushes. Some of the women, the ones who train the men, they get to do some real soldier stuff."

"The women really train the men?"

"Sure," Timna said, reentering the

165

kitchen, her jeans, Sima noticed, that much tighter from the dryer. "They watch over a unit during basic training, organize things. A bunch of my friends did it. But it's difficult — you're supposed to care for these guys like a mother, but they're your age. And when someone gets a crush —"

Sima nodded, her head lowered as she watched Timna pull on a pair of lavender socks, her ankle bracelet disappearing under the cotton. "I always liked working just for myself," Sima told her, "not having to answer to anyone else."

"And Lev?" Timna asked. "He seems lonely now, no?"

Sima looked up. "What does Lev know of lonely?"

Timna didn't respond.

"I mean, it's not like he has friends —"

Sima paused, ashamed by the look Timna gave her: a frown like that you'd give a child caught acting badly. Though she usually reacted defensively to such judgment — what does she know, Sima might have once said — she couldn't bear to have Timna disappointed with her.

"You know what," Sima said, standing, "why don't you stay here with Lev, keep him company a little while. I need to catch up on the books, but you might as well sit, relax until the storm passes." She noted with pleasure Timna's approval — she smiled, said call me if you need anything.

In the basement Sima listened to their laughter, swallowed her jealousy as she congratulated herself on making him happy, just this once.

■ ■ ■ ■

NOVEMBER

■ ■ ■ ■

14

Sima heard the laughter just before Timna's friends entered, touched her hands to her hair to check for smoothness. Timna had asked a week ago whether she could bring Shai and Nurit to the shop. "I tell them so much about it, they want to see for themselves." Sima had agreed, assuring Timna she'd love to meet them, though she knew she was being duplicitous — she didn't trust these new friends, this new life. She looked up only after Timna called hello, pretended surprise — "Oh, I wasn't expecting —"

"Sima," Timna said, still flushed with some joke, "This is Shai and Nurit."

Sima stepped out from behind the counter, shook their hands, said what was expected: an exchange of I've-heard-so-much-about-you, so-nice-to-finally-meet-you. She tried not to look too closely at Shai — he was good-looking, tall and broad with brown, curly hair that hung just a little into his eyes — for fear of being too impressed.

Sima looked up every now and again as Timna, speaking quickly in Hebrew, showed Nurit and Shai around the shop. Nurit, Sima decided, was not a nice girl. As a rule she never trusted friendships between unattractive women and beautiful women, and Nurit, bony, awkward, her dyed-red hair flat against a pale, narrow face, was too plain not to envy Timna. There was that, and then Sima did not like the way Nurit touched a slip here, a nightgown there, rubbing the fabric between her fingers as if she was entitled to it. Still, she had to admit that Nurit and Timna seemed close — they touched each other when they talked, and sometimes one or the other would bend her knees in laughter, smile wide with pleasure.

Shai stood awkwardly during those moments. Like Sima, he seemed separate from the two, and in the shrugs and apologetic smiles he tried to exchange with her when the girls laughed was a vulnerability that, Sima had to admit, was appealing.

But she drew the line at returning his smile. There was Alon to think of, and if Timna couldn't be loyal — well, she could be.

"Sima," Timna asked, grinning, "Should I show them the old people's lingerie?"

172

Sima cringed as the two girls giggled over the thick canvas of the corsets. It was her fault — she'd made fun of the pieces herself one of Timna's first weeks there. "I told Connie," she'd told Timna, "when it comes down to me wearing one of these, shoot me." Timna was speaking in Hebrew, maybe repeating the exact line for Nurit.

"Look at this, Shai," Nurit called, and Sima turned to see Nurit seize a training bra left on the sewing table, drape it across her chest. Sima frowned: the truth was Nurit had only a little more than that — if she were Nurit she wouldn't call attention to that fact. Timna, laughing, pulled a purple silk bathrobe off the rack, slipped it over her clothing, and modeled with one arm out like a game show girl. Sima wanted to object — customers would come soon — but as she looked at Timna, sharing the gaze with Shai and Nurit, she lost the words: the purple fabric fell against Timna's body in soft sweeps; she looked too wonderful to resent.

The door opened, and Rivkah Shapiro entered. Timna hurried to replace the robe on the rack while Sima approached Rivkah, taking her hands in her own. "Mazel Tov," she told her, "your sister was here last week and told me the news." She pulled back, glanced down Rivkah's body. "I'd hardly notice if she hadn't warned me — you're barely showing. How far along are you again?"

"Four months," Rivkah told her, glancing at Shai. "You really can't tell? I think I look huge."

"You're tiny. But never mind, the first time women can't wait to start showing, then by the end when you're carrying around this pumpkin everywhere you go" — Sima held her hands before her, rounded across an imaginary belly, "you'll wonder why you ever wished for it." She turned to Timna, who was making plans to see Shai and Nurit after work. "Timna, why don't you go too? Rivkah can always pick up any alterations later —"

Rivkah nodded.

"And this way you can show them around the neighborhood a bit."

Timna hesitated, but Sima insisted, urging her to show them the local businesses: the groceries and bakeries, the discount shoe stores and upscale clothing shops. "You can do better here than anywhere in Manhattan, and they have every Israeli product you can think of. Go, go," she said, waving them off, "and take your time."

As the three stepped out of the shop, Sima

could hear Nurit say, "Nice boss," and she felt proud, for a moment. But as she moved the stepladder along the shelves and climbed three rungs toward the boxes, she realized what a pushover she'd been, so desperate to win the approval of Timna's friends that she'd sent her out the door just as a customer arrived. She remembered how Lev used to complain about teachers who tried too hard to be popular and ended up behaving worse than their students. She was becoming no better.

Sima was surprised to see Timna return ten minutes later, just as Rivkah was trying on the first of three support bras.

"I can't believe I've gone up an entire cup size already," Rivkah said, clearly pleased.

"And when the milk comes in, you'll go up another. Come back two, three weeks before your due date and we'll fit you for a couple of early nursing bras. You want a few that are really soft and stretchy — as comfortable as can be for those first weeks."

Rivkah nodded, drawing in her breath slightly as Sima pressed her hands across each cup.

"Then, when everything's settled down again, say when the baby is six weeks, come back, and we'll take these bras you buy today and make them into nursing bras for the long haul." Sima stood back, looked at Rivkah. "That fits well. You like it?"

Rivkah nodded.

"Okay, slip back on your shirt and see how it looks."

"I didn't realize," Rivkah said, buttoning her blouse, "that you made nursing bras —"

"This one," Sima said, pointing at Timna, "does it. She just cuts the shoulder strap where it meets the bra, adds a hook and," she waved her hand in small circles like a magician unveiling a rabbit from a top hat, "Voilà. Right, Timna?"

Timna grinned. "Right."

As Sima rang up Rivkah, Naomi Cantor stopped by looking for underwear, followed by Florence's daughter-in-law, Tamar, who bought three camisoles with support shelves, and then two women Sima had never met who came, they told her, all the way from Toronto. When the shop finally cleared in the early afternoon, Sima turned to Timna, asked if she wanted anything from the kitchen. "I need a cup of coffee," Sima said, moving toward the stairs, "I haven't stopped for one second all morning —"

Timna looked up from behind the seamstress table. "Sima," she said, "before you go —"

Sima paused, one hand on the banister.

176

"About this morning —"

"Don't worry about it," Sima said. "I didn't mind you bringing your friends by, and thought it'd be nice —"

But Timna shook her head, said she felt bad leaving work like that. "This is the best job I've ever had," she told Sima, sweeping a few loose threads from the sewing table into her palm. "When I came to New York, I was so terrified, I've never been so nervous in my life. But since getting this job, it's like everything fell into place: I had work, so then I could relax and meet people, have fun too." She closed her hand around the threads. "If it wasn't for you, I'd still be crying on the phone to Alon every night."

"That's nice to hear," Sima said, though she was unsure whether to be flattered or alarmed — her shop the stable base that gave Timna the courage to explore.

"Anything else?"

Mario himself served their table, one hand clapped casually on Art's shoulder. Sima and Lev had been meeting Art and Connie at Mario's for nearly two decades. The restaurant had not changed much in that time: red carpet, stone-mural walls, white stalactite-stucco ceiling trimmed with plastic grapevines. On a shelf beside the kitchen entrance stood three old-fashioned wicker wine carafes and a terra-cotta donkey pulling a cart; at the take-out counter a crystal bowl of pastel mints, the silver spoon always mid-plunge.

They sat in the corner. They drank red wine, ate baked pastas. A Saturday night every six, eight weeks — Connie liked to joke that each meal kept her full until their next visit.

"More coffee?" Mario asked.

They all demurred, and Mario promised the check.

"Where was I?" Sima asked. She had been telling a Timna story: how she had celebrated a friend's birthday on the Staten Island Ferry with a bottle of champagne. Five of them had ridden it back and forth for two hours; totally free and the same view as the cruise lines. "I didn't know anything in New York was free these days," Sima said.

"Aren't all the best things free?" Art asked, running a hand down Connie's arm.

Connie turned to him, rolled her eyes. "Thanks, Art. That's really romantic."

He laughed.

"Anyway," Connie told him, "you don't know how this Timna character has shaken things up. In what, just two months — ?"

"Three —"

"Three months and Sima's selling stuff she's never carried before. Bikinis, in November no less. Bikinis!" '

"From the men of Boro Park," Art said, "let me say thank you. You have taken things up a notch. That peach outfit, with the red trim —"

Connie looked at him, considering. "What peach red trim?"

"You know, the lacy number."

Sima saw it emerge, this new truth. She didn't want to see it, but there it was: gleaming, exposed, undeniable.

She felt calm and detached, the world slowing as it had once when an oncoming car had sped through a red light as she advanced through green. She'd seen the car, thought: it's going to hit me. She braked hard; wrenched the wheel. In the end it just grazed her bumper, but it was a close enough call that when she pulled over to catch her breath, a knot of pedestrians gathered beside her, shaking their heads.

She looked to see what Art would do, strangely curious. He could laugh. He could say he was just teasing, it was a dream, it was a joke, it was a fantasy. But instead, he stammered. Blushed. Looked ridiculous the way only a man caught cheating could.

"It's Alzheimer's, isn't it?" Connie asked, smiling.

Art looked at Sima. Please, he was saying, his eyes wide and terrified, Don't. She looked back at him, the high screech of the brakes still reverberating in her ears.

"What?" Connie asked, catching their silent exchange. "What's the big secret?" When they didn't respond, she tried again. "What, did I ruin a lingerie birthday surprise?"

Mario approached with the check. He laid it on the table with his usual flourish but then, sensing something, quickly retreated.

Sima nodded at Lev: it was their turn to treat. She knew even he had caught on by the speed with which he reached for his wallet, counted out the cash.

"Sima?" Connie asked, her voice high, needy. "Am I supposed to ask you who's been buying peach bras or something like that?"

Sima looked straight at her. There was still time to brake, but Timna's voice was in her ear. Be brave, it said, tell the truth. Don't let fear win.

Sima whispered, "Suzanne."

A whimper from Connie. Art lowered his head.

"I'm so sorry," Sima said, already feeling

the inadequacy of her words. At her mother's funeral the rabbi had handed her a shovel, and though she'd thought she couldn't take it, she had. She held the shovel, scooped up dirt, listened to the tinny sound of small rocks bouncing against her mother's coffin.

The things we do, she'd thought then.

She'd done the same, now, to Connie.

Sima stood; Lev followed. They left them in silence.

"Come on," Connie had said, rocking Nate's stroller with one hand while she stirred her coffee with the other, "Let's go shopping or something. You deserve a treat, after what you've been through — all those tests and damn appointments." Connie waved her hand absently, as if conjuring up the times Sima had been made to lie naked but for the green gown on a cold table, legs bent. Nate grabbed the sugar spoon from her hand as it passed close, put it in his mouth. "You know my cousin Frieda, the one with the hip problem I told you about —"

Sima nodded, yes, as Connie retrieved her spoon from Nate. He cried out to see it go, but Connie moved it quickly from the sugar bowl to her coffee back to his mouth —

silencing him. Watching, Sima decided that later she'd throw out the remaining sugar, refill the bowl. It disgusted her, actually, to think how the infant saliva would clot the sugar; she was, she realized, becoming hard, bitter.

Connie smiled at Nate. "He's a screamer, huh?" she said, lightly tickling his toes, which curled just a little on contact. "Howie was so quiet I used to worry whether he was mute. Sometimes I think Nate's a punishment for that worry, for not appreciating a good thing when I had it." She brushed a sweaty curl off his forehead.

Sima tapped her fingers against the side of her coffee mug, a little impatient for Connie's interrupted story. "Frieda's the one who used to come in for Passover each year, right?" Sima asked, prompting her.

"Exactly," Connie said, bending down to kiss Nate's forehead, "because her parents became communists," she whispered the word, "and stopped observing. Anyway, she couldn't have a baby for the longest time and they tried everything, all sorts of tricks —"

"What tricks?"

"Oh, nothing really. Nothing I can remember. Vitamins or something, I think. But anyway, the point is that nothing worked and meantime she's getting crazy — Max says she was screaming about something different every night. At the bris he said — it was hilarious — 'Either she was going to get pregnant or I was going to kill her — no two ways about it.' Anyway, they go on vacation to the Bahamas, and boom, she relaxes and a week later she's pregnant."

"What? From relaxing?"

"Yeah."

"That's the big secret, relaxing?" Sima leaned back in her chair, disappointed. Though she told herself there was no magic word, no special trick to discover, still she kept searching for the answer, the thing that would bring the baby. A few months before, she'd been grocery shopping on 13th Avenue, negotiating her way between the women pushing strollers and the sidewalk displays of fruit, shoes, fabric, when an old woman had passed her, close. The woman's wig was jet black despite her wrinkled face, and it sat too far back on her head, exposing her cropped hair, but her eyes, deep gray, stared at Sima with something like recognition and, Sima thought then, something like a promise. Sima had smiled, helped the woman, who struggled to navigate a shopping cart of groceries, to cross the street, and then to her house and up the brick steps to her door. The old woman hardly spoke but nodded her thanks as they walked, and Sima was reminded of the stories she'd read as a child, angels coming down to earth disguised as beggars, bringing riches to the young woman who helped at the well or the poor couple who shared their last cup of wine. Maybe, Sima had allowed herself to think, this woman will bring me a baby.

When Lev returned home that afternoon, Sima was waiting for him. As he joked over dinner that night, obviously pleased, she'd pounced.

Though her period came again, despite the old woman with the black wig, despite her own clenched-hand wishes, a few weeks later she was on her knees helping a young boy in yellow overalls retrieve his cat from a fenced-in front yard, and then, just a few days after that, almost rushing to help a young mother push a twin-stroller over the curb. She found a panhandler in the subway, matted hair and blackened nails like an ogre from a child's nightmare, to whom she gave money in proportion to her revulsion: a nickel for averting her eyes, a dime when she held her breath on approach. Although Lev had shaken his head when she admitted the game to him, told her she was being ridiculous for allowing "this whole baby thing" to consume her life, still she did not stop. Lev could object all he wanted — she told herself she didn't care. At worst she was doing some good, and at best it comforted her to walk with her eyes peeled for angels in disguise who would make the barren woman bear.

Her own superstitions she accepted, but the rushed, thoughtless advice of others, as if it were her fault she were not pregnant, her weakness, this she rebelled against.

Connie looked at Sima, raised an eyebrow. "Don't get all huffy with me," she said, leaning forward on her elbows. "The truth is you've been tense lately, not that I'm blaming you" — she raised her hand as Sima opened her mouth to protest — "and I think it'd do you good to try to forget about it for a while, enjoy yourself."

"Right. Even if relaxing was what I needed, you think Lev would be willing to spend on a vacation to the Bahamas? Not in a million years."

"No one's saying you have to go to the Bahamas," Connie told her, bending down to retrieve the spoon Nate had thrown onto the floor, "but maybe you can pamper yourself a bit, take a vacation somewhere close by."

"Sure. Like to the supermarket."

"Sima!" Connie wiped the spoon on her shirt before returning it to Nate. "I'm not trying to fight you. The truth is I'd like to spend a few days together. You may not need it, but I do. Since this one's born," she began again to roll the stroller back and forth, "we haven't seen so much of each other. My fault, I know," she said as Sima moved to object. "What can I say — with two boys in two years, I know I haven't been there for you like I could. But you've been my friend for what, fifteen years? I'm just saying I know when you're not happy, and I want to help."

Nate threw down the spoon again, and this time Connie returned it to the table, handed him instead a proper teething toy, colored plastic keys around a white circle. Sima watched with envy the ease with which Connie handed it to Nate, fascinating him with such a simple, absent-minded gift. He kept his eyes on his mother as he chewed the red key; Connie smiled down at him, lightly touched his cheek. Sima stood, feeling if she did not move she would scream. She walked over to the coffee percolator, poured herself a cup of coffee she did not want.

"Okay," Sima said, turning back toward

the table with the warmed mug in her hand, "I promise to try to relax. You name the day, and I'm yours." She sat down at the table, concentrated on the milk and the sugar, tried not to see Nate drop the keychain in his flapping-hand eagerness to be held by Connie. "I didn't know I was that bad," Sima said, as Connie lifted Nate from his stroller, brought him to her.

"You're not bad," Connie told her, "But I miss you, and I'm taking you shopping."

"Well, if you insist —" Sima stood up again, this time to retrieve a tin of butter cookies from the counter. "Hey, you know who I heard about the other day?" she asked, placing the tin on the table with an extra emphasis. "Elaine Weiner."

"Elaine Weiner? My God, I haven't thought of her in ages. What is she —"

Nate cried out for a cookie; Connie handed it to him without looking. Sima knew she finally had her full attention, such was the need they both had to hear about people they had lost touch with, did not want to be in touch with, but wanted to keep a finger on, literally to point to and say here, you are here, not somewhere, God forbid, I might envy.

Two weeks later, they met for their shopping date. Sima had imagined it'd be just the two of them, but Connie had brought Nate and Howie. Of course, Sima thought, as the station wagon pulled up outside her house, why did she think she wouldn't?

At Bloomingdales Howie ran ahead, hiding behind clothing racks and slipping his feet, sneakers off and tossed to the side, into ladies' shoes. "If Art saw him, he'd die," Connie said, as Howie reached for a pair of mock-alligator heels, and Sima couldn't help but think that, after all, it wasn't fair to the saleswomen to let the child run about like that, making a mess. She slid a few inches farther away from Connie on the leather bench, and when the manager came over, his gold Bloomingdale's badge glistening under the fluorescent lights, she focused on removing the paper stuffing from inside a pair of rain boots, did not come to Connie's defense.

"Let's get out of here," Connie said, furious and wishing aloud she hadn't bought that pocketbook, given them her money, and though the boots were just what Sima had been looking for and she'd never owned anything from Bloomingdale's before, still she followed Connie out, reminded herself she could get them cheaper in Brooklyn, anyway.

"My doctor's office is right near here," Sima told Connie as they walked up Madison Avenue, looking for a place where the boys could eat. "Sometimes I walk here a little after the appointments."

Connie was not listening. "Howie," she said, pulling him away from a coiffed black dog, "Stay beside Mommy."

Sima didn't attempt to speak again until they were settled in a diner booth, had found something on the menu for Howie — grilled cheese, no tomato — and opened four saltines for Nate. "It is a nice purse you bought," she said, beginning.

Connie nodded. "Still, I wish I hadn't —" She glanced over at Howie, whose forehead was growing increasingly furrowed. "Howie!" she yelled, pulling him from the booth, "Don't!" She pushed Nate's stroller toward Sima. "Watch him, will you?" she asked, as she steered Howie toward the bathroom. "We'll just be a sec."

Sima watched Nate. A beautiful baby, she thought, saying the words slowly in her head as she watched him chew the saltines, his hands and face covered with wet remnants of the cracker, a few pieces even in his hair. He kept his eyes on her as he ate, as if enforcing his mother's request, ensuring that Sima watched him. She smiled at the

189

seriousness of his wide-eyed stare and allowed herself to wonder, as the last of the cracker fell onto his lap, whether he was the one.

Can you bring me a baby? Sima silently asked, one just like you?

Nate kicked his legs, sent his tiny leather shoe onto the floor. He clapped his hands while Sima bent to retrieve it, he sang out sounds in a drumbeat tune. She slipped his foot back into the shoe, carefully tied the red laces, lifted his denim jeans to the thigh, and kissed his dimpled knee. A beautiful baby, Sima thought, wanting to breathe in deeper the powdered smell of his skin but, knowing he was not hers, pulling back.

"Oh Connie," Sima said, after she'd returned with Howie and they'd finished their Cokes and a plate of French fries smeared with ketchup, "I want one so much."

She hadn't meant to say it. She'd accidentally caught sight of Nate in the mirror alongside the booth, watched him smile a perfect O as Howie, giggling at his own game, pretended to steal Nate's nose. The words had slipped out before she thought to say no.

Connie didn't need to ask one what. She pressed her lips together, smiled. "Have faith," Connie said, "and patience. That's all you can do." She didn't look at Sima as she spoke, instead bent over her bag, removed a blanket with which to cover Nate.

Nate kicked at the blanket: he was warm, did not need it, but Connie persisted, slid it behind him and over his legs and chest. She's protecting him, Sima thought, hiding him from my desperation, my longing. "Shh," Connie said as she smoothed the blanket across his body, "Shh," she said as she hid him from Sima's view. Sima watched Nate disappear beneath the thin cotton, thought, well, who can blame her, I only wish it were so easy as that, a blanket to provide refuge from the evil eye, a hidden space beneath its tented warmth from which to emerge healthy, healed.

15

She looks terrible, Sima thought, as Timna entered the shop. Her hair was unwashed and parted unevenly; she wore no makeup. Sima watched as Timna took off her coat, turned to ask what was needed, what should be done. Sima saw the red in her eyes, felt an empty-inside amazement: Timna had been crying.

"Did the new shipment come in?" Timna asked, rubbing her nose with the back of her hand.

Sima shook her head no, stepped forward from behind the counter.

She'd been waiting to tell Timna about Art and Connie. She felt raw inside, wasted — aching not just for Connie but for the loss, too, of their love in her own life. It was a love that had warmed her and Lev as well. At the same time, she couldn't help but anticipate the thrill of good gossip; though she hated herself for it, she'd been relishing delivering the news, imagining the shock on Timna's face. But seeing Timna so sad, she put Connie aside.

"What happened?" Sima asked. "Everything okay?"

"I know, I look like hell," Timna said, half-smiling. "I didn't sleep so well."

"Is it Alon? Did something —" Sima placed her hand on her chest, clutching where it spread suddenly ice-cold inside.

Timna looked at Sima, paused. "No."

"Oh." She sighed with relief, lowered her hand. "I can't tell you how you scared me just now, what with all the fighting in Israel and you coming in looking —"

"Yeah?" She sat down, shrugged off her cardigan. "It's funny that you say that," she said, "about being afraid. I've been thinking about fear a lot lately."

Sima nodded. "You're worried about Alon, of course."

"Yes, but not —" Timna placed her elbows on the table, stroked each arm with the opposite hand. "It's actually that I've been wondering if it's not fear that keeps me with Alon."

Sima felt the cold return, a dampness moving across her like rain across the window of a fast-moving car. First Art and Connie, now this — she couldn't allow another love to disappear. "But you're fearless," she told her, "of all the women I know —"

Timna walked toward the dressing room, her purse in one hand. "That's not true," she said, gathering her unwashed hair into a loose bun, darkening her lips a deeper red. She talked while fixing her makeup, admitted, as she wiped away the gray remains of old mascara with a creased tissue, that she'd cried like a kid when Alon signed up for another year of army, told him she couldn't live without him. "I was so weak," she said, "so terrified of being on my own —"

"But Timna, here you are in New York, having come all this way alone." Sima watched as Timna turned toward her, amazed at the transformation she'd so quickly undergone: a little makeup, her hair swept back, and the evidence of sadness completely erased. "If that's not bravery, I don't know —"

"It wasn't bravery. I got in a fight with my mother, and I bought the ticket to spite her." She walked to the table, sat back down, told Sima that her mother had converted her bedroom into a den while she was in the army and then, when she was finally out, refused to allow her to move back. "I screamed until I was hoarse,"

Timna said. She shook her head, smiled. "So I called my cousins in New York, arranged an extended visit. And then it was Alon and my mother's turn to be angry, which was maybe what I wanted."

Sima looked at Timna, trying for an expression of patience, wisdom. "Timna, it doesn't matter why you decided to travel," she said, "but that you did decide, and came all this way alone. Anyone would be nervous to just up and move somewhere new —"

"But the thing is, I'm still just waiting for Alon." Timna undid the bun, shook out her hair. "I act like I'm all about travel, but my whole life is on hold while I wait for him."

Sima looked at Timna, hiding behind her hair. How young Timna was, she thought, how ignorant — the fear subsided as Sima thrilled to her new responsibility: knowing, better than Timna could, what was right. She clucked her tongue, chiding, reminded her how she'd just been to Philadelphia, was planning a trip to D.C. "Timna," she said, "you're always on the go, traveling all the time. You don't know how I envy you."

Timna frowned. "Don't envy me, Sima. That's not fair."

"I only meant —" Sima said, ashamed that her deepest offer, her own envy, was so quickly rebuffed.

"It's too much weight, other people's envy. I never asked for that." Timna pulled her hair back again, sharp enough that Sima could see the pink rib of her hairline. "I know what you're saying is true, that I'm not just sitting around," Timna brought one hand to her ear, touched lightly the soft of her earlobe, "but I think, maybe, I need to be free a little while." She ran a finger along the edge of the sewing needle. "Why do you want me to stay with Alon, anyway? You've never even met him."

"The things you tell me," Sima began, "I can sense —"

Timna watched her, waiting.

"What can I say? I guess I just think, when someone makes you happy, you don't throw it away." She looked down, focused on an old yellow stain on the linoleum. "It's like everyone says," she said, reaching back for the words, "it's no good to grow old alone."

"Yeah?" Timna tapped her finger against the needle, once, twice. "But that's just fear, isn't it?" She looked up at Sima. "I used to feel that if I lost him, I'd lose everything. In Israel, my family —" she trailed off. "But here I feel good in a way I haven't in a long time. Working with you, and then meeting new friends — I didn't think I could do it, and I have. I like being on my own, and I don't want to stay with him out of fear." Timna paused, looked at Sima. "You understand that, Sima, don't you?"

Sima held her own hands, cold to her touch. "You think Lev and I are together from fear of being alone?"

"Why do you think you're together?"

Sima shrugged, her lips a thin line. "What should I tell you?" She thought of Art and Connie. "Who would've predicted it'd be them?" she had asked Lev in the quiet of their bedroom, and he had nodded in agreement. She knew without asking that he shared her thought: it should have been us.

She walked behind the counter, bent to collect a bottle of oil soap and a red square of rag. "Art cheated on Connie. Suzanne — that bra we sold her. It was for him."

Timna brought her hand to her mouth in surprise. It was the move that Sima had anticipated, but rather than excitement, she just felt exhausted. There was both too much and too little to explain; love ends, was all.

"How? When?"

Sima told her about the dinner, how she'd been the one to tell Connie.

"Oh, Sima, I'm so sorry —"

"Me too. The romance of a lifetime — they had it. Well, I thought they had it."

"You did the right thing," Timna said.

Sima bent her head as she poured a circle of oil onto the counter. She was surprised by the threat of tears, hadn't realized how much she needed to hear those words. "Maybe yes, maybe no," she said, concentrating on keeping her voice even. "Lev said I did what I had to do, but I think we both wish that I was the kind of person who wouldn't. Anyway, what's done is done."

She dipped the rag in the oil, paused. "I'll support you, you know," Sima told her, "whatever you do, I'll support you."

"I know that," Timna said. "You're the only one who really does."

She raised her eyes, caught Timna's a moment before looking back down, spreading the oil thin across the false wood. It was more than she'd known she had to give, more than she thought she had left.

"The way this next test works," the doctor told her, "is that we blow some carbon dioxide," he pursed his lips, blew out some air, "like that, into the tubes. That'll tell us if the tubes are patent, or if there isn't some blockage there stopping things up."

Sima nodded, resigned to this new image of her body: just a series of dull metal pipes in need of cleaning.

"Now, you may find the test uncomfortable. I always believe in warning my patients —"

"It's okay," Sima said, "it's what I'm here for."

The doctor smiled, mentioned how easy a patient she was — never rushed, never complaining. Sima accepted his compliments, did not explain that for her the pain was necessary to prove her worthiness.

Again she'd given the dime to the beggar: the coin ready in her hand as she approached, her eyes on the cigar box before him. She gave a quick nod when he looked up in thanks, her eyes just catching his own — the baby, bring the baby — before she stepped back into the flow of exiting passengers.

Again she'd rode the elevator to the office, listened for her name to be called, followed the receptionist — "Beautiful day, huh? Makes me want to play hooky and go to the beach" — to an examination room.

Sima folded her clothes on a stool, carefully hiding her hose, bra, and underwear underneath her shirt — a small attempt at modesty even as she once more drew her arms through the worn cotton gown and, leaning back against the metal table, clenched her feet along the stirrups. He nodded when he entered the room, and she smiled back, thinking, as he slid the cold speculum once more inside her, the closed beak opening within her, hungry, what an old hat she was at all this, what a pro. But then the door opened and two nurses came alongside her and a young doctor appeared at her head, and while the talk went on around her — the restaurant down the street, the police this morning — her doctor inserted a tube into her body and switched on a machine. And this time, as the young doctor moved to place a stethoscope against her abdomen and the nurses reached for her arms and her doctor flicked another switch and the carbon dioxide stabbed through her, she looked up at the water-stained ceiling and screamed.

We'll repeat it, he told her afterwards, when she sat in his office in her hose, bra, and underwear, in her wool skirt and sweater set and navy pump shoes — as if it mattered, anymore, what she wore, as if she weren't always naked on a metal table, all her failures exposed beneath the white orb of a standing lamp. "We'll repeat it, and then if it still shows blockage we'll take an x-ray, with colored dye to trace —"

Sima nodded, made the appointment, took the card. Waited.

■ ■ ■ ■

One week after Art left, head bent, a suitcase in each hand like some sad stereotype of the fallen man, Sima knocked on Connie's door, a bag of food at her feet. They'd been talking on the phone several times a day, but the last few times she'd called, Connie hadn't picked up.

Sima knocked three times, counted to ten, and then reached for her key.

She'd had a key for decades, given so she could water the plants and take in the mail when Connie and Art went on vacation. She'd always resented it, wedging open the rusty back door to toss that day's newspaper into the recycling bin (Connie always forgot to cancel; Sima inevitably missed, had to stoop to pick it up again), while Connie and Art splashed in green waters somewhere.

"Sorah's teenaged daughter across the street," she'd recently complained to Lev, "how cheap are they that they can't pay her to do it?" He would give a shrug-shouldered suggestion that she simply refuse next time, but she was always unable to do so. The truth: she got some pleasure, too, from time alone in Connie's house. She'd walk slowly through the house, admiring shoes, lotions, new pieces in Connie's powder-blue Wedg-wood collection. But best of all was Con-nie's night-table drawer: every now and again she'd find stashed there a love letter from Art. A real love letter, written for a birthday or anniversary and details she didn't think a man would remember to notice: a joke Connie had made, a blouse she had worn. The letters sometimes made her eyes water, sometimes her body flush. Like nothing Lev had ever written her, even back in that dim-distant time that hurt to think about when she knew they'd been happy.

Sima turned the key in the lock. Hard to believe, but of course it still worked.

"Connie? You there?" Sima placed the grocery bag on the kitchen counter.

From the bedroom, a groan.

Connie lay in bed, a soft dark shape Sima could just make out in the dim room, the curtains drawn and a sour smell in the air. "It's like a horror movie in here," Sima said from the bedroom doorway.

Connie pulled the covers over her head.

Sima drew back the white pointelle cur-tains, securing them behind ornate faux-bronze hooks. Light streamed in, illumi-nated motes of dust that swirled softly toward the beige carpet below. "I'll be right back," she told Connie, switching on the light as she left. Connie groaned again in response.

Sima returned with a glass of water and a just-damp olive green tea towel. She shushed softly as she lowered the covers, gently touched the towel to Connie's forehead, cheeks. When Connie opened her eyes, Sima helped her to sit up, held the glass to her lips.

Connie drank. As her body awoke to thirst, she took the glass from Sima's hand, held it, slightly trembling, with both of her own.

"Look at me," Connie said when she'd emptied the glass, "wallowing in bed like someone died." She offered a weak smile.

Sima took her hand.

"Someone did."

While Connie showered, Sima heated chicken soup, unpacked bakery rolls, put on a pot of a coffee. When Connie appeared in her bathrobe, Sima nodded for her to sit at the table. "I know it's a cliché," Sima said, placing a bowl of soup before her, "but sometimes things are clichés for a reason."

Connie looked up at her. "You're the best."

Sima smiled, turned quickly away. Connie's hair, always perfectly blown, hung damp; her skin was pale and blotchy, not a spot of foundation. For all their closeness, Sima had never seen her without makeup; Connie was one of those women who, when making plans, did not shy away from saying, "Just give me a few minutes to put my face on."

It scared Sima to see her this way.

As Connie ate, she described how she had hardly left the bed in three days, no hunger and no reason, she felt, to wake, and yet for all those days in bed still she was constantly exhausted. "You know that expression," Connie said, "'pulled the rug out from under me'?"

Sima nodded.

"It feels just like that. Art cheats on me, the most typical thing in the goddamn world, and it's like the floor is gone, the walls, the roof. A cyclone, the whole planet spinning and I'm like Dorothy — remember? Only my bed felt safe."

Sima pushed a poppy roll toward her; Connie took it, ripped off a small piece to press into butter.

"And my boys. My wonderful, devoted sons. Selfish bastards. They call, they talk a big game: 'How could Daddy do this?' they say. 'We'll kill him when we see him.' Then two days later they're begging me to take him home, saying he's so sad, he's lost without me. They don't care about me, they care about themselves. Two grown men, Howie with a family of his own, and they're like little boys again, simpering for Mommy and Daddy."

Sima stood to pour herself a cup of coffee. "But to them, you'll always be —"

"Sure, sure, because all these years I made them my world. So now, when I kick Art out, when I make a choice for my own life — as if I had another choice to make, cheating on me with his secretary, for God's sake, talk about original — they can't handle it. They have one stupid beating hope: that Art and I will stay together. Well, I'm too old for compromises."

"You're exactly right," Sima said, though just an hour before she'd been telling Lev they had to get back together, didn't make sense apart. "Look at you — three days in bed and you're like a woman reborn."

Connie raised a fist in mock salute. Then her face fell: mouth, cheeks, eyes, all the quick brightness gone again. "Oh shit, Sima. How am I going to live alone? Tell me — what do I do now?"

Sima looked down, opened and closed her fingers around the coffee mug. Of course Connie didn't mean it like that, but Sima was the one who knew how to live without love. Only there was nothing to tell. You just did.

16

Once again, Sima sat on the subway, not quite reading the novel she'd brought along: four generations of Jewish matriarchs, from Odessa to Palestine to New York City. She dozed between stops, sure enough of her route to know she would waken on time, her head sagging toward her shoulder, jolting up and down as the train vibrated along its steel tracks.

She woke up with one stop to spare, forced her eyes awake. When the train reached her station, she stepped out, already opening her purse, removing one dime for her beggar. It reassured her to see him there, sitting, as always, straight-backed against the white tunnel wall; she kept her eyes on his profile as she approached, but barely looked at him as she tossed the coin into the cigar case, the light thud of landing a comforting sound: there, that's done at least. She continued on, approaching the dark end of the tunnel, the sharp turn toward the exit staircase.

"Sima!"

She knew it was him, though how could he know her name? A chill coursed through her body and she couldn't move and meanwhile he came closer — footsteps, breath — the tunnel suddenly and inexplicably empty.

"Sima."

Her eyes widened, her heartbeat quickened, her mouth went dry.

He placed a hand on her arm, like a handle moved her toward him.

As in a movie she tried to shout, but found only her own breath, shallow.

"You dropped this, it's yours —"

A postcard. Her name on it. An image of Hawaii on the front, her friend's ridiculous bubble writing on the inside: thinking of you!!! A high school girlfriend she hadn't heard from in years, married and then divorced (lower your voice), and now married again and on honeymoon and needing to plaster the world with images of palm trees, proof of her normalcy. Sima looked down at her handbag, realized she hadn't closed her purse after taking out the dime. Somehow it had been pushed up and out.

"I didn't know," he said, "if it was important."

She still stared at him.

"Your name was on it."

Up close, he was younger than she'd thought. Not some noble beggar after all, but a young man sharp with the scent of liquor, and no excuse not to be working.

She nodded, took the postcard from him, careful to grab only the corner farthest away from his hand. "Thank you," she managed, before retreating down the tunnel, taking the stairs two at a time.

They repeated the gas insufflation and scheduled a hysterosalpingography: a length of dye injected inside her, the x-ray tracing its path as she lay in the dark and prayed, make it all right, make it okay.

But it wasn't.

"Sima," the doctor asked, closing the door behind her, "do you know why you might have tubal scarring?"

She shook her head, no, watching him for the answer.

He sat down, smiled weakly. "This is a rather delicate subject, but —" he leaned back, drummed his fingertips against the table. "The kind of complete scarring you have seems to point to your having been exposed to —" he shifted forward, "a venereal disease."

Sima looked down to the tan carpet, watched the individual weaves of knot blur beneath her eyes.

"Sima, have you asked your husband about his own," he coughed, "proclivities?"

She focused on her feet. Her toes were visible in the buttonhole of the shoes; unpainted, yellow like the doctor's teeth.

"Mrs. Goldner, I know how difficult this must be for you —"

"It wasn't Lev."

"I know you might feel that, but the facts remain that you've been exposed and —"

"It wasn't Lev."

The doctor drew in his breath. "Well then, Mrs. Goldner, how can you account for the fact that —"

She looked up. "It was me, it must have been me."

He looked at her longer than she could stand, long enough that she envied the plaster bust on his bookshelf, wished she could be like that — without flesh, without feeling. She mutely accepted his censure, proud at least that she had defended Lev: he had done nothing wrong, and she wouldn't let him be judged.

"Well," the doctor said, taking a manila file from atop a tidy pile, "that's that, then. The infection has run its course, so there's no need for antibiotics for you or your husband." He opened the file, glanced at a note scrawled within. "On the way out, please see Terry about the bill."

Sima nodded. "And the next appointment?"

He looked up.

"To get rid of the scarring? To open up the tubes, right, we need to get rid of the scarring?" Sima paused, watched his face sharpen. "So I can have a baby," she said, her voice wavering as she tried not to see the glint of his eyes, the long muzzle of his nose.

The doctor put down the file, brought his fingertips together like the schoolyard game — Here is the church, here is the steeple, open the doors, see all the people — leaned his chin on top. "Sima, I'm sorry if this wasn't clear to you, but —"

The words ripped through her, cutting like scissors someplace secret, deep inside.

17

Lev knocked on the bathroom door. "Sima? You're taking a bath?" She could hear him outside, shifting his weight, his hand on the doorknob but hesitant to enter. "Everything all right?"

"Of course, I'm taking a bath," she said, speaking above the rush of water, though it was true it'd been years since she'd done so. She crouched to open the crowded cabinet beneath the sink, pulled out perfumed bath products from years of birthdays and anniversaries: bath salts and soaps and scrubs, bubbles and pearls and beads nestled in bright bottles; gifts from Lev and occasional customers that she'd smiled over and stored away, saving for an occasion. Well, she decided, ripping the dusty wrap off a wicker gift basket, this was it.

The doorknob rattled again. "Sima, you sure —"

"Lev, what do you think I'm doing, slashing my wrists?"

"Sima?"

"A joke, Lev. Listen, just give me twenty minutes and then I'll make dinner."

She could hear him hesitate a moment before he answered — "Fine then, whatever you say" — listened to his slow-shuffle retreat: the television turned on, the newscaster's voice rising.

She'd sent Timna home an hour early — too hard to keep up appearances in front of her — and when Lev looked up from his place at the table as she came up the stairs, the question, Why are you home so soon, forming on his face, she'd found herself overwhelmed, unable to answer. She'd rushed to their room, slamming the bathroom door behind her, quick as she'd run in years but not fast enough that he wouldn't have seen her face collapse as she hurried past.

Sima stood, looked in the mirror. Heat steamed the glass, obscuring her reflection and muting the wet-redness of her skin. She unscrewed the cap on a mini-bottle of raspberry bubble bath, poured it into the tub.

It was hard to act normal after what Timna had told her. At least they might have mourned together, her own tears

disguised as sympathy rather than selfish-
ness, but Timna had insisted she was fine,
and indeed had looked terrific, radiating
energy as she moved about fitting shoppers,
making small talk.

She's in shock, Sima thought, as she
slipped her hand under the water to check
the heat, she doesn't have the tools to deal
with this loss and so she's overcompensat-
ing.

Sima wiped her hands on a towel, sat on
the closed toilet seat to unbutton her blouse,
unroll her pantyhose, remove her bra.
Standing, she lowered her skirt and underwear, folded her clothing into a neat pile,
and placed it atop a digital scale. She lifted
her bathrobe from its Lucite hook, wrapped
it round her body, and sat on the edge of
the tub to survey the bath.

The bubbles were a disappointment —
thin, concentrated only around the edges.
Sima unsealed a canister of dark blue and
green bath beads and tossed them into the
bath; from a pastel box unpacked a lavender starfish-shaped soap and, dipping her
hand into the water, let it sink to the bottom. With her teeth she bit open a bag of
bath salts and poured them slowly into the
tub, watching the water grow cloudy. It
smelled like the soap shops in malls —

something antiseptic in the air not quite hidden by the cloying sweetness as the bubbles crowded the water and the skins of the bath beads floated along the surface, limp.

Sima untied her bathrobe and shrugged it onto the tile floor. Holding on to the wall for support, she lowered one foot in the tub. The water was hot, burned along the edges of her skin. She hesitated a moment, remembering how Timna had asked for the sugar and just after — as if it only occurred to her then, as she ripped open the pink packet — said, "We've broken up." Sima raised her other foot, placed it square in the tub, and edged herself slowly into the water. Some suds splashed onto the floor; she reached with a soapy hand outside the tub to pull the bathmat closer, as an afterthought removed her wedding ring and placed it in the center of the small green rug.

She'd thought for a minute that Timna was speaking of Shai, "broken up" a euphemism, an admittance that she had been seeing too much of him. But Timna had kept talking, said something about the time difference, about leave, and Sima realized it was Alon — he was gone. Though she kept her face controlled, she felt for a moment what it would be like if her jaw could drop,

215

exposing that empty place inside that gathered wind, garbage circling, as someone else she'd loved, another ghost she'd turned to, was taken from her.

Of course it was different than with Art and Connie. She'd been friends with Art and Connie a lifetime; losing them as a couple felt like losing a part of herself. And yet: somehow it was this new loss of Timna and Alon — a man she'd never met, a fantasy future she would never even share — that had truly brought the tears.

She leaned back against the cold porcelain of the tub, lowered her shoulders beneath the water. It was hard to think he was gone. She'd wanted to scream, yell at Timna — how could you, what were you — but had stayed quiet not from propriety but from fear: she was afraid to cry in front of Timna. Instead she'd raised her mug to her lips, waited for Timna to tell her story. But Timna only said, "It was time," as if every intimacy had an expiration date.

She's scared, Sima thought, she's a coward.

She felt the lavender starfish press against her calf, lifted it out of the water, and began to clean her body. She dipped the soap into the hollow of her armpits, the crease beneath her breasts, the space between her thighs. She knew her feelings were laughable, bizarre. Lev had said all along she had to remember she was not the girl's mother — even then, hadn't she told her customers for years and years not to take their child's life for their own?

The water cooled around her and the drain gurgled — she turned the hot tap on a steady drip, lowered her ears beneath the water not to hear it. He was gone, and maybe Timna would leave soon too; despite Timna's insistence that she loved the work, she had no reason to wait around anymore, and those friends of hers would probably be willing to take off, quit their jobs at any moment. You could depend on no one. She'd given Timna a job, a community, she'd given her what was left of her own heart, and Lev too, and now she'd find herself waving goodbye as Timna pulled away in someone else's car.

Sima turned off the tap; closed her eyes to take in the quiet. Maybe she had maps somewhere, maybe some old maps that, if the highway names hadn't changed too much, might be of use for Timna's journey.

■ ■ ■ ■

DECEMBER

■ ■ ■ ■

18

Sima stood outside the jewelry shop, gazing at the window display. Strands of gold and silver, pearls and diamonds curved delicately around imaginary necks, arched above soft gray molds. Sima studied the jewelry, concentrating on the earrings: gold knots, diamond studs, pearl drops. She imagined Timna sweeping her hair back into a ponytail, revealing each pair in turn.

She'd walked by the shop three times in the last five days, each time pausing before the window. Since deciding to buy Timna something special for Hanukah, she'd taken to strolling all over Boro Park, staring at the shop displays: flower-pressed pastel paper journals in one window, brightly colored French cooking pottery in another. "Why don't you just get her whatever it is you usually get your assistant?" Lev had asked, when she complained to him that nothing she'd seen so far was right. She'd looked at him, rolled her eyes: as if Timna were just another seamstress.

It was true that she usually just gave the seamstresses a fifty-dollar bonus and two days off: never a gift, and certainly not jewelry. But in search of a wedding gift for Esther Adelman's daughter, she'd wandered through the silver shop the week before — glass counters stuffed with candlesticks and spice boxes, silverware and serving platters — and overheard a saleslady explain to a customer that the candlesticks she held, seemingly skeptical of the price, were an heirloom. The saleslady said the word slowly, letting it linger a moment, floating above the white glint of silver and the deep blue of the plush carpet. "Every time she lights the Shabbos candles," the saleslady continued, "she'll think of you. And after you're gone, she'll always have those candlesticks to remember you by."

A standard sales line, Sima knew; if she could convince women that bras were heirlooms, she'd use it herself. And yet she couldn't be cynical when she saw how the candlestick customer blinked away a low brim of tears, knowing the vision the customer saw: her daughter bending over a halo of candlelight, remembering her as she brought her hands to her eyes, closed them in blessing.

Yes, Sima had thought, that's what I'd want for Timna: something that would remind her, every now and again, of our time together.

There was no telling how long she'd have Timna. Though Timna had insisted, when Sima finally worked up the courage to ask, that she wouldn't be leaving before the spring, still Sima felt she might disappear at any moment. It was all the more crucial, then, to make this gift special. As Sima gazed in the window of the jewelry shop, the tips of her gloved fingers just touching the glass, she hoped to find among the metals and gems spread before her the gift that Timna would wear over a lifetime, the piece she'd reach up and touch, absently, for years to come.

Sima rang the bell, waited while a well-dressed woman in an auburn wig evaluated her through the glass. After buzzing her in, the woman returned to a customer — a young man, a tray of diamond rings on the counter beside him — while Sima paced before the display cases. Immediately she felt disappointed: the jewelry was too staid for a young woman like Timna, the rows of Stars of David and heart-shaped pendants were designed for a different breed.

She paused before the watches, feigning interest — it would be rude, she felt, to leave too quickly. But as she watched the young man shyly point to a princess-cut diamond ring — the saleslady assuring him, "It's our most popular setting" — she hesitated. Occasionally women would come to her shop looking for transformation. They'd criticize everything Sima brought them — this one didn't hold in the belly enough, another made their breasts too flat — until she reminded them that while good lingerie made a difference, it wasn't plastic surgery. There wasn't a shop in all New York City, she realized, that would sell her what she wanted: a combination of gold and jewel that could capture Timna's own beauty, bind her forever close.

The saleslady walked over to Sima as the young man wrote out a check. "See anything you like?" she asked. Sima looked again at the earrings. In the center, a pair of gold hoops was on display: wire-thin at the top, gradually thickening toward the center. She pictured Timna running a finger along the sharp edge of metal, light glinting off the gold and catching in the soft waves of her hair.

"Those," Sima said, "I'll take those."

Sima gave Timna the gift the next day. "Before I forget," she told her, as if it hadn't been on her mind all morning, "I got you a little something —"

Timna opened the card first, a little square that matched the rainbow-candle wrapping paper and said only: "Happy Chanukah, thanks for all the hard work!" Sima had meant to write a real letter, but she gave up after ruining six sheets of the pink sheared stationery Connie had given her for her sixty-fifth birthday. "Dearest Timna," she'd write each time, pausing for a moment before losing herself on the unlined paper, the words coming too quickly as she struggled to explain how different it felt to get up each morning — even with winter outside and the bedroom cold because Lev always insisted on a window half-open — since Timna had come to work with her; how much richer her days felt, how much more joyful. "I want to tell you," she'd write, "I have to say" — but as she reached the end of a page and traced back to the beginning, she'd see it was all wrong: her praise too heavy on the pale paper, like her envy an unwelcome burden. She crumpled the pages, took out the recycling herself so that Lev would not see her pastel drafts.

"I wasn't expecting —" Timna said as she peeled back the wrapping paper, opened the cardboard box beneath, "Thank you so much —"

Sima looked down, nervous for Timna's reaction. "I didn't know what you liked," she said, "but you had silver hoops, so I figured —"

"Sima, they're beautiful." Timna held the earrings up to the light, took off her own turquoise studs and placed the hoops through. "What do you think?"

Sima looked. There was only one word for Timna, always. "Lovely," she said, "Absolutely lovely."

Timna began to thank her again, but Sima cut her off. "Come upstairs," she told her, "we'll eat some latkes, celebrate a little. And then you can go home early, enjoy half a day off."

Timna slipped her old earrings into the front pocket of her jeans. "Let's go."

Sima had to push aside stacks of Tupperware — take-out containers cleaned and saved — to find the electric frying pan. She'd grated the potatoes and chopped the onions the night before, pausing frequently to rub her hands, ease the stiffness.

While Timna told Lev about her trip to D.C. — Sima had hardly asked, hadn't wanted the details — she added eggs, baking soda, and flour. Pressing small scoops of the mixture flat, she released them, careful of the hissing oil, into the frying pan.

"We did mean to go to the Smithsonian," Timna was saying while Sima opened the fridge, took out sour cream and applesauce, "but then we got up so late —"

Sima browned both sides of the latkes before placing them on a paper-toweled plate in the oven, dropping more of the mixture in the pan. When she'd worked her way through the mixture, she removed the latkes from the oven and carried them to the table.

"So, Lev," Sima said, placing a bakery box of jelly doughnuts beside the latkes, "Mrs. Klein was in before, talking about her son-in-law like you wouldn't believe. Turns out he's not a doctor at all, just has some pharmaceutical degree from someplace in South America." Sima spread a thick layer of sour cream on a latke, lifted it to her mouth.

"Someplace in South America?"

Sima nodded, chewing. "One of those countries, yeah. So they get married, you know, and —"

"Who gets married?"

"Mrs. Klein's daughter and this doctor."

"But you just said he's not a doctor," Lev said, tearing off a piece of the latke with his hands, dipping the edge in applesauce.

"Are you listening to me?" Sima looked at Timna, pushed the doughnuts toward her. "Try them, they're from the good bakery. We never eat jelly doughnuts, but someone told me in Israel —"

Timna motioned to the latke in her hand. "In a minute," she said, one finger on her lips to hide the chewing, "these are excellent."

Sima beamed. "So, anyway, at the time they thought —"

"Who thought what?" Lev reached for a doughnut.

"The Kleins thought that their son-in-law was a doctor."

"Okay, Okay. So then what?" Lev bit into the doughnut, releasing a squirt of pink jelly onto his chin.

"So then what, what?"

"What happened?" Lev wiped his chin with the back of his hand.

"Nothing."

"What do you mean nothing?"

"That's it."

"What's it?"

228

"Why do you keep interrupting? Just that. That he's not a doctor at all. The police came and closed his office, and now they're threatening to move to Miami." Sima turned to Timna, who had taken a doughnut. "Good?"

Timna nodded.

"Who's threatening to move to Miami?"

"You know, you're really driving me crazy." Sima dipped a corner of her napkin in seltzer, passed the napkin to Lev. "Wipe your chin, there's jelly all over it."

Lev took the napkin, rubbed at the spot. "Sima, who's moving to Miami?"

"Who do you think? Mrs. Klein's daughter and the doctor."

Lev looked at Timna. "You understand this?"

"You two are the ones who have been married all those years. You're supposed to understand each other."

Lev lifted his glass; Sima, noticing wet rings on the table, reached forward with another napkin. "How many times do I have to tell you you'll ruin the wood? Use the place mat."

Lev turned to Timna. "That's how well we understand each other."

Timna drummed her fingers on the table while Sima searched desperately for something to say. She was trying to remember if she'd told Timna about Helene and her latkes — she'd forgotten the eggs at a party for her daughter's engagement and they'd all fallen apart on the tray, but everyone was too polite to say and Helene hadn't noticed until the end because she was too busy to eat, can you imagine — when Timna stood up, and walked over to a picture hanging on the wall behind Lev. "Is it you guys in this picture?" she asked, looking at a couple on a boardwalk bench on a windy day, the ocean stewing behind them.

Sima nodded. "Art took that, when he first started doing photography."

Sima was laughing as she struggled to hold her coat closed against the wind; Lev had one hand on his hat.

"I never noticed it was you before," Timna said. "It's a great photograph."

"Yeah? Art gave it to us framed like that, so I put it up. Personally, I think I'm the least photogenic —"

"Oh Sima, you are not," Lev said, "we have lots of nice pictures of you, when you used to let me take them."

"I used to let you? What, you need permission?"

Lev looked at Timna, opened his hands. "She didn't like being photographed, so I guess I stopped."

Sima saw Timna glance at her watch, but instead of making an excuse to leave, she asked if they had more pictures she could see. Though Sima suspected Timna was just being polite, still she found herself crouching before the den bookshelf to sort through a pile of old albums, unable to resist Timna as an audience.

They sat on a brown leather sofa trimmed with rivets: Lev and Sima on either side watching as Timna turn the yellow-edged pages. There were snapshots on the beach, at the Catskills, outside their home: Sima in a white cotton dress with a handkerchief round her head, proudly clutching a striped purse and blushing at the camera; the two of them at a cousin's wedding, Lev in a pale blue tuxedo, Sima in a sparkling black dress; Sima and Lev on the porch of a bungalow, a puppy propped into a sitting position on Lev's lap.

"I didn't know you had a dog."

"I bought Poncho for Sima. What was he for — your birthday?"

Sima nodded. "He was cute, but he just wasn't made for an apartment. He tore up everything, peed everywhere. We gave him to a couple moving to a farm in Connecticut."

"You never got another?"

"Too much work. We thought kids would like a dog, but then, for just us —"

Sima didn't finish the sentence; Lev groaned softly.

Timna quickly turned the page. "Look — you've been on the Cyclone? I went last weekend with my cousin."

Sima and Lev stood with their arms round each other beside Connie and Art. The men had horn-rimmed glasses; the women wore their hair piled high on their heads.

Sima sighed loudly. Art and Connie, her sigh said, such a shame.

"You guys look like fashion models," Timna said. "Seriously, all that stuff is back in style now — you could be a *Vogue* spread."

"No," Sima said, "We weren't much to look at."

"How can you say that, Sima?" Lev asked. "You were lovely."

"Now you say it?" She looked at Lev, disgusted — he was posing for Timna, pretending to be the devoted husband. "I never heard that then."

"You still look nice," Timna told her, turning another page. "If I look like you at your age, I'll be thrilled."

Sima raised an eyebrow. "You, look like

232

me? You must be insane. Anyway, your life will be completely different. My body was ruined by hormone therapy, whereas —"

Lev sighed.

"What are you making noises for?" Sima asked. "I'm just saying —"

Lev shook his head. "Enough." He looked at Timna. "Sima can show you the rest of the album, she prefers that anyway. I'm going to go lie down."

Sima didn't watch him leave. Instead she studied a gray and white photograph where the two of them, bundled in heavy coats, scarves, hats, cried out for the lowering of the ball in Times Square: a new year to celebrate. After she heard the click of the bedroom door — quiet, of course, Lev would never slam — she closed the album, and stood.

She smiled at Timna. "Well, now you know the worst of it."

"I'm sorry, I didn't mean —"

Sima dismissed the apology: "Nothing to be sorry for." She patted the album, returned it to the bookshelf. "Maybe you were right, Timna," she said, her hands on the shelves as she pulled herself up, "maybe it is better to end things sooner, better not to let it last until all the love is gone."

■ ■ ■ ■

"I won't adopt," Sima told Lev. "I don't want someone else's children. Those kids have problems — brain damage, delinquency. I won't have it."

What she didn't say: she no longer felt she deserved to be a mother.

Lev barely protested. "Give it time," he told her, "you'll feel differently after a while."

Sima waited, wishing it true, through the nights and the mornings and the shut-in weekends — Lev no longer rushed through his paperwork so they could spend time together, go on a walk, instead pored over essays and exams and committee meeting notes for hours while she read in the kitchen, met with a friend — hoping for him to see how she hurt, assure her of his love.

In the dark of the bedroom she longed for his touch and, sometimes, Lev tried, because he had no words, to open Sima instead with his body. He stroked her belly, breasts; he bent to kiss her cheek and ear. But, despite her longing, she did not turn toward him. It was always all wrong: his breath too thick in her ear and his hands too heavy on her skin, and though she allowed him to part her legs and move forward into her, when he asked her how she was, when he tried to meet her eyes, she kept quiet, her face turned away toward the pillow.

At night when she could not sleep, she curled her body tight, clenching her eyes shut against the years ahead with just the two of them on the beach and no children to crowd the blanket with bright, plastic toys. At night, desperate, she reached for Lev to hold on to, but he rarely awoke, comforted her through closed eyes when he did, "Sima, in the morning. We'll talk then." At night, alone, she suffered, raged, blamed herself, wished to be held and recoiled, all the same, from the weight of his arm around her.

And always the fear: he would find out the truth, he would discover her secret and shun her, hate her as she deserved to be hated.

As the disappointment stretched into months Lev seemed to resent her martyred breathing. Sima could hear him some nights, turning, and though they were both awake neither asked the other why.

Like that, they withdrew from each other: just a couple rolling toward either side of the bed, away from the center, backs faced in protectively, guarding.

19

Sighing, Sima lowered herself into bed. "I'm exhausted," she bragged to Lev. "Between Connie and Timna, you have no idea." She squeezed a dollop of peppermint moisturizer onto her hand, rubbed it into her feet.

She couldn't remember the last time she'd been so needed.

It was both terrible and wonderful.

Connie had stopped by the shop that morning. She had cried; Timna had moped. "They both looked like hell," Sima told Lev, raising her voice so he could hear her in the bathroom. "And there I was, running from one customer to the next, needing double the energy to cover for Timna's monotone, like a zombie that one, and then stopping to dry Connie's eyes in between —"

Of course, she hadn't really dried Connie's eyes. Lev knew that. But the cheap exaggeration hid a real sorrow; Connie was broken, and Sima ached for her. Sima had watched the familiar way in which Connie reached into her purse, carefully drew out one tissue, wiped her eyes, blew her nose. Her Connie: her brash, loud, always-envied Connie. A well-practiced, pathetic gesture. It stung.

Connie had taken possession of a folding chair, occupied it for most of the morning. When Sima wasn't busy — and sometimes when she was — Connie spoke about the separation: updates on Art, ensconced in some overpriced hotel beside the Brooklyn-Queens Expressway, and insights from her lawyer. Himself married three times, he'd told Connie: "You get through it."

"Sure," she told Sima, "but how?"

There was nothing to say, but still Sima couldn't stop herself from trying. "Treat yourself to something," she offered. "A massage, new boots."

Connie had nodded, blotting her eyes.

Sima brought her water, coffee.

Connie cried.

Sima comforted.

Meantime, Sima led the customers one by one between the changing room and the cash register. All the time listening, agreeing, intervening — this one's crazy daughter-in-law, that one's weight-loss regimen.

In and out of bras, bathrobes, nightgowns, corsets. Yes. No. Yes. No.

"If only I'd died two months ago," Connie had said, reaching for her coat. "A car accident, an explosion. Think of it: I'd have died loved. But now —" she raised a hand dismissively, "nothing."

"Don't be crazy," Timna had said, "you're still loved."

But Sima had thought: she has a point.

"What'll become of her?" she called out to Lev. "How should we help her?" She rolled over, sighed. "We should have her over more often. Only I'm so tired at the end of the day that the thought of serving someone else dinner —"

"She'll be fine." Lev shut the bathroom door behind him. "She can take care of herself. She'll land on her feet."

"We're talking about a woman, Lev, not a cat."

"So have her over more often."

"I know, it's just —"

"It's just what?"

"Nothing." Sima reached for her book from the bedside table. A page-turning novel, only she'd cheated by reading the book club questions at the back and now she knew how it all turned out. Still, a little worry niggling in her head: to be so needed by both Connie and Timna — she almost didn't want him to be right.

"It's fine, it's fine," Sima said, though Timna, on the phone, had not really asked for approval, "just get some rest, and make sure to drink lots of water. I'll call later to see how you're doing." Sima twisted the phone cord a few times round her wrist, picked up a pen, and tested it against a yellow legal pad, "Yeah? Okay then, just in case you're asleep, I won't call. And if you need anything, soup or whatever, let me know." Sima sketched a cube on the paper, two connected squares with reaching lines like she'd been taught in junior high. "Uh huh, sure. So listen, will you be around this weekend? Because if you want —" The door opened, and Sima smiled at a mother and daughter, held up her hand to signal, one minute. "Okay," she said, shaking her head no, "but I don't know if you should go to the concert if you're not feeling —" She nodded at Miri, in an auburn wig, who had motioned toward the rack of nightgowns, waved her hand for them to look through them. "All right, if you say so. Sure. Call me if you need something." Sighing, Sima hung up the phone.

The older woman looked at Sima, her

eyebrows raised with a question. "If I didn't know better, I'd think you were speaking with your own daughter. Who was that?"

Sima forced herself to smile. "Just my employee," she said, "I don't think you've met her."

"But I've heard of her. Reva told me, 'Such a beauty Sima has hiding in her basement,' she said. Nu, so what's the problem?"

Sima ran her nails lightly against the counter, raising her fingers at the knuckle. "No problem. She's sick is all, she's Israeli; she's not used to the weather changes."

"No? It snows sometimes in Jerusalem."

Sima smiled: of course she knew it snowed in Jerusalem, every business in the area used the same snowy shot of the Western Wall as the January image on the free calendars they gave out. She was tempted to tell this to Miri, point out that she was not after all a complete idiot, but, glancing at Miri's daughter and seeing some nervousness there, paused instead. "Who's shopping today?" Sima asked, looking at the slight swells beneath the girl's cable-knit sweater, "Is it for you, Netya?"

Netya blushed, looked at the ground. "You think it's time?" Miri asked. "She wants one, but I wasn't sure. The girls start earlier and earlier —"

"How old are you Netya, twelve?"

Netya nodded.

"It's the perfect time," Sima said, pleased at herself for remembering Netya's name and age, wishing Timna had been there to see. "Tell you what, I'll bring you a few styles, and you can see what you like best, okay? Go wait in the dressing room."

"You really think she has enough?" Miri asked as Netya walked toward the curtain.

"Of course there's enough, Mirela." Sima grabbed the stepladder, turning her back to Miri. "You can't keep her a baby forever, you know," Sima said, reaching casually for a stack of cotton bras.

"What do you mean?"

"I mean," Sima said, "you have to let her grow up sometime." She set aside one white and one beige cotton bra, pretended absorption.

"You think I'm one of those mothers?"

"Everyone's one of those mothers."

"Maybe so. But believe me, if anything it's more the other way — I'm always pushing her to try new things, grow up. With five others at home I can't keep them all children, that's for sure." She paused, considering. "Do you remember when I used to bring her here as a baby, and everyone said she looked unreal, like a painting?"

Sima nodded. All babies received the same overblown compliments, she thought, when would these mothers realize that?

"But I worry about her. She seems younger than the other girls. In a few years we'll be looking for a husband, and sometimes she plays with dolls still. Can you believe? A girl old enough for a bra."

"Of course she plays with dolls — she has three younger sisters."

"But in a few years —"

"How few? Seven, eight? Think how you changed from twelve to nineteen."

"I had Netya by then."

"So, you see, you never gave up playing with dolls." Sima lowered herself carefully down the ladder, though she felt like dancing at her own jab. Miri followed her to the dressing room.

"I'll ignore that comment," Miri told her.

Sima laid a hand on her arm. "I'm just teasing," Sima said, "like you do." Before Miri could respond, Sima added, "Is that new hair?" and when Miri nodded yes, "it looks like it was made for you. I love the color."

Miri smiled, appeased.

After they left — Netya with three new bras, white, beige, and pink though she'd wanted black ("Who's going to see it?" Miri had asked, and of course Netya had no response) — Sima glanced at her watch, debated going upstairs for coffee. Lev would be up; he would ask after Timna.

Anticipating Lev's question — where's Timna, he'd want to know, the coffee ready, cream on the side the way Timna liked it — Sima asked it herself. Where is she, Sima thought, smiling at her own game, and pictured Timna not home sick under the covers, where she clearly wasn't, but outside somewhere, with friends. She'd be ice-skating in Central Park, Sima decided, and she closed her eyes to think of the way Timna would giggle as she stood unsteadily in her skates, a cup of hot chocolate and the boy who bought it for her close by on a bench.

She sat down behind the counter, taken with her game. Maybe Alon would be at the rink, and he and Timna wouldn't have to say anything because just looking at each other, they'd know. Timna would crawl into his lap, and he would grin to feel her warmth against him as he reached his arms around to keep her close. How he would laugh as he brought the hot chocolate to her lips, held it while she blew on it and then, leaning forward, the cup still in his hands, took a sip —

Oh, Sima thought, as she imagined the warm sweetness passing Timna's lips, to be her, to be her.

Sima turned off the TV when Lev walked into the room, but she knew he could see, just before the picture went black, that she'd been watching a talk show.

"I thought you'd given up on those," he said, sitting on the edge of the bed to pull off his socks.

"I did. But I was bored."

"Where's Timna?"

Sima looked up at him, annoyed. "How should I know? It's Saturday, she doesn't hang out here on Saturday."

"Sorry. I just thought —"

"You thought wrong." Sima lay back on the bed, put a hand to her forehead. "My head is killing me."

Lev didn't answer, walked over to the bathroom, and closed the door. A moment later he returned, a faded chart in one hand. "What's this?" he asked.

Sima watched the blank screen of the television set, concentrated on not revealing the fear that gathered in her stomach.

"What do you think it is? It's an ovulation chart."

"From when?"

"I don't know. 1964 or something, I guess."

"But where'd it come from? Why is it here?"

The anxiety in his voice surprised Sima, but she didn't show it. "It was under the sink, all this time. I finally finished cleaning away all those old bath products, and there it was, just waiting. So I dropped it in the sink and —"

"Turned on the TV?"

Sima nodded. She could tell him it was nothing, just that she found it and then paused to watch a show — no big deal, no grand connection. Instead she sighed a thin stream of breath, allowed the clouds to gather above, the thunder, the lightning.

"My God, Sima, what is it with you? Is this because of Timna, this obsession again with not having had children?"

Sima stared at the screen. She longed to hide under the blanket, pillow, under the very bed itself with the dust-ruffle tent safe on all sides, but, running her hands along the sheeted surface of the mattress, nails digging slightly, forced herself to stay still, speak. "What do you mean, 'again'?" she asked. "Has there ever been a time it hasn't consumed me?"

Lev looked toward the door, but did not retreat. Sima saw that his face was flushed; he gripped the paper so tightly that it creased in the middle, the edges curling in toward the center. He's pushing too, she thought. They were like children in a school-yard, circling, wanting to strike but afraid to step forward first, stand exposed.

"Oh Sima." Lev shook his head, glanced down at the chart. "It's such a waste, isn't it," he said, taking the graph gently in both hands, smoothing out the creases, "to throw our own lives away just because we couldn't have children?" He walked over to the side of the bed, sat down softly. "It wasn't our fault," he said, placing his hand on the bed between them, "we didn't fail. Look at Art and Connie, at all they had and still, now, nothing. We're still together — doesn't that count for something?"

Her rage disappeared before his quiet protest, but the hollow it left was more frightening than the anger. She thought of Art leaving Connie, Timna leaving Alon, separation as easy as a push away from the concrete edge of a pool, strong strokes into the open. She wanted, too, to be free.

"Why this punishment, Sima? Why all this —"

Sima clenched her fists, enough. "Lev,"

she said, "Lev." Her face creased, gathering his pillow to her she turned on her side, wrapped her body around its bulk. "Lev." She thought, even then, to turn back, but she was like a cartoon character who, having walked out on the sky, now understood it was time to fall. "It was my fault," Sima said, speaking more into the pillow than to him, "It was my fault."

"No, Sima," Lev said, moving his hand full on her knee, "I never thought that, not once. These things happen, bad luck. You know I never blamed you."

Sima spoke quietly. "Yes. I know you never —"

"Blamed you."

Sima nodded. "But the thing is," she looked at Lev a moment, covered her face in her hands. She rubbed her eyes and looked up again, breathing deep. "Lev, it was my fault. I was sterile because of a disease that I got," she paused just a moment, "from another man."

Lev shook his head. "No, that makes no — what are you saying, Sima?"

"When I was sixteen," she bit her lip, her face contorted. "Oh God, I was so young. I was a camp counselor, and there was this boy —"

"A boy?"

"A boy. He was eighteen; I thought he was a man. But he was just a boy, too. It took years for me to forgive him, but now I understand how young he was."

"Forgive him for what, Sima?"

"Lev," she said, "I couldn't have a baby because my tubes were scarred."

"I know."

She shook her head, smiling. "Do you know, you never asked why? That whole time I was going through the testing, and then after, you never asked where the scars came from?"

Lev looked at her, not responding. He brought his hand back toward his own body, cradled it against his stomach.

"We only had sex the once. Like they taught us in health class, it only takes one time and —"

"And what Sima, what?"

"It's so stupid, you know? One time. One" — she paused, her voice wavering — "one fucking mistake when I was sixteen and I can never have a child. Like that, just like that."

Lev looked down at the pink, plush carpet, the dark of his footsteps from moments ago still visible. "You had sex with someone, that's what you're saying?"

Sima nodded.

"Before me?"

"Before I ever met you."

"And he gave you what? A disease?"

She nodded.

"And so —"

"So it made me sterile. Scarred the fallopian tubes." It was easy, this part, answering his questions; she hoped he would continue asking until it was all solved and stored away.

Instead Lev shook his head, stood.

Sima felt suddenly terrified. He couldn't leave — she couldn't stand to be alone, abandoned on the bed with the false warmth of the winter sun casting triangles on the comforter and unable, she felt, to stand even to close the curtain, turn off the light. It wasn't freedom she wanted, she realized, but forgiveness. Sima reached out her hand. "Lev, don't leave," she said, the words heavy in her mouth, "I know I should have told you, but I was so ashamed. For forty-six years I didn't speak, and now, please don't —"

"Yes, you should have told me," he said, standing, looking down at her. "It wasn't worth ruining our marriage over, Sima. It wasn't worth it."

After he left, she curled back to her side, brought her hands to just under her knees and held in the shaking. It was over. She'd leaned up against that terrible secret for so long that she wasn't sure she could stand without it. A brain aneurysm, she thought, a stroke — anything to make her disappear. Lev would return to find her dead, suddenly cold like her own mother, pale above the bedspread.

But dark came and hunger and she was still alive. She went into the kitchen, prepared enough ravioli for both of them, delayed until the pasta turned cold before taking the food to the table, eating. She placed his leftovers in Tupperware, cleaned the dishes, retreated to the bedroom, waited. He can't leave me, she thought, he can't survive on his own. She'd always envied the way Art cooked and cleaned, but now she comforted herself with their differences: Lev doesn't know how much laundry detergent to use, doesn't know how to roast a chicken — she repeated the complaints that brought laughter from her customers, recited them in her head like a well-worn prayer.

He returned after she'd lain down for bed, worried, though she wouldn't admit it, over where he'd been — stabbed in a gas station; pushed onto the subway tracks. When she heard the door open, she closed her eyes, whispered thanks.

There was enough light in the room that she knew he could see her, but he was silent as he undressed, brushed his teeth, urinated. She felt the rush of cold air as he peeled back the covers and then the warmth of his body beside her and still he said nothing. She had to speak.

"Well?" Her voice was not as gentle as she would have liked.

He was silent another moment while she listened to the shallows of his breath. "Goodnight, Sima," he finally said.

"That's all you have to say, 'Goodnight'?" After hours of worrying over his response, she couldn't stand to be ignored: he was cruel and uncaring, so indifferent to her feelings, so oblivious to her needs, that even her darkest secret was not worthy of anger. "What's my punishment? What are you going to —"

"There's no punishment, Sima."

"Well, there has to be something. Doesn't there have to be something, after all this time?" She hated him for making her beg for his rage.

His voice was even. "You're the one who made the choice, Sima —"

"I was sixteen!"

"That's not the choice I'm talking about." He paused a minute before speaking. "You chose not to tell me, Sima. Decades you didn't tell me. So what is it you want me to say now?"

Without thinking, she told him: "That you understand."

"What would it mean, to understand? What would it change?" He folded his arms across his chest, each hand on the opposite elbow, holding. "It doesn't matter anymore. You could have told me five, ten years ago — it's all the same. But if you'd told me then, if you could have let me in then —" He paused; she could hear his breath become fuller. "We might be better people now, Sima. We might have had a better chance."

It was the cruelest of all, his regret. She was the one who regretted, she was the one who mourned — never Lev, never before.

"Who wouldn't?" she asked. "Who wouldn't have been better, if only?"

"I don't know, I don't know anyone but us. It's just a shame, is all, it's all just such a shame."

Sima had been to the mikvah, the ritual bath, only once before. Two days before her wedding she'd rung with a trembling hand the yellowed bell, immersed herself in water to enter the marriage clean, purified. Ten years later, she returned to the mikvah — a sort of goodbye.

An old woman, a paisley kerchief covering what remained of her hair, opened the door, led her inside. It smelled of damp and sourness; a blue-striped towel Sima remembered from five years before was still dangling from the ceiling, half-protecting a torn pipe. The walls were the green of hospitals and elementary schools; the floor a white tile faded gray round the edges.

The woman pointed toward a small room with a few lockers and some wooden benches. She spoke with an Eastern European accent, "Undress there, yes?" Sima nodded, entered the room.

Sima hadn't intended, when she awoke that morning, to come to the mikvah. It was in line at the butcher that the sight of a yellow-haired child hiding behind her mother's leg had made the envy rise up in Sima's throat so that she felt, surrounded as she was by the torn, plucked bodies of birds, her own neck twisting, choking.

"I can see you," Sima had joked to the hidden child. The girl, a look of fear on her face that Sima remembered from her own childhood when strange, smiling women would lean over to twist her cheeks, burst into tears.

"I'm so sorry," Sima said to the mother who, pleased to be needed, bent down, whispered into the child's ear something that made her laugh, "I didn't mean to upset her."

"What's to be sorry for?" the mother answered. "You know how it is."

Sima found herself saying, yes, of course she knew, her own child after all — so that she missed the butcher calling her number.

She passed the mikvah on the drive home; circled the block once and parked, leaving the meat on the front seat. Maybe if she'd gone regularly, she couldn't help but think, after each period as prescribed, things would be different. At the very least she'd go now. Close up shop, she told herself, not smiling at her own dark humor.

Sima removed her clothing slowly, folding it in a neat pile on the narrow bench, and placed her jewelry — wedding ring, pearl earrings, cracked-leather band watch — in the pocket of her shirt. She walked naked to the sink, surveyed the various toiletries scattered beside it: a half-empty tube of toothpaste, perfectly rolled from the bottom up; one box of Q-tips, slightly worn from water around the blue cardboard edges; a cup filled with cotton balls; a pink bottle of nail polish remover; and a dozen or so plastic-sealed toothbrushes gathered into a loose pile. Sima brushed her teeth, cleaned her ears, and scraped with one nail the dirt from the others — not caring about the cold that blew in from the air duct. After spitting into the sink, she splashed it with water, then entered the shower. There was a sliver of green soap and a bottle of pink shampoo — she worked both into thick lathers before ducking under the water, closing her eyes as it ran hot down her back.

Sima walked dripping into the mikvah room. For once she did not cringe to hide her body as the attendant bent down to check that her toenails were unpainted, lifted her hair to confirm her earlobes were unadorned. The old woman assessed her briskly, professionally, and Sima relaxed under her disinterested gaze: she was just one more naked woman among the hundreds the attendant had seen, and what a relief to be so reduced. Without jewelry, makeup, polish, Sima descended the seven steps to the bath.

The water wasn't as warm as she remembered; Sima shivered slightly, hesitated. She looked up at the old woman a moment, a tiny woman, shrunken, and, realizing for all their difference in age they were the same — thick inside with the green fur of mold, useless, over. She bent into the water.

She immersed herself completely so that not even a strand showed on the surface, once, twice. Arms and legs out, eyes open. Rising, she recited the blessing that praised God for the commandment of immersion. Without pausing, she recited the prayer she'd spoken as a bride: "Blessed are you, Lord our God, Ruler of the Universe, who kept us alive and preserved us and enabled us to reach this season." As she came to the final words, this season, *Lazman hazeh,* her voice cracked. The tears were warm on her wet face, and she bent down once more to blur them into the pool of water, hide them as she did late at night while Lev slept and she wept to her reflection in the bathroom mirror, taking some sympathy from the pained face that looked back.

"What's the matter, dear?" the old woman asked when Sima stood again, her voice softer than Sima expected, soothing.

Sima shook her head in response, clenched her eyes shut.

"You're married?

Sima nodded.

"Children?"

Sima placed a fist to her lips and bit, lightly, for control.

"Next time maybe. Every woman has that

loss. How far along was it?"

"Two months," Sima told her.

"Two months? Yes, it's hard. Next time my dear. You're still young." The woman patted her head, absently, as Sima stepped out.

Sima dried herself carefully in the dressing room. She touched the scar on her abdomen, the purple mass. The woman must have been almost blind not to see it, her check for nail polish and jewelry a sham. Sima felt angry for a moment, wanted to report her. It was a ritual, after all; the attendant needed to be competent — things could happen, women could drown. But no, she was just an old woman in need of work. The children she'd had, at any rate, had left her on her own.

It'd been two months since the surgery. The nurse had told her to massage cocoa butter into the scar to keep the keloid down, but Sima had not bothered. For the first few weeks the scar was just a sharp surgical line, cutting from her belly button to her pubis — another red line, pointing. As it thickened and deepened in color, its drama seemed to justify her sadness.

She wanted the physical scar as a symbol of her loss.

"You don't need it now," the doctor had

told her, "and with childless women there are all sorts of problems, cancer the worst of it, of course. Given your fibroids, I'd feel more comfortable just taking everything out. And these days a hysterectomy is really a very simple procedure."

She was thirty years old.

Sima had nodded, signed the right forms. Lev ventured once to ask if she was sure about it. "Sure I'm sure," Sima told him, unwilling to admit fear for worry it would stop her.

Lev did not press further.

Of course, she thought, he wouldn't.

A few days after the surgery Lev wheeled her out of the hospital. The wheelchair was difficult to maneuver; Sima felt herself coming dangerously close to walls and corners at every turn. "Lev! Watch it!" she'd cried, surprised at how damaged her body felt, how vulnerable. She held her breath in the crowded lobby until, just outside the hospital doors, she was again allowed to stand.

Sima leaned against the windowed entranceway while Lev ran for the car, brought it up beside her. In the front seat was a stuffed animal, a small white bunny with pink eyes, ears, and nose.

"A bunny?"

Lev nodded. "For you. A gift."

"It's Eastertime. They sell these at the drugstore."

Lev didn't respond.

Sima rolled down the window, dropped the bunny into the parking lot. Despite herself, she watched it as they pulled away: it lay sideways on the cement, a few whiskers bent toward the sky.

Sima paused on her way out of the mikvah to open her purse, leave some money in the jar by the door. The kerchiefed woman did not close the door after her, and Sima, remembering her own mother, did not say goodbye.

■ ■ ■ ■

JANUARY

■ ■ ■ ■

20

Sima frowned. It was bad enough Timna had abandoned Alon, looking for some bright-edged future that, Sima knew, would always be out of reach, but now she looked ill — her skin was pale, her lips chapped, dark roots were beginning to creep along the edges of her scalp. "Hello, doll," Sima said as Timna entered the shop late that morning, pretending not to notice when Timna barely responded, draping her coat — some suede thing she got at a thrift store, not right for this weather when all the other girls wore ankle-length wool coats, proper — over her chair, though Sima had asked her before to hang it up.

"Were you out late last night?" Sima tried to sound casual, but she heard in the echo of her voice that ring of disapproval she'd always recognized in her own mother's questions.

"Mmm. We went into the city, to the bar

where Nurit works. We didn't even stay so late. It just took forever for the train to come." Timna crossed her arms on the table, laid her head down atop them.

"You took the train home?" This time she didn't attempt to hide her judgment. "Timna, it's not safe to take the subway alone at night, and so far —"

Timna turned her head so she faced Sima, but kept her eyes closed as she spoke. "I wasn't alone. Shai and Nurit were with me."

Sima nodded. She wanted to warn Timna that maybe these friends weren't the right sort — going out late at night, returning by subway at all hours — but wasn't sure what to say. "You're just jealous," Lev had told her when she complained to him that when Timna's friends called the shop they never said hello to her, always asked for Timna with that flat, uninterested voice so many young people had these days, "it's normal for a young girl to make friends."

"I know what's normal," Sima said, making a show of unpacking the groceries, banging the cabinet closed, "but they aren't nice, they aren't friendly."

Since her confession she and Lev had returned to the usual dull exchanges, and Sima didn't know whether she was relieved or disappointed by that; she was forgiven, at any rate, but after so many decades of silence she wasn't sure what forgiveness meant. She'd imagined fury, renunciation, but that kind of passion had disappeared, along with all others, years ago.

"They're fine. It's just a cultural thing, Sima. You know how Israelis are — sabra, remember?"

Sabra: the tough cactus hide, the juice of the fruit: prickly on the outside but sweet on the inside, as if a people could be reduced to a plant. "I don't begrudge her friends," Sima said, moving aside a carton of milk to make room for an orange juice container, "and I'm not just judging them on whether they say hello or not."

"So what are you judging them on?" Lev asked.

She ignored the question, complained that he hadn't told her the milk was almost gone and now she'd have to go back to the store. She was acting cowardly, she knew, but she couldn't explain to him why she objected to Timna's friends — that it just felt wrong, to replace Alon with a whole new crowd. If Timna could really do that, what sort of person was she? And if she couldn't, and was just protecting herself by pushing him away — Sima knew this had to be the case — then it was her job to help Timna find her way back to him.

Timna opened her eyes wide, stretched her mouth in a yawn. "I'm sorry, I know I shouldn't come in so tired. I'm not sure why, but lately I'm just exhausted."

"If you want to go home, rest —"

"Sima, you're too nice to me. Maybe I just need some coffee. Is there some upstairs?"

"Of course, of course. Go, Lev will be thrilled to share some article with you."

Timna stood and stretched her arms above her head, her hands clasped and her back curved. Sima watched as Timna leaned back, letting the stretch curve up and out through her body before bending over, wrapping her hands around her ankles, pressing her chest toward her knees. Like a Degas dancer, Sima thought, though she was aware of a tightness in the way Timna grasped her ankles, holding on, that she hadn't noticed before.

Timna straightened. "And now for the coffee," she said, smiling. "I have to admit, I think it beats yoga."

Sima watched Timna disappear into the kitchen, listened to the warm hello, the rustle of Lev's newspaper closing. She wiped the counter clean with a dry cloth, checked the change in the cash register drawer. In twenty minutes the shop would be crowded for the next five hours: women vying for Sima's attention, calling to her from behind the dressing-room curtain. The bell rang as Timna walked down the steps: one hand on the mug handle, the other cradling the cup for support.

"You ready?" Sima asked.

Timna yawned, nodded. "Let's go," she said, and Sima pretended not to hear the exhaustion in her voice.

"How's Debra?" Sima asked as she rang up Rose's purchases, her voice just a hint louder than usual so that Timna, who was assisting a new customer, would hear.

"Oh," Rose said, "The usual craziness. First she calls, says she's moving back to Brooklyn, can we help her find a place. So, fine. Herbie spends the whole week driving around, making calls, looking at listings. Finally we find just the thing, a perfectly clean one-bedroom in a young area, right near Seventh Avenue. He calls her, and guess what? She changed her mind. Now she says maybe L.A.; she has friends there."

Sima opened the neckline of a camisole, checked the price. "What friends, from here?"

"Who knows? I think she just wants to drive us crazy." Rose sighed, placed her purse on the counter. "What do I owe you?"

Sima punched the numbers on her calculator. "One thirty-five," she told Rose, "with the discount comes to one twenty-one, fifty."

Rose opened her wallet, a black leather weave, and counted out the bills. "The last time I saw her," Sima said, folding a camisole, two bras, and three pairs of underwear into a plastic bag, "was what, five years ago? She was just starting college and she bought that push-up bra, remember?" Sima saw Timna was turned just slightly toward them as her customer looked through the nightgowns, comparing colors.

Rose smiled thinly. "To think, we once fought over push-up bras. What I wouldn't give to have arguments like that again." She handed Sima the worn bills, let her wallet fall back into her purse.

"How long has it been?"

"Since college, actually. There she was with that impressive scholarship, and then —" Rose paused while Sima put the money in the register drawer, waited for the ring of the purchase to fade. "She stopped showering at one point. I never told you, but when Herbie and I first went up there, she had dreadlocks. Actual dreadlocks, from not showering."

Sima glanced at Timna. "And how did you

know to go there?" She raised her voice another notch, wanting Timna to know: sometimes an older perspective was necessary to see what was wrong.

"It didn't take a brain surgeon. She stopped calling, and then when we called, she sounded distracted. And then —" she paused a moment — "that's right, her roommate called, said she was worried."

"My God." Sima remembered Debra as a child, the way she'd sit cross-legged under the nightgown rack while her mother shopped. "You look like a gypsy," Sima used to joke, smiling to see how the brightly colored silks and satins spilled around Debra's shoulders, sashes coiling against her dark hair.

"Debra was hardly leaving her room, and the roommate thought maybe she was suicidal —"

"Oh, Rose." Sima pressed her hand to her neck, felt her pulse echo lightly against her fingers — a gesture of sympathy, a wish for protection.

"Remember how I used to bring her here," Rose asked, "and you'd let her try on those silk nightgowns?"

Sima nodded.

"I never thought I'd be one of those women moaning about where does the time go," she said, pulling on tan cashmere gloves, "but here I am, wishing so fiercely I could just turn back the clock."

Sima nodded again, aware from the presence of a certain warmth that Timna was approaching.

Rose took the bag Sima handed her, walked to the door. "Anyway," she said, her hand on the doorknob, "I'll send you the chicken recipe I told you about, the one with the mustard. It calls for cream, but I leave it out and it still tastes wonderful."

Sima waved goodbye.

"Old customer?" Timna asked.

Sima nodded.

"She seemed so sad."

"She is." Sima looked at her.

Timna turned back to her customer. "The navy and the ivory?" she asked, "Are you going to go with those?"

The woman nodded. "I think so."

"And what about you," Sima asked, following Timna, "are you feeling better since you had the coffee?"

Timna didn't answer, instead took the two gowns from the customer, said something about care, color. "This is Natalie," Timna said as she handed Sima the nightgowns, "she just started working around the corner, at that big children's store."

Sima shook her hand, absently praised her choices. She rang up Natalie's purchase, waited for Timna to respond to her question. When she didn't, she tried again. "You're feeling okay?" she asked as she swiped Natalie's credit card through the machine. "Because you seem so exhausted —" Sima tore off the receipt, handed it to Natalie. "I know it's winter and all, but —"

"I'm just tired," Timna said, as she folded Natalie's nightgowns into a bag. "I swear — you're worse than my own mother."

Sima smiled, though she wasn't sure what to make of the comment — Timna's mother wasn't much to be compared with, after all.

"And Shai?" Sima asked, as Timna walked back to the sewing table, "What's the story with him? Are you two dating?" Her words came out high, unnatural; she felt herself warm to pink.

Timna looked over, a blank stare Sima couldn't read. "Why does everything need to have a label? I just left a relationship, I'm not looking for another."

Sima nodded. "Sure," she said, thinking of the nighttime subway car, the touch of a stranger's body as the train curved along the tracks, everything dark and hidden outside. "Just so long as everything is safe —" She looked at the counter, avoiding

Timna's gaze. "I mean, I know you can take of yourself," Sima said, knowing she thought nothing of the sort, "but things can happen so fast —"

She hesitated, tempted to tell Timna her own story, a once-upon-a-time fairytale with a moral as clear as those they'd read in grade school — the wolf in the forest, do not stop — but though she wanted to warn Timna how much might be lost for one mistake, she felt ashamed, too, to expose herself. As terrible as it was to admit her flawed history, it would be worse still to observe its effect: the disbelief with which the long-ago stories of the old were inevitably met, the pain of watching Timna realize, so you were young once too.

"You sound so serious, Sima," Timna told her, before she had a chance for the warning. "Everything is fine — I'd tell you if it weren't."

Sima looked at her. Let me take care of you, she wanted to say, let me be there for you. The words burned the back of her throat, but she did not let them out, and then Timna was already walking away, returning to the nightgown rack to put back in order what had been misplaced.

Sima followed Timna again.

What was the point, she told herself even as she walked behind Timna to the bus stop, what was the point in standing there silent and stupid as Timna once again boarded a bus, pulled away. As if in witnessing she could change anything, as if she could protect by watching.

But then two buses pulled up together — "Make us wait fifteen minutes," a woman in fuchsia lipstick complained, stamping out her cigarette, "and then come two at once" — and Sima found herself reaching for her purse, counting out quarters.

"Transfer?" the driver asked, and Sima nodded yes.

She kept her eyes on Timna's bus ahead, feeling like a character from one of those late-night action films Lev occasionally watched. "What are you wasting your time with this for?" she'd ask him, pausing in the doorway as something blew up on screen, but sometimes she came inside, sat down beside him, asked "Who is he? Is that the bad guy?" listening while Lev, in the pauses between the action, explained the story, his voice a whisper between them in the dark room.

When the buses pulled up to the subway station, Sima got off, waving her transfer like everyone else. She could hear the

273

squealing brakes of a train pulling in; let the crowd surge around her, pushing her along so that looking back she might say, I didn't choose to follow her, really I just found myself there, and then —

And then underneath the streets of Brooklyn and over the bridge to Manhattan and under again like some hide-and-seek game and then whispering "Excuse me" as she struggled off the train after Timna, whom she'd been watching nervously from across the subway car.

Timna took the stairs two at a time. So that's how, Sima thought as she scrambled after, those thighs. She followed Timna down a corridor and then up another flight and into the sky and the night and the city.

They emerged into Union Square, where the market was closing down for the evening. Sima looked around, amazed. She seldom went into Manhattan. There was the lingerie trade show once a year, and then every now and then she and Lev met another couple for dinner, or attended an event — a wedding, a bris — but she couldn't remember the last time she'd simply walked around the city at night. It felt immediately romantic: the dark winter sky, the tremendous buildings, the open space of the square. A woman in a pink coat packed beeswax candles into cardboard boxes and Sima paused a moment, looking at the candles and dried flowers and jams, thinking how beautiful, and why had she never thought, and maybe she could come back on a Sunday, with Lev. But Timna kept walking, and so she did too, crossing in front of a taxi, hurrying past a Starbucks, following Timna down darkening streets of beige brick buildings. As they walked east, the buildings showed their age — grayed brick, pock-tiled entrances — but the restaurants were all wood and soft lighting and the clothing shops bright-white, lines of colored dresses on narrow racks. Where am I, Sima wondered, knowing the street numbers and the hospital and so yes, it had to be the same neighborhood — Connie's cousin Marty had grown up here, and they'd visit on weekends sometimes — but so much had changed and could it have been so long ago?

Timna stopped in front of an old tenement and pressed the buzzer. Sima watched from across the street as Timna spoke into the intercom and then leaned against the glass door.

The city swallowed, and she was gone.

Sima scanned the building, wondering which apartment Timna had disappeared into. There were windows curtained in leopard print, in neon pink, in yellow and orange flowers Sima knew would be called retro; there were silver micro-blinds and cheap white shades and one bare window that revealed a sliver of white wall, black metal bookcases.

It was impossible to know which window hid Timna.

She began walking. Dinnertime already and she was cold and hungry like a kitten, a line she knew from somewhere that now rang in her ears. She called Lev on the cell phone, always in her purse for an emergency that never came, and directed him to defrost a few perogies. She hung up before he could ask where she was.

Every block had a gleaming restaurant, but where, Sima thought, seeing the chalkboard menus, the prices, does one eat around here? She was tired. It was freezing. Seeing a small clothing store before her — three steps down into the basement of a tenement — she entered, thinking only to get warm.

A woman looked up from behind a glass counter, smiled. She was in her forties, dyed red hair and big jangly earrings. She wore a vintage pale blue cashmere sweater half-buttoned over large breasts, a rhinestone snowflake pinned to one side. "Let me know if you need anything," the woman said, flashing a bright lipstick smile. A newspaper was spread open before her, a salad in a plastic take-out container on the side. Sima smiled back.

There was a rack of camisoles in candy colors; of course Sima went to them first. Some were similar to the ones she sold, but she realized immediately they were old. The white lace yellowed; the pink nylon loose around the armpits. Sima reached for a pale green polyester camisole — thick straps twisted through an old buckle, a tiny ribbon above the rounded neck.

"Do you want to try it on?"

Sima shook her head. "It's just — it's the same as one my mother used to wear. Same brand it must be, though the color is different. She had it in blue and pink."

The shopkeeper smiled. "That one's a favorite of mine. Sure you don't want to try it?"

Sima touched the worn fabric. "I don't think I could handle wearing my mother's lingerie. But where do you get them?"

The shopkeeper ("Liza," she had said, shaking Sima's hand) came over, dragging her stool behind her ("my back," she said by way of apology, and Sima looked down at her old-fashioned heels and thought, well, what do you expect), explained how it worked. She waved her hands as she talked, indicating the buildings all around them — the old tenements and the 1960s high-rises — how she collected clothing when the old people moved out. So much great vintage clothing for the taking, and with just some cleaning, maybe a bit of mending, they were better quality than most new things. "I get from a supplier too, of course, but the stuff I love best is what I find on my own. Otherwise these things would have just been tossed out. Such a sad waste, don't you think?" She gazed fondly at the green camisole.

Sima nodded. She didn't ask where the old people went, but understood now why the neighborhood felt so changed. It had been purged.

"Did you grow up here?" Liza asked.

Sima told her no, told her Brooklyn, and Liza nodded eagerly, as if that made sense. She told Sima she came from a small town in Ohio, had wanted to live in New York since she was a kid. "But enough chitchat," Liza said, as Sima glanced up and out to the street, "what can I get for you?"

Sima was about to say nothing when a rack of coats caught her eye. "I know," the woman said, following Sima's gaze, "it's that time of year. At the beginning of winter last year's coat isn't so bad, but midway through I find myself just yearning for something new, you know?"

The lines were familiar but different too — she would never say yearning, would never employ such bright-eyed dewiness. Sima pulled out the coat that had caught her eye, black wool, midcalf, with gray paisley lining. Taking off her own black coat, worn thin already at the wrists and the pockets bulging, she tried on the new one. It fit nice: a little slimmer than her old coat. The yellow tag at the wrist said $75, and though Sima had never spent such money on anything used, still it wasn't much for a coat —

"It's a great cut, classic, but it's just like the one you had," Liza told her. "Can we try something a little different?" Before Sima could object, she was being handed a green coat. Viridian, Sima thought, imagining it in a catalog.

"Oh, I prefer black."

"Try it."

Because Liza was so nice and because she'd been Liza, too, in her own way, Sima tried it. It came with a belt that tied across her waist; Liza pulled it inches tighter than

Sima would have. "Like something out of *Breakfast at Tiffany's,*" Liza said, and Sima thought, now that kind of exaggeration I never do, but she smiled all the same, because it looked all right, in a dress-up kind of way. With the belt pulled, she did look thinner.

"Now this one needs a scarf, because of how the neck opens up." Liza handed her a polka-dot silk scarf, pale green with pale blue dots.

"Oh no. I look like a clown."

"Okay, this one's simpler." It was black with tiny pink roses. Pretty, though not something she'd wear. Sima looked at herself one last time in the mirror, admiring the original effect even as she thought: not me, never. But then the woman was so kind and the store so empty and Sima knew days like that and how it wasn't even so much the money from the sale as it was feeling that someone had wanted what you had to offer. "I don't know," Sima told her. "Now I have visions of someone like you ransacking my closet after I die, taking this coat straight back to sell."

Liza laughed. "I should sell them with some kind of homing device. But think of it this way — it's coat reincarnation. Good karma. Maybe with you the coat is moving up the soul-ladder."

Sima smiled. Though she had no idea what Liza was talking about, she did know that in this coat Timna wouldn't recognize her. Her spy get-up, she thought, pivoting before the mirror.

"Do you take checks?"

"Big news," Connie said, shaking her hair loose from under her hat. "I have a date!"

Timna paused mid-yawn. "No! Who? Tell us everything."

Sima gave a stunned smile, listened while Connie ran through the details. She and Estie were in the dressing room at Loehmann's together, talking. As she was zipping up, Estie ran into someone she knew.

"Myrna Silver," Connie said, turning to Sima. "You know her?"

Sima shook her head no.

"Me neither. But she and Estie carpooled together a million years ago. Well, one thing led to another, and it turns out this Myrna has an orthodontist brother who's widowed two years. At first I say no way, I'm not ready, but Estie says, 'How many years do you have left that you're going to take your time?' So I figure what the hell and give her my number —"

"Good for you!" Timna grinned her approval.

Connie nodded. "Get this: he calls that evening. We talk, we laugh, so on and so forth. Long and short of it is, he's taking me out for dinner Friday night. Manhattan."

"Go, Connie!" Timna gave her a hug.

"Wow," Sima said. "That was fast."

Connie looked at Sima, but then turned away. Taking Timna's hand, she pulled her toward the dressing room. "Come, give me everything you've got. This is my first date in almost fifty years — I think it calls for some new lingerie."

Sima watched as Timna, giggling, escorted Connie to the dressing room. She didn't follow.

Connie had been her customer for as long as she owned the shop. A good customer: she liked lingerie, always chose what was pretty, hardly minded the cost. For years Sima had envied that about Connie — that she still cared. About her body; about Art.

But now —

There was no question of loyalty. Lev had met Art for lunch, and it went without saying she wouldn't come. She and Connie even laughed about it — what would they talk about, anyway, just the two of them?

And yet, to fit Connie for the dating scene felt like cheating. She loved Art, after all; he was like family. If she wasn't ready to leave him behind, how could Connie?

"I'm thinking that watercolor number," Timna said as she took hold of the step stool.

Sima nodded, distracted. She remembered the first time they'd met Art. "That one's cute," Connie had said, pointing him out to Sima from across a crowded bus. He was a college boy; they were still in high school. Here we go again, Sima had thought, as Connie dragged her through the crush until they were beside him.

Connie had turned to Sima, mouthed a command: "Watch." Then, smiling, she'd boldly clasped the center pole so that her fingers touched his.

Art had looked up, surprised. He smiled when he saw Connie. He asked Connie her name; Connie feigned aloofness. He pressed; Connie made him guess. Sima couldn't believe that something so obvious, so insipid, could work so well. "Alice?" Art had asked, "Grace?"

They were both beaming.

It was Sima who had given Connie the pen with which she'd written her name and number on the back of Art's hand. Sima could still see Art's shy grin as he watched Connie draw a perfect cartoon heart over the letter "i."

How could it be, Sima thought, that their lives had changed that day and only to lead here: Connie in the dressing room, calling across the shop floor to ask if it was really true that garters were back in style? From the dressing room came laughter, whispers. High school again, she thought. Here We Go Again. And she was supposed to be ready with the pen as always.

21

Sima closed her eyes, tried to press away the thought that had appeared, a sentence fully formed, in her mind. She saw it like the story in the Bible, the Babylonian king whose walls had been covered with writing from God, each letter alive in flames. The thought was that hot, that searing; she covered her eyes with her hands.

Timna did not notice. She was assisting Leah Korngold, who wanted a corset for her niece's wedding. Sima knew the rivalry between Leah and her sister from decades past; knew Leah would spend any amount of money to look an ounce thinner than her sister. "Show her the Dior," Sima had told Timna, and Timna, understanding, had immediately picked out the top of the line in lingerie. "It's the latest thing," Sima could hear her saying to Leah, and Sima smiled despite herself. How unself-conscious the phrase was, coming from Timna's lips —

she'd learned it from Sima, noticed the power it had to convince, and repeated it without the slightest sense of mimicry whenever a customer expressed hesitation.

Timna had come in late again that morning, and Sima noticed, as she always did these last few weeks, how unwell Timna looked — her skin blotchy, her face drawn. As Timna removed her coat, Sima saw that she was wearing a pair of black cotton drawstring pants that she'd bought from the store a few weeks ago, saying they were for yoga. Sima realized it wasn't the first time she'd worn them to work; it'd been at least twice this week, and in between not the blue jeans or black cords, both of them tight, faded down the thighs and across the back, that Sima was accustomed to admiring, but instead a pair of shapeless gray slacks.

There was that as evidence. And then Timna had been so tired lately, going so far as to lay her head on the table between customers, sometimes in seconds falling asleep. Sima had blamed Timna's late nights — who knew what she did, or with whom — but when Timna again refused a second cup of coffee despite the darkness under her eyes, Sima wondered if evenings out were only half the story. Timna had taken out a bottle of water instead, said something about a celebrity diet, and indeed she had gained weight: her breasts pulled at her lavender sweater, the wool creasing under her armpit.

While Timna stood beside the dressing room, waiting for Leah to pull back the curtain so she could check the fit, she ran a finger beneath the drawstring waistline of her cotton pants, loosening them.

My God, Sima thought, the words on fire: Timna is pregnant.

"See how it holds in your tummy," Timna said, smiling as Leah turned before the mirror. "Especially if your dress is beige, you want something like this, because there's nothing for the dress to catch on — it's smoother than your own skin could be."

Leah frowned with approval. "It's very nice," she said, running her hands along her sides, "no lines or anything. My sister always has panty lines — it's so embarrassing, I hope her daughter checks her before the wedding so she doesn't ruin the pictures."

"Well, you'll look perfect, at least," Timna said, and Sima wondered again at how she knew just what to say. "You need anything else? Bras? Panties?" Before Leah could answer, Timna continued, "We just got in some wonderful stuff from Olga's, and I think we have in your size this great set, just a hint of lace and so comfortable —"

Sima watched as Timna walked over to the shelves, stepped up one level on the ladder, and grabbed a box. She was a good worker. Better than good. She took naps, coffee breaks, she didn't like to clean — but the women fell for her, bought whatever she recommended, because she was young and beautiful and when she smiled, they felt they'd won something.

But if she were pregnant they'd whisper, stare, look from her face to her ring finger, searching. It was not acceptable, it was not okay — an unmarried pregnant woman could not work in her store. Never.

Leah liked the bra and the underwear, chose one set in beige and one in black. Timna carried the purchases to the cash register; Sima, without speaking, took them and rang them up. "Cash or charge?" she called to Leah, wondering how she should tell Timna that she knew.

"Cash," Leah answered, and appeared a few minutes later, dressed, counting out the twenties from her wallet, full of gossip for Sima about the wedding plans — "Can you believe a buffet, not sit-down? The lines will take forever, and for that food, who would bother?" Sima nodded, clucked in sympathy, but concentrated on Timna — noting how quickly she went to sit down again.

"You're tired, huh?" Sima asked after Leah left.

"I guess. I haven't been sleeping well lately."

"Maybe you're sick? Your skin is blotchy."

"Maybe. I think it's the winter — I'm just tired all the time. I'm not used to this weather."

Sima looked at her. Was she lying, or could it be she hadn't noticed? She'd heard stories — women taking months to realize, as much from denial as ignorance, and Timna had every reason to hide from such a truth. It wouldn't be Alon's, of course; Shai was the only other man Sima knew by name, though she suspected there were more. Timna went to dance clubs, concerts, and looking like she did, having resolved to explore, there would be no lack of opportunities. Just one night, one time, and her whole life would be changed. Ruined.

Timna was pregnant.

Sima was furious.

Here was a life so young, so capable of doing so much. The travel, the education — all the things Sima could not have, would never have. And to throw it all away. The man was probably already out of the picture, or would be soon enough — it was an old story, ending Timna's too soon.

She was too irresponsible, Sima thought, watching as Timna lifted her head, checked the polish on her nails for chipping. She wasn't like the neighborhood women, raised to raise children. She wanted too much — she'd feel the disappointment of all she would not be, could not do, too cutting. And who would help her, her own mother distant, her father preoccupied with his own family? She needed support; she'd have none.

No. It couldn't be. But then the alternative —

Sima imagined for a moment Timna on a cold metal table, saw her old doctor standing over her, smiling through yellow teeth. She sat down, rested her head in her hands. The alternative was unthinkable.

The bell rang, and Sima started, jumped quickly to her feet. "You were resting too?" Timna asked, as Sima stepped out from behind the counter. "How about I go make another cup of coffee for both of us?"

"And your celebrity diet?"

"Screw the diet. I need a cup of coffee."

Sima watched her go; said nothing.

After the hysterectomy Sima was put on a

hormone regimen. She took the Premarin pills each night and watched her body change: she gained weight, her breasts, belly, and thighs expanding as they had when she was a teenager while her hair, previously thin, thickened into stiff waves to be forced back into a bun each morning, bobby pins pressed between her lips. The changes were internal as well. She became quick to anger, the feeling rising as a heat inside her until it burst out like steam from beneath a pocked and potholed city street. She yelled at Lev for forgetting to buy stamps, misplacing the car keys, leaving the newspaper spread on the kitchen table. "You always screw things up!" she screamed when he'd overwatered the spider plant so that it dripped in five thin streams onto the carpet below, "Why can't you do anything right? Why is everything such a mess with you?"

He didn't respond.

She wished, sometimes, he would, wished he would scream as she did and with hands on her shoulders pull her back to a place where they'd been happy. But he didn't. He allowed her, instead, to care for him — sacrificed his role as husband for that of child.

She didn't have the words to say, I need you.

He didn't know how to hear her through the silence.

22

"What should we do?" Sima asked Lev, watching him as he captured a piece of cauliflower from the soup with his spoon, brought it to his mouth.

"I don't see we can do much of anything. It's her life."

Sima looked at him. "How can you still say that, now that you know she really is in trouble?"

"You haven't proven that," Lev said, pointing his spoon at her. A drop of soup fell to the table; he quickly wiped it up with his napkin.

"How were you ever a vice principal," Sima asked, "given you see so little?" She shook her head, began to count on her fingers. "First, she's tired all the time. Second, her skin is blotchy —"

"Since when is blotchy skin and tiredness a medical symptom?"

"Third, her breasts are larger. Fourth, her

roots are showing. Fifth, she hardly drinks caffeine —"

"But you said she did the once, no?"

"So, once is okay. The point is —"

"Okay. Go on. What's the other evidence?"

"Sixth," Sima paused over her new hand. Was there any more evidence than that? "Lev, look at how you got soup on your shirt," she said, pointing to an orange stain along the button-line. "I should get you a bib or something."

Lev half-stood. "If you just want to pick on me —"

"No," Sima said, waving him back down, "stay." She wanted his advice; needed him on board. "What do you think?" she asked, "what should I do?"

Lev shrugged. "Timna might be pregnant," he said, emphasizing the might, "or she might be tired or sick or depressed or anything else. Maybe she has that new disease, that seasonal depression syndrome."

Sima clucked her tongue in disapproval. "Timna's not the type to have a syndrome."

"There's a type?"

"There's a type of person prone to depression, and Timna's not one of them. Believe me," Sima said, taking away the soup plates, "I should know."

She returned with two dinner plates —

fish and a side of rice — served Lev and then herself. They ate quietly; it wasn't until she stood to again clear his plate that she spoke. "You love Timna," she said, saying it and knowing it was true and how odd, she thought, that they should love the same girl when she couldn't really say if they loved each other. "Don't you care what happens to her?"

Lev looked at her. "If she wants to let me in, she will."

"If she wants to let you in, huh?" Sima tasted a bitterness in her mouth, an anger rising. "That's your excuse for never asking, never pushing to help anyone." She put the plates in the dishwasher, not bothering to rinse them clean. "You just sit around and wait for an invitation while ignoring the suffering right in front of your face."

"That's not true, Sima — you're the one who locked me out. You sacrificed everything to keep your secret, and then blamed me for not being there." He stood, faced her. "Now Timna has a secret, maybe has a secret, who even knows for sure, and you want to expose it. Why?"

"Because of that, because of that exactly." She closed the dishwasher door, smoothed the puffed pockets of her housedress. "Because I know what regret can be, I know how it can strangle and kill —"

"Do you think we'll get her baby?"

"What?"

"Do you think Timna will give us the baby?"

She looked at him. His face was pale; the veins on his neck just purple. "Lev, now you're the one out of his mind." Even as she dismissed it, her heart jumped at the thought — a baby, Timna — but she swallowed, pushed the longing deep down.

"Come on, Sima, admit it: the daughter we never had, the grandchild we never even dreamed of —"

You never dreamed of, she thought. She glanced at Lev's hand lightly resting on the counter: the fingernails a little long, the hair turned to white — when? "I have to help her, Lev. It wouldn't be right not to."

He shook his head, turned away. "Whatever you say, Sima. Whatever you say."

"You have got to do something," Connie said when Sima called that evening. "She needs you. Here she is all alone, thousands upon thousands of miles from home, and now pregnant —"

"So you think, based on what I told you —"

"God, yes. Haven't I always said, Sima,

296

that you're one of the most observant women I know? That's how you run such a successful business. Notwithstanding that you destroyed my own marriage —"

"Connie, I —" Sima felt her heartbeat quicken.

"Kidding, kidding. The point is you see things, you notice what your customer needs even before she sees it herself."

"Yeah?"

"Remember Shirley, how you told her she needed more support before she even said anything about it, and then it turned out she was about to get reduction surgery before your bras made the difference?"

Sima nodded, sat down on the bed.

"She's pregnant. My God. Do you know whose?"

"No. I don't know anything, we haven't spoken about it." It was cold in the room; she brought the comforter up above her legs.

"Can you imagine — it could just be some guy. I swear, if Nate ever did anything like that —"

"What? What would you do? Because this is what I'm trying to figure out, what my role is, whether I should interfere or not." Sima leaned back against the pillows.

"Well, keep in mind I'm his mother, so of course I'd have a role. I'd call the girl myself. I'd take her for lunch, explain how disappointed I was in my son, but between her and me things would be open. She was carrying my grandchild after all, I'd say, and I wasn't about to let my grandchild be raised in poverty —"

"I don't want the speech, Connie, just what you think I should do."

"Sorry, I got caught up. Listen, as far as Timna, I think maybe you should call her mother, explain your suspicions —"

Sima sat up, moving a pillow to the small of her back for support. "Really? Just like that, call her mother?" Sima tried to keep her voice even, hide her disappointment — she wanted to be the one to save Timna, didn't want to defer to Timna's mother.

"Of course her mother. Why not?"

"Because they're not that close. Timna told me —"

"So they're not close. All the more reason for you to call, because Timna probably won't." Connie paused. "Listen Sim-sim, I know how much you love this girl —"

Sima pressed her eyes closed, tears hot behind the lids.

"But this is too big a job for you. If she's not going to call her mom herself, then you need to do it."

"But she'll be furious —"

"Maybe so. But it's the right thing. You can't just stand by and do nothing while she destroys her life. Sima, you of all people —"

"But is it my place to interfere?"

"If not you, then who? Here she is, young and alone in New York City, of all places. Imagine she has an abortion and never tells her mother — think of that, the distance between them."

Sima nodded, smearing away tears with the back of her palm.

"Sima, it's up to you to heal that relationship. All along I've said to Art —" Connie paused, and this time Sima could hear the catch in her throat, "I've said, there's a reason Timna was given to Sima. Now I see why."

After Sima hung up the phone, she sat in bed, quietly smoothing the covers across her lap. It wasn't the role she'd wanted — the bridge between Timna and her mother, stepping back as they reached forward — but perhaps it was the only one she could claim. The important thing wasn't her own desires but Timna's needs. How to protect Timna, how to keep her safe, how, she thought as she ran her fingers along the quilted comforter, to preserve for Timna wonder and joy, the happiness that, so long ago, she herself had lost.

■ ■ ■ ■

FEBRUARY

■ ■ ■ ■

23

Sima put her hand on the phone receiver, felt the curve of the plastic beneath her palm. She lifted it up slowly, tucking it between her ear and shoulder while she carefully dialed the numbers she'd found written in Timna's date book. She'd felt all the stereotypes of the thief when she opened Timna's purse, searched for the book: fast-beating heart, pricked ears, every noise outside the approaching footsteps of witnesses ready to condemn.

She had waited for Timna to go upstairs for lunch with Lev, a tradition that took place a few times a week, before circling Timna's desk, readying for the attack. She counted twenty, thirty seconds, listened closely to the noises upstairs: the kiss of the refrigerator opening, closing; the scratch of chairs pulled out and in; the rising whisper of voices: Lev's rushed, tumbling out the thoughts he'd saved for this one bright listener — "You'd be interested in this," and "I came across that" — Timna punctuating his stories with "I never realized" and "Isn't that amazing?" offering discrete scenes from her own past, a plastic-dome still life — plastic palm trees, blue ink sea — for him to marvel at, shake softly in his hand.

At the count of fifty, Sima grabbed Timna's purse.

She kept her eyes on the staircase as she felt for the date book, reaching between lipstick, tissues, and a leopard-print wallet before running her fingers along the spiral spine, pulling it to light. A tiny book, the kind sold at bookstore checkout counters: Monet's water lilies on the front cover, one of Picasso's clowns on the back. Sima opened it, fumbled to "S."

She found him right away: had first noticed a name of just two Hebrew letters and then, sounding them out, spelled Shai, her mouth open with the whisper of his name. She copied the number into her own date book, hiding it below October's reminder to clean the leaf-filled gutters.

She watched Timna carefully all afternoon, noted the way she sat down between customers, her yawns never quite hidden behind her hand, her gaze distracted. She let her off a half-hour early, feigning a headache as an excuse — "Go, I need to rest a little" — afraid that if she waited too long, she'd lose her nerve.

Despite Connie's advice she'd decided to try Shai first — she'd met him, at least. He might be able to help approach Timna's mother, and he might even be the father — an outcome Sima both hoped for and railed against. She prayed for an answering machine — she'd hang up, try again some other time.

On the third ring someone picked up.

"Hello?"

"Hello. Is Shai there?"

She heard the man calling Shai's name and then footsteps coming closer. She felt like a teenager, calling a boy from the hallway phone while her mother prepared dinner, mouth close to the receiver, ready to whisper.

Shai picked up the phone. "Yes?"

"Shai," Sima said, her voice coated with an enthusiasm she did not feel, "It's Sima, Timna's boss."

There was a pause. She could feel the press of his palm to the receiver, hear him whispering something to his roommate.

"Sima, hi." She could hear a question in his voice.

"Hello," she said, trying to sound friendly,

warm. "How are you?"

After an exchange of small talk — the usual comments about February in New York, how cold, how gray and wet — she forced herself to move the conversation forward. "I'm calling about Timna," she told him, wrapping the cord around her wrist — of course he'd know she was calling about Timna. "I was calling," she said, choosing her words carefully, "because I was wondering, if, well, does she seem sick to you lately?"

"Sick?"

"Yes. She's tired, and —" Sima paused, unsure how to explain without revealing too much. "Her stomach is upset a lot I noticed," she said, pleased at her subtlety.

There was no response; immediately Sima worried she hadn't been subtle enough. "I wouldn't call," she explained, a sense of shame growing, "but you know Timna, she refuses to see a doctor, and I don't get the feeling her cousins really pay attention, and I didn't want to just sit by if there really is some problem —" Sima paused, why wasn't he jumping in? — "if I could be of help."

"You think something is the matter with her health?"

"Well, I don't mean to set off an alarm —" She drew the cord tighter, so that it

306

pulled at her skin.

"You think she needs a hospital or something like that?"

"No, not exactly." Sima hesitated. She'd hoped that Shai would confide in her, relieved to have someone to share the weight of Timna's secret; she'd imagined, as she'd watched Timna assist a customer that afternoon — noting how she ignored the woman's baby tucked in its stroller, though usually Timna was sure, like any good saleslady, to coo over every child — that together she and Shai would solve Timna's troubles. "Thank you, Sima," she'd pictured him saying, "I couldn't have done it without you." And though what "it" was, she hadn't decided but that Timna would be left safe and happy — which might in fact entail Shai's removal — still she smiled to think of how she'd wave away his thanks, say it was nothing, it was just what anyone would do.

"What I was wondering —" Sima began, determined to make one last try. "Is whether you and Timna have talked about this at all. About her not feeling so well?"

Shai took a moment to respond. "I don't think she mentioned it."

"Just because," Sima said, taking his pause as a wearing down of defenses, "I know you're one of her, umm, closest friends in

New York, so I thought she might have said something to you —"

"No. Actually, I haven't seen her in a while."

Sima let go of the phone cord. Timna had reported going to the movies with Shai a few days earlier. "When was the last time you saw her?" she asked.

"A few weeks ago."

Sima lowered her voice. "Did something happen?"

She didn't need to hear the silence to know she'd overstepped a boundary, shown herself not for the concerned friend she'd hoped to appear but instead a gossiping, meddling old lady. "No. Just busy," Shai said, and Sima made an excuse to end the conversation — well, sorry to bother you, I should get going — before he could.

She had to sit after hanging up the phone, sort out the questions running through her mind. Shai might be lying: as the father, he would have reason to. She imagined Timna crying as he raged — this is your problem, he'd say, this is your fault — pressed her own hand to her lips as she pictured Timna curl beneath his anger, Timna's face flushed and her breath uneven as she rocked herself back and forth, back and forth.

Or maybe it was Timna who rejected Shai,

told him, her voice low and thin, don't ever touch me again, don't ever call me again, and though he'd pleaded — I love you, he'd have told her, we can do this — she'd walked away, knowing she was alone and his best promises inert as the future rose before her wide and dark and terrifying. Sima saw Timna turning down dim city streets, the same stale questions circling in her head as she moved alone among strangers, and no one placing a hand on her shoulder, no one saying, as Sima longed to, "I'm here now, I'm here for you."

Sima bit her fist lightly, touched by the image before her. Timna needed her; she would say something first thing tomorrow, no matter what. She placed a hand on the counter, steadying to stand, when another thought made her pause. Timna might not be alone. Shai might have been replaced weeks ago by some other boyfriend Timna hadn't even bothered to mention to her. And was it this stranger who had taken Timna to the movies the other week, or did the movie excursion cover a darker one — a health clinic somewhere, lavender trim against the ceiling and the intermittent beep of glass doors sliding open?

Sima dialed the operator. "Yes, I need help finding an international number. Israel,

Herzeliyah. The last name is Shachar."

She didn't hang up after the operator gave her the number, held the phone against her chest, one finger pressing it off, and surveyed the shop — all the spaces where Timna wasn't. She glanced at the notepad beside her: a series of numbers to awaken Timna's mother from across the world, a curled cord to pull her in, spiral Sima out. Timna would likely quit as soon as Sima told her what she'd done, and even if she didn't, even if she ended up saying thank you, you were right, even if Sima reunited mother and daughter with one phone call, even then — Sima knew she'd lose her. Replaced. Redundant. Waving goodbye, wishing she'd write.

Sima looked over to Timna's sewing table, thought of that earlier conversation when they'd agreed that the bra shop, like Timna's supermarket freezer, was Sima's refuge, safety. She wondered whether that was still true. In the past months she'd been aware of all she'd gained from Timna: the joy, the excitement, the flush of watching her beauty, winning her laughter. But with that gain had come loss: she'd loved her days in the shop not because they were her own but because she'd shared them with Timna.

Sima hung up the phone and glanced,

briefly, at the smooth curve of the chair that did not hold Timna before walking up the staircase, turning off the light.

Sima would say, afterwards, that she didn't come to the bra business — it came to her.

"You need to keep yourself busy," Connie told her. They'd run into each other outside the green grocer, where Sima had responded to her suggestion that they get a manicure together with an indifferent shrug. "I've been thinking about it," Connie continued. "You need to get a job. Something to get up for every morning, something that'll be fun."

"A barrel of laughs, I'm sure," Sima said, dropping three tomatoes into a plastic sleeve.

Connie ignored the comment. "A legal secretary maybe, or a saleslady at A&S or Gimbels — just think of the discounts."

Sima tied a knot at the top of the baggie, frowned. She didn't know many working women her age: most of her friends had married straight out of high school, and though a few earned degrees as teachers and nurses or entered the family business — textiles, electronics — they stopped working when the babies were born, staying at home at least until all the kids had entered school.

311

"Come on, Sima," Connie said, following her over to the oranges. "You know if you'd been raised anywhere but the Boro Park ghetto we came from, you'd have gone to college, gotten a real job. You're so smart and so capable — you saved us from poverty, for God's sake."

Sima pretended to concentrate on the oranges — the pale ones, she'd recently read, were the sweetest — not wanting to admit how the compliment flattered. "I did not save you from poverty, Connie, I just taught you how to keep a budget."

"Poverty, Sima. My boys would be in rags if it weren't for you."

Sima looked up. "Are you being fresh with me?" she teased, repeating a question she'd heard Connie put to Nate and Howie.

Connie laughed. "Think about it, okay? Just do me that favor."

Sima became the bookkeeper for three neighborhood shops: Faye's Fashions, Michael's Film and Processing, and Holy Land Travel. She'd been concerned about Faye's Fashions before she began. Changing outfits three times before the interview, she was sure she wouldn't be as elegant as they'd like, but it quickly became her favorite place to work. At the film and travel shops she sat away from the customers: at Michael's she

312

shared an old metal desk with a barely mustached teenager whose job it was to sort the photographs into the correct envelopes, and whose beet-red blushes gave away every bikini-clad woman — worse, Sima didn't let herself think — he came across, and though Holy Land gave her a mahogany desk complete with olive desk-set, the leather cylinder always flush with pens, they expected only that she would sit quietly for the time it took to balance their accounts, then leave.

But at Faye's she sat beside the counter with one of the shop girls, or with Faye herself — her hair dyed blond, her nails long, her voice husky from three decades of smoking, her smile always conspiratorial, always making Sima feel it was her and Faye against the world. Faye paid her for only five hours a week, ten at tax time, but Sima often stayed longer, standing beside Faye as they looked through the samples the salesmen brought or debated what to put on sale, and for how much.

"You," Faye once said, "are the typical Boro Park woman. I'm here to give that woman flair, but I can only push so far — you're like my litmus test."

"If I'd wear it," Sima laughed, "then anyone would, right?"

Faye smiled. "Only thirty-five, and already the most conservative woman in Boro Park."

"Except for the Hasidim."

"Except for the Hasidic men, maybe. You wear short sleeves and pants, sure, but have you seen how nice some of those women dress? I'm thinking of designing a line just for them. Every spring we'd do a High Holy Days fashion debut. Can you imagine what I could make on hats alone?"

Faye became a friend. Sima loved sitting beside her, coffee and cookies always within reach, as she gossiped with each woman who entered the shop. "We sell them something better than themselves," Faye would tell her. And though the clothing was mostly cotton and polyester, Sima felt, as she watched a woman grin at her reflection, turn before the mirror, that Faye really was a fairy godmother, capable of making even the dullest women gleam.

Sima confided in Faye, as all the women did. She told her that she was barren, to which Faye replied that barren was a terrible word, horrible, and she never wanted Sima to say it again. "Barren is a desert where nothing grows. That's not you, Sima. That's the opposite of you."

Sima believed her when they were together, in the shop with the women laughing under cream-colored lights ("No one wants to be naked under fluorescents," Faye told her), or smoking cigarettes in the backroom while Faye updated her on the gossip ("You didn't know Hazel has mafia connections?"). But at home she felt barren, just as Faye understood the word: empty, useless. She and Lev had lost each other, and though sometimes the space she felt between them made her angry and sometimes ashamed, more and more she became resigned to what she imagined was not uncommon: two people living together who did not exactly love each other, but who had no reason to leave each other either.

All the women at Faye's Fashions complained about their husbands, and though Sima suspected that the distraction of children made their marriages happier than hers, she also knew her own parents had not loved as she'd once hoped she and Lev would. How many did, she asked herself, and how much, after all, could one expect from life? The country was at war; the evening news full of images of dead soldiers, burned jungles. Her own sorrows were insignificant beside that reality, the barren desert Faye conjured no larger than a brushing of sand in the weeds that grew against

315

the public bathrooms at Brighton Beach.

Sima had been at the store two years when Faye announced her retirement. It was not just surprising; it was a betrayal. "You're barely fifty," Sima argued, concentrating to keep her voice calm, "who retires so young?"

"I want to be a lady of leisure while I still have time to enjoy it."

"Time? You'll have fifty years."

Faye placed her hands on either side of Sima's face. "My own dear child," she said, smiling, "I'm off on a new adventure. Can't you be happy for me?"

Sima thought a moment. The answer punched her in the stomach: "No."

Faye had a cousin who sold shoes from her basement and was looking to expand; she came by the store before it closed, bought what was left of Faye's handbag and belt stock. "Talk about ideal," Sima told Faye after the cousin left, "a business in your own basement. You don't even have to walk two blocks to work."

"You know how she got it?" Faye asked.

Sima shook her head no, though Faye had told her before.

"Well," Faye said, sitting down. "So —"

Sima listened again to the cousin's story: her father had owned a shoe store on 13th

Avenue and kept his overstock in their basement a few blocks away. Eventually his regulars realized the basement contained the best bargains and began to go straight there.

"Why pay rent when you've got a basement?" Faye asked. "For a small operation like they have, it's perfect."

"I have a finished basement," Sima said, as if she'd never realized it before. "Actually, since we're just one block off Thirteenth, it's a great location for a store, right near everything."

Faye looked at Sima. "Are you thinking of going into business yourself?"

"No, no," Sima said, shaking her head. "I just meant I have a good basement for that sort of thing is all."

"Well, but have you thought of it? I haven't sold off my all my stock yet. The lingerie —"

Sima had thought of it — her own shop, women asking her advice — but didn't want to admit the fantasy for fear of Faye's reaction. "What would I do," Sima said, "just up and open a shop?"

"That's what I did."

"I thought your father owned it first."

Faye waved her hand. "He sold junk. I changed everything when I took over."

"Still," Sima told her, "it probably wouldn't work."

Faye didn't respond, and Sima took her silence as agreement. She wanted to protest — though she wasn't much for fashion, it was surprisingly easy to order the basics and follow well-established trends, and as for customers, the truth was she knew some of them preferred her matter-of-fact approach to Faye's exhausting need to entertain. But instead of arguing, she rejected the possibility herself, before Faye could. "It was just a thought," Sima said, "nothing serious —"

"I've got it!" Faye spread her hands apart as if unveiling a marquee. "Sima's Showcase. Sima's Showcase — is that not perfect?"

Sima grinned.

24

Sima meant to call Timna's mother before breakfast, but instead she lay in bed making excuses; the room was so cold and the bed so warm and probably her mother wouldn't be home then, anyway — she'd call later. But then the shop was busy all day, and Timna was there, and she didn't feel it was right to leave her alone while she snuck upstairs to call her mother. Twice she tested her, "How's Shai?" she asked once, and "What movie was it you and Shai saw again?" another, but Timna just answered fine, and named some comedy, and Sima could not think how to question her further.

At lunchtime Timna stood and stretched, mentioning a few errands she needed to run — buy a birthday card for her mother, pick up a jacket from the dry cleaner. "No problem," Sima told her, grateful for the time alone, "go, take your time."

As soon as Timna left, Sima sat down

behind the counter, tucked her head against her arms. *You need to say something,* she told herself, *you can't let her leave tonight without trying to help her.* She tried out lines in her mind — "We need to talk, Timna," she might say, or "There's been something I've been meaning to ask you" — but each sentence echoed lamely in her head. Timna would dismiss her concern again, and Sima would be left without words to express her fears.

When the doorbell rang, Sima smiled at the woman who peered tentatively into the shop, glad for the distraction. "If you're looking for bras, you've come to the right place," Sima told her, moving out from behind the counter.

The woman smiled. "I am," she said, taking off her coat. She wore a black sweater dotted by white cat hairs; she tucked her hair behind her ears in a shy, self-conscious gesture.

"Thirty-four-D," Sima said, glancing at her bust. "So what can I get you?"

The woman raised her eyebrows. "I heard you were a pro, but —"

"It's easy to be a pro in this field," Sima told her, walking them both toward the dressing room. "There's not much competition." She stepped aside before the curtain, watched as the customer walked in ahead: a tall woman, she moved with a slight stoop. "So what's your name?" Sima asked, warming, as always, to displays of insecurity. "What can I get for you?"

"Louise. And I'm looking for anything that minimizes."

"Are you sure? I get women here, they'd pay for those."

"I'd pay to get rid of them."

"Well," Sima told her, "we'll see what we can do without surgery, okay? Just wait here, and I'll bring you some choices."

Louise tried on the bra Sima brought — "Our best-selling minimizer, you'll love it" — grinned at her reflection in the mirror.

"It fits perfect," Sima told her, tugging at the shoulder straps, "but a young woman like you should be showing off a little. This bra is good for work, but let me get you something for evenings, for when you want to feel a little sexier —" Sima left the dressing room before Louise could protest. "A little black, a little cleavage, something nice, not too much." She spoke quickly as she moved up the stepladder, reached for a box. "I've got just the thing," she called, removing a bra. "You've got to at least try."

Louise tried on the bra — black, with two stitched birds that met just below the rim of each cup — paused in front of the mirror. The bra lifted her breasts, creating cleavage that swelled above each cup. "Look at that," she said, angling her body before the mirror, "I never knew they could do that."

"Oh, they can do plenty." Sima smiled at Louise, remembering how Timna had shrieked over the bra when it arrived at the shop. "Have you ever seen something so nice?" Timna had asked, shifting her shoulders before the mirror as she modeled it.

No, Sima had admitted, taking in the black lace stretched across Timna's skin, she hadn't.

"Still," Louise told her, "I don't think this is really me —"

Sima crossed her arms across her chest. "So, what's you?"

"I just, I like to keep my body to myself."

"Louise," Sima said, "you're too young for that attitude. Me, I couldn't pay a man to look. But you — here, put your shirt back on."

Louise slipped on her sweater, stepped back to see the effect.

"Is that not sexy?" Sima asked, gesturing with her chin at Louise's reflection: just the faintest hint of cleavage was visible at the top of the V-neck, but her breasts swelled against the fabric. Sima knew she was being too aggressive, but couldn't resist. This small rescue — just to help one woman enjoy her body every now and then — this she could do, had to do.

Louise laughed. "Okay, okay. You've convinced me; I'll take it."

"Yeah? Good for you. Really, it's good for you."

Timna came back just as Louise was leaving. "I sold her your favorite push-up," Sima told her, and Louise laughed as Timna asked, "The one with the birds? You'll love it."

Sima watched Louise disappear up the steps, a brown plastic bag, filled with three minimizers along with the push-up, swinging from one arm. She waited for another customer to appear, hoping for an excuse to delay confronting Timna, but none did. *Now or never,* she told herself, turning away from the empty staircase.

Timna sat down at the sewing table. "I have to tell you," she said, putting her purse on the floor beside her, "why I left just now — it wasn't a birthday card I had to buy for my mom."

Sima looked at her. "Oh?"

Timna placed her hand in her chin, frowned. "Her birthday isn't until April."

Sima waited for what would come next.

Timna would tell her the truth: she'd been at a pay phone pleading with Shai; she'd been to the doctor for a blood test; she'd been at the children's boutique, fawning over soft pastel nightgowns. She held back a smile as she anticipated the confession, thrilled that Timna had come to her in the end, she hadn't had to force it. Just like that, she imagined telling Connie, she opened right up to me, told me everything.

"I bought her a card because we had a fight," Timna said. "She broke up with her boyfriend, Udi. You saw his picture — the man making breakfast in our kitchen."

Sima watched Timna as she spoke, described what had happened — her mother calling for the first time in months, alternating between tears and giddy laughter as she recounted the breakup. "Nothing she said made any sense," Timna told her, "first she was hysterical and Udi was a bastard, then she'd met someone else who I was just going to love." She pulled her hair back into a ponytail, sighed. "I'm so sick of it, you know? He was the first guy in so long who made her laugh, made me laugh. They were together almost two years, and I just really hoped —" Timna took a deep breath, smiled weakly at Sima. "It's just — no matter how much I try to distance myself, no matter how far away I go —"

"Oh, Timna," Sima said, fully won over now to the delicious attraction of her tragedy. Without thinking, she crossed the shop floor, wanting to gather Timna to her, but once in front of the sewing table she paused, unsure of how to move — Timna was sitting down, her body unavailable. "If there's anything I can do," Sima said, "if there's anything you need —" She placed a hand on Timna's shoulder, lightly squeezed the narrow bone beneath.

Timna rubbed her eyes. "Look at this," she told Sima, removing a brown paper bag from within her purse. Sima reached into the bag, pulled out a greeting card. On the cover yellow sunflowers bloomed in a green field, inside it was blank. "It took me thirty minutes to decide on a card. Thirty minutes for a blank card. And now I have to figure out what to write." Timna sighed as she crossed her arms on the desk, rested her head on top of them.

Sima reached forward to stroke Timna's hair, unable to resist its soft pull. "It's nice of you though, to write her —" she offered, aware of her own jealousy at Timna sending her mother a card, worrying over what to say. She smoothed Timna's hair once, twice, before forcing her hands back to her own side.

Timna shrugged, explained that she bought it out of guilt — they'd had a fight, her mother had accused Timna of caring more about Udi than about her. "And maybe it's true," Timna said, sitting up. "Maybe I would rather keep him in my life than her."

Sima held her hands together, unsure what to say. She was thrilled, partly, to hear how little respect Timna held for her mother: there was nothing to envy in that relationship, and as for the phone call — even Connie would agree that Timna's mother shouldn't be brought in at this point. At the same time, Sima couldn't help but feel sorry for Timna's mother; she imagined her as a customer in the shop, shaking her head sadly as she told Sima, "I don't know why she hates me, I can't imagine what I've done."

"I just hope I don't end up like her," Timna said. "It scares me sometimes, the thought that I might."

Sima was about to dismiss Timna's fears — of course she wouldn't end up like her mother — when something stopped her. "You're afraid of that, then," she asked, "of being like her?"

"Terrified."

Sima nodded. She thought of everything that had changed for Timna in the last few months — breaking up with Alon, staying out late with Shai and Nurit, and finally the changes of the last few weeks. "What about being like her do you fear?" Sima asked.

"I don't know; it's not easy to say, exactly." Timna reached for a spool of navy thread beside the sewing machine, began to roll it back and forth across the table. "The way she needs men, I guess, but then always pushes them away."

"And do you ever think," Sima asked, excited now as the clues fell neatly into place — so observant, she could hear Connie say, so insightful — "that this thing with Alon, breaking up with him because you felt too settled, too dependent —" she paused, looked at Timna. "Do you think maybe you pushed Alon away from fear of becoming your mother?"

Timna tapped the top of the spool, turned it over. "What?"

Sima hesitated, once again knowing she should stop but unwilling to do so: everything had changed when Timna left Alon; bringing him back might return her to joy. "You told me," Sima said, "back when you showed me those pictures, that your mother was afraid to be alone, that she always needed a man."

"Maybe. I don't really remember —"

"But at the same time she's unable to really commit to a relationship. She needs men, but then she pushes them away, right?"

Timna waited a moment before responding. "Right."

"Timna," Sima said, her gaze soft — how young Timna was, how in need of guidance. "When you broke up with Alon, saying you didn't want to stay with him out of fear of being alone — do you think maybe you were afraid of being like your mother, of needing men?"

She felt like one of the experts on the talk shows, how quickly, how clearly, she exposed the truth, the audience breaking into applause.

Timna rolled the navy spool back and forth beneath her palm.

"Because to be so afraid of being dependent on someone else that you push them away — that's what your mother actually does, that's how she hurts you." Sima had to concentrate to keep her voice calm. She felt both terrified and triumphant as she explained: out of fear of becoming her mother, Timna had acted just like her, pushing someone wonderful away.

"It's not that simple, Sima," Timna said, her voice strained thin, "I was with Alon for years —"

"I don't mean to make it simple," Sima told her, "believe me, I know how far from simple it is." She looked at Timna, smiled. "I just want to tell you, so you should know — you're not your mother, Timna."

Timna nodded.

"I know it's hard to hear this, and maybe it's not fair for me to say —" Sima hesitated a moment, but only for display. "You broke up with Alon so you wouldn't fear being alone, but it takes as much courage, maybe even more, to stay with someone."

"Sima —"

"Timna, your mother may lack that courage, but you have it. I know you have it." Sima crossed her arms before her, holding on. She wanted to tell Timna she understood her secretiveness, sympathized with how ambivalent she must feel about becoming a mother, but hesitated, hoping Timna would come to her first. "Timna," Sima said, imagining for a moment the joy of the months to come — Timna taking her hands and drawing them to her belly as they felt together the swell of her baby's kick — "you haven't been yourself lately. How come?"

Timna kept her gaze steady on the spool

of thread. "I don't want to talk about it."

Sima nodded, checked her disappointment: she'd have to wait for Timna to make the final move. She reached again for Timna's hair; let a few strands cascade through her fingers. "Think about it then, will you? Remember that what you had with Alon, that was brave."

Timna looked up. "Maybe," she said, "maybe so."

Sima leaned back in her orange-plastic chair at the Dairy Delicious, registering what Connie had just told her. How many times had they sat here, the two of them, how many times a cup of coffee, an omelette, a slice of cake shared with two forks, the food the grease for their conversations: Lev, Art, Howie and Nate, this one, that one, have you heard, and wow, I never knew? But now Connie was whispering, was rushing her words, and Sima had to ask twice until she understood: Connie had contacted an escort.

"Escort, shmescort," Connie said. "This wasn't some phone-book advertisement. I found him in *Jewish Week*."

Sima stared in amazement. "What did the ad say?"

"You've probably seen it. Or you would, if

you were looking. He calls himself the Chasana Man. Available for all occasions: weddings, bar mitzvahs, brit milot, et cetera." Connie waved her hand. "How did he put it? Middle-aged divorced CPA, fit, willing to dance."

"Oh." Sima had an impulse to turn away, even leave; she didn't know what to make of Connie's exploits. She fingered her purse, an excuse already forming in her mind: the car was due an oil change, she'd been meaning to take it in.

But then she glanced at Connie.

Connie was watching her, waiting for her response. But what could she say?

My best friend just contacted an escort, Sima thought. She imagined telling Timna, solemnly repeating the words in her mind. But before she could finish the sentence, the hilarity of the situation struck her.

"A Chasana man out of *Jewish Week*," Sima said. "Only in New York."

When a wide grin spread across Connie's face, Sima realized how much Connie had been hoping for her approval.

"I know, I know," Connie told her, laughing. "And when I first saw the ad, well, I never thought. But then —"

"What do you have to lose?"

"Exactly."

Sima smiled. "Tell me everything," she said, allowing herself to give in to curiosity, even excitement. Connie needed her, after all. "What did you say when you called? What did he say?"

Connie leaned in, told the story. She'd left a message, he'd called back, and they arranged to have him accompany her to her great-niece's bat mitzvah. "I just couldn't do it alone," she said. "All those relatives, all those looks of pity and the unwanted advice. You know me, Sima — I'm not up for being single."

Sima nodded. She did.

"So — it was nice. He was nice."

"That's it, nice?" She sensed there was more, and wanted to hear it.

"He's better than the orthodontist, that's for sure."

"Anyone's better than the orthodontist." Myrna Silver's brother had turned out to have both an eye twitch and a jumpy leg; Connie had said he made her seasick.

Connie laughed. "That's true." Then she whispered, "I took him home."

"No!"

Connie nodded. "Well, I mean, he drove me home. And it seemed rude not to invite him in —"

"Did anything —"

"Oh, Sima." Connie covered her face with her hands, but Sima could see she was smiling. "I feel like a kid again, to be even talking about this —"

"Me too," Sima said. It was a good feeling.

"There's not much to say. We sat on the couch — the bed felt too creepy. We kissed. Remember that, kissing on a couch? How long has it been?"

Sima shook her head, amazed.

"I'd forgotten how uncomfortable a couch can be, to tell you the truth —"

Sima looked at her again, and laughed again, and this time Connie joined in, and before she knew it, they were giggling like schoolgirls.

But then Connie's laughter caught.

Sima looked on as Connie cried, knowing there was nothing she could say.

"What a mess, huh?" Connie asked, when her breath had evened out again.

"You know what?"

"What?" Connie pressed a napkin to her eyes.

"I'm so proud of you."

Connie paused, and then put down the napkin. "You know what?"

Sima waited.

"That may be one of the nicest things

anyone has ever said to me." Connie squeezed Sima's hand; their eyes met and held.

Four months after Faye sold her business, Sima opened Sima's Undergarments for Women, financed by the money in the purple tallis bag plus a decade's banking interest. It was not, Sima considered as she waited in line at the bank, how her mother would have wanted the money spent. The savings was not a gift to enjoy or money to take a risk with but a lesson in thrift: all this I saved on the few dollars a week your father gave me. It spoke of denial rather than wealth, and as Sima tucked the cashier's check into her wallet — almost all of which would go to buying Faye's stock from her, along with the cash register, counter, some chairs and the dressing-room bench — she flushed with pleasure to think how the money would buy her independence, a life fully different from her mother's.

In the first few months Sima felt like an impostor, just some woman feigning authority and expertise. She worried she'd made a terrible mistake; the customers wouldn't come, she'd be left alone, buried, she half-joked to Connie, by all the boxes in her basement.

But the customers did come. Every time the doorbell rang, she felt flush with the miracle — they were here for her, and just some flyers she'd paid a neighborhood boy to distribute and word of mouth from Faye to account for it. And although she'd worried, too, that once in the shop she'd disappoint them, she soon found that the authority of shopkeeper gave her a new confidence to make small talk — a joke here, a compliment there — she'd never had before. As Faye's stock ran out and she began to replace it, getting to know the salesmen and developing her own opinions of brands — what was worth the price and what wasn't — she began to feel that her authority was earned. One afternoon Sima returned to Bloomingdale's, this time as a spy, and was shocked to see the shoddiness of the lingerie they sold, the ignorance of the saleswomen, the complete lack of concern for fitting a customer properly.

"I could have walked out of there with a bra completely the wrong size, and no one would have cared," she told Connie. "Is that not appalling?" Though Connie was not as shocked as she might have been — "You went to Bloomies? Why didn't you call me?" — Sima knew she no longer needed Connie's confirmation to make a thing true.

Compared to department store clerks, she was an expert, and so an expert she became. She became more confident fitting women, pulling aside the curtain to check size and shape, forgetting, in the moments she evaluated the bra, that it was another woman's body, as imperfect and insecure as her own, that she observed. Because she forgot, they forgot, and when the women smiled at their reflections Sima was proud to think that like Faye before her, she gave each woman just a little more comfort, a little more happiness, than she'd had before.

One day a customer surprised Sima by touching her on the arm, telling her it'd been a year since the shop opened, hadn't it, and where had she ever gone before?

It was August, the air outside thick with the sort of still summer heat that made it impossible to believe the ocean bordered the borough, dark blue waves and pebbled sand and the rounded edges of glass shards worn by the sea. Sima thanked the customer, flush with pride — a feeling she had not known since the earliest days with Lev. After the customer left, Sima reached under the cash register for a photograph Faye had sent when she first moved to Florida: Faye on the beach in white slacks and a blue-striped sweater, her hands thrown open as if to say — here it is. "Thank you, Faye," Sima whispered to the picture, "I owe you."

The shop grew. From bras and underwear Sima expanded to slips, nightgowns, bridal wear, swimsuits. Sima's Undergarments for Women became a neighborhood fixture, word of mouth spreading sales through and then beyond Boro Park. Women came from Bensonhurst, Brighton Beach, Coney Island, Crown Heights, and Flatbush; retirees visited from Miami and Boca Raton; children returned from Houston, Chicago, and Los Angeles to shop at Sima's, stock up until the next trip home.

It was from one of the visiting retirees that Sima learned of Faye's death. She hadn't even known Faye was sick — they'd lost touch years before — and even as she sighed and clucked through the details — breast cancer, a double mastectomy and chemotherapy, a two-year fight, a hospice at the end with a sliver of ocean visible from her bed — Sima folded the news away, waiting for a free moment to think it through.

She didn't remember until she washed her face for bed that evening — the cold pull of water unfurling the knowledge of Faye's death from a gray fold somewhere. Sima saw Faye as she looked in that picture, long since thrown away after being stained with diet soda: her arms spread wide on the beach, an endless expanse of sun and sand and sea cradled within that embrace.

Sima recalled Faye's faith in her, her insistence that she was not barren. Her shop had given her purpose and pride, as Connie had predicted and as Faye had assured her. But Sima knew purpose and pride were not joy, did not send one spinning on the beach, arms flung open in full view. Remembering Faye, Sima remembered a time when she still mourned the death of that prospect of happiness — a time before resignation, before acceptance, a time when she was raw with the loss of love, aching.

Sima wished she could tell Faye how she'd admired her, wished the words didn't always come only after those they were meant for could no longer hear. I lost her, she thought, holding her own gaze in the mirror, I lost her, and I will never have her back. Tears gathered, but as she opened the cabinet door, her face sliding away before her, she recalled too the other woman she'd lost — her own young self, the one filled with long-ing — and pressed them away. Thank God, she thought as she removed Lev's choles-terol pills, closed the cabinet shut, thank God that's all over.

25

"I listened to you," Timna said, turning to Sima after closing the door behind the last customer of the day.

"About the pantyhose? I told you for older women the control top are the best —"

Timna laughed. "Not about the pantyhose," she said, taking a red silk handkerchief from her pocket and knotting it around her neck. "About Alon, about the breakup."

"Oh?" Sima sat down behind the counter. "You called him?

Timna nodded. "I told him I was sorry," she said, dipping her finger in a new jar of lip balm before sliding it across the counter to Sima.

"So what did he say? Is he coming here?" Sima reached for the lip balm, a sense of triumph settling: Timna would have the baby, and she and Lev and Alon would go with her to the hospital, sip bitter coffee from Styrofoam cups as they waited, heart in throat, for the wonderful news —

"He said —" Timna paused, grinned at Sima. "He said he'd been waiting for me to call every day since we broke up."

"Oh Timna —" Sima couldn't wait to tell Lev, plan for Alon's visit.

"We're going to meet out west like we originally planned, travel a bit. It won't be just the two of us: Nurit will come, and some friends from Israel, so we'll have time to see —"

Timna kept speaking, but Sima did not listen. She brought her finger to her lips, slowly drew the balm across. She closed her eyes a moment, blackened out the image she'd had of the waiting room, the stacks of magazines they'd be too nervous to read. She felt surprised, and then foolish — wasn't it always this way with young couples, and why had she led them back together only to push Timna farther away from her? With Connie, too — she'd cared for her until Connie was strong enough to leave her behind. "It's wonderful, Timna," Sima said, a thin smile pushing at her cheeks, "it's just wonderful news."

"Well, thanks. But it's no big deal. We'll see, that's all."

Sima nodded. Whatever was wrong with Timna, she now had someone close to help her through. What a relief, and what a painful disappointment — she'd lost what little importance she envisioned for herself: Timna's champion, Timna's protector.

And then there was Shai.

"Have you and Alon talked about everything that's happened recently?" Sima asked.

"What do you mean?"

"About everything that's been going on. The way you've seemed so ill lately."

"Sima," Timna said, pulling on her coat, a jean jacket lined with curls of white wool, "how many times are you going to tell me I look sick?" She bent her head, buttoning the jacket. "I swear, you're going to give me a complex."

"Well, but it's the truth. In fact, you had me so worried" — she looked at Timna, suddenly furious to be cast out, after all she'd been willing to sacrifice — "that I spoke to Shai about it. I told him about how you haven't seemed well."

Timna's hands stilled. "You spoke to Shai?"

"I found his number in your address book —"

"Sima —"

"I went looking when you were upstairs with Lev the other day —"

341

"What?"

Sima looked at Timna, awakened to what she'd done. She'd finally made a difference for Timna, helped her back to Alon, only to immediately ruin everything forever.

"Sima, what do you mean you told Shai? What did you tell him?"

Timna stared at her, waiting for a response. Sima waited too, wishing she could disappear, turn back the clock, undo all she'd done. If only, if only.

"Sima, tell me —"

"Timna," she said, forcing herself to speak, "Timna, I was worried." She took a breath, her body hot — beads of sweat above her lips, a wet warmth beneath her arms.

"You were worried, so you —"

"I was worried, am worried. You haven't looked well, Timna, and you were so tired all the time, and you wouldn't answer my questions —"

"I can't believe you're serious, Sima. Why would you do that?"

"I just said, because —"

"I'm not a child."

"And you're all alone here —"

"I'm not your child."

Sima looked down, her eyes on the empty buttonhole, the navy stitch along its almond-shaped rim. "I know, I know." It was a whimper. Come back, she wanted to say. Come back to me, don't go, don't go.

"You called Shai. I can't — what else have you done? Called my parents? Followed me home?"

Sima opened her eyes wide. Terrified, she thought only to protest. "No," she said, "No, I never —"

"So, what did you tell him?"

Sima tried to hide her relief: Timna hadn't been serious, hadn't known. "All I said was just that I was worried because you didn't seem well, and had you mentioned it to him, and was there anything I could do to help. I just wanted to help, Timna, I just —"

"And what did he say?"

"Nothing. He didn't know what I was talking about." She paused. "And then, he said he hadn't seen you in a while. Timna, please, I was only —" Her lower lip trembled like a child's. Like that, just like that, and Timna's baby, Timna's love, had been stolen from her.

Timna turned to go. Sima said nothing as she watched her leave, but Timna paused at the doorway. Turn around, Sima thought, her eyes on the tremble of Timna's back, look at me.

Timna turned back.

"Sima, I know you wanted to help me."

Sima nodded — yes, yes. She felt a warmth rising — Timna understood, would forgive her, would not abandon her to that awful empty ache.

"You were right about Alon — I was afraid. But you know what?"

Sima waited, desperate even for Timna's criticism — whatever she would give her, whatever she could take.

"So are you." Timna opened the door, turned once more to Sima. "Stay out of my life, Sima. Stay out of my life, and look at your own instead."

Timna disappeared into the evening: the sidewalks covered with stained snow, dotted with salt and sand. When the door closed behind her — a sharp pull but not a slam — Sima walked to the staircase, sat down stunned. Timna had left, angry. Sima placed her hands in her lap, studied the raised path of the blue veins that pressed against her pale skin. She closed her eyes, cupped her hands over her face, curled the tips of her index fingers toward the corner of her eyes, and breathed deep, in and out, like Timna had told her they did in yoga. She felt it work: all her fears leaving with the exhaled breath. Timna had left furious, but what mattered was that she'd won: Alon was back, and Timna was safe.

Still there was an emptiness inside that the rushing breath did not fill. Think something happy she told herself, and she tried to remember the ice-skating scene, the photographs of Timna and Alon in the park. She concentrated to conjure the images and the feel of their flesh — soft, but with the round of muscle beneath, warm and ready to grip. But their bodies were just colors swirling, and though she tried to steady the vision — the beauty mark on Timna's stomach, Alon bending to kiss — it escaped her.

She felt again the impact of Timna's words: *Stay out of my life, look at your own instead.*

Sima brought her fingers across each eyelid, stroked lightly back and forth. It felt nice, the flesh so delicate there. She smoothed her eyebrows, the soft hairs shivering against her fingertips, and then traced a circle from the narrow of her nose to the curve of her brows and then under to the loose skin beneath her eyes, a slight pull as her fingers skirted across. She repeated the circle, feeling the touch move through her.

Sima brought her fingers up the middle of

her forehead, separating her hands to follow the hairline along each side of her scalp before leading them down the sides of her face, stroking behind her ears. She remembered dabbing on perfume when she was a young wife, going out for an evening still flushed with her new role. She traced a path from the edges of her face to the soft pocket under her chin, rubbed with the back of her hand back and forth, back and forth, and then up the hill of her chin and lips to the bone of her nose. Her fingers followed the thin line of cartilage before leaping out to circle each cheek, paint mustache swirls above her mouth.

She parted her lips, ran a finger across each lip and then between where it was wet. She touched her tongue to her fingertip, bit lightly. Her finger moist, she returned it to her lips and spread the wetness across, felt her lips expand and darken with a rush of blood.

Not allowing herself to hesitate, she unbuttoned her blouse.

Sima rubbed the smooth expanse of her breastbone and then, breathing deeply, cupped the full warmth of each breast. She pressed lightly, her hands circling slowly before, following her body's pull, she lowered them to stroke her belly, hips, thighs.

She thought of Timna, the softness of her body, the promise of it, and of Connie on the couch, kissing. And then she thought of the intimacies of her own life, years before — the time she'd pounced. With a deep intake of breath she leaned back along the steps, drew her skirt up above her waist. Closed her eyes.

Head bent back against the basement steps, neck exposed, Sima gripped the banister with one hand and let herself remember with the other, holding on until she felt the shudder pull her from the place she'd locked herself in so long ago.

■ ■ ■ ■

MARCH

■ ■ ■ ■

26

The mother and daughter entered arguing. Sima could hear the daughter's question, "This?" saw the mother nod in response, her lips a tight line.

"What did I tell you?" Sima asked, turning to Sylvie. "It's been like Grand Central Station here today."

"No cause for complaint there," Sylvie said, placing her hand on Timna's arm. "You go help them, I'll take Timna." She smiled at Sima, winked. "Maybe I'll finally let her sell me that green bra, huh?"

Sima nodded, her eyes lingering just a moment on Sylvie's hand — the skin of Timna's arm soft between each finger — before approaching the mother and daughter. She and Timna had hardly spoken that morning, the first they'd been together since the fight.

Timna hadn't come to work the day before. Sima was miserable, convinced

Timna would return only to collect her final paycheck, reclaim abandoned scarves and sweaters. In her absence Sima rehearsed unsatisfying lines — I want to apologize, I hope you understand — but when Timna entered the shop that morning, Sima had just stood there, hands clasped before her, mouth empty.

"Timna," she'd finally said, as Timna started up the stairway for coffee, "I'm so sorry."

She surprised herself with her own sincerity. As she spoke each word, she felt the sharpness of her sorrow. "I'm so sorry," she told Timna, and meant it: each word rounded with the weight of her regret, lassos she wished might circle round Timna, pull her close.

But Timna had simply shrugged off the apology. "I know," she'd answered, continuing up the stairs. "Let's just forget about it for now, okay?"

Sima nodded, unsure what else she might say, while the longing in her words circled back to her, limp and wasted. As Timna disappeared into the kitchen, a warm hello, as always, for Lev, Sima swallowed the permanence of their separation. "She's gone," Sima had thought. "She's gone, and she will never come back."

Sima turned toward the mother and daughter. "How can I help you?" she asked, her voice bright, seemingly innocent of the tension she knew was between them.

The mother answered. "My daughter needs something for under her wedding dress. You sell that, right?"

"I should hope so," Sima said. "Mazel tov."

Once again the mother responded. "Thank you."

Sima turned to the daughter. "What's your name? When's the date?"

"Rachel. It's not until June, but my mother —"

"She needs the lingerie now," the mother told Sima, "for when she goes for the fitting."

"This is an idea my mom has," Rachel said.

"This isn't just some idea — it's common sense." Her mother looked up at the ceiling, sighed.

Sima kept her expression blank. "First things first. Rachel, could you describe the dress for me?"

"Um," Rachel paused. "You want me to describe it?"

Sima nodded. There were two types of brides: those who couldn't stop talking about the dress — "and then it has just a few, not too many, but just like really nice crystal beads around the edge of the skirt" — and those who were slightly embarrassed by the whole idea of it. Her sympathy was with the latter, but her envy for the former.

"It's pretty simple, I guess," Rachel said. "Sort of fitted on top and then fanning out on the bottom. Not like a ball gown or anything, just —"

"A-line," her mother said. "It's a classic A-line. And it's ivory, with cap sleeves — Rachel doesn't do it justice. It's not so simple really, it has embroidered flowers that cut diagonally across the chest with tiny crystals for petals, and —"

"It sounds gorgeous," Sima said. "It really does." She stepped back, glanced at the daughter's body. "You're small," she said, taking in Rachel's black sweater, blue jeans worn on the hips. "I say, what, thirty-two twenty-eight thirty-six?"

"I'm not sure."

"I am. And with a body like that, you don't need anything but a good bra and nice panties." She turned to Rachel's mother. "We sell what you're looking for, but not in her size — she's too skinny, she doesn't need anything sucked in."

"Really? Even for a wedding dress?"

Sima nodded. "If it was a sheath dress and she really wanted a onesie then we could order something for her, no problem. But since it's A-line there's no need." She smiled at Rachel. "A-line's a terrific cut. I always say, for most Jewish women it's the best: it works fantastic with curves, and you don't look lost if you happen to be just a little short."

"See, Mom?" Rachel said. "I told you it wasn't a big —"

"Oh, but your mother's right," Sima said, steering Rachel toward the dressing room with a light hand on her shoulder. "The cut of the bra will affect the shape of the bodice, so you want to go to your fitting in the bra you'll be wearing on the wedding day." As Sima pulled aside the dressing-room curtain, she looked over to Sylvie. "That bra was made for you," she said.

"I know," Sylvie told her, smoothing the fabric. "I have it in white and beige already and it always feels great. We have a bar mitzvah in a few weeks that I bought a black dress for, so I figured, why mess with perfection, I'll get the same bra in black. Timna chose it for me — she's my personal shopper."

Sima looked over at Timna, who shook her head at the compliment. Sima grinned, thrilled to share such an easy, knowing exchange, but Timna turned away a moment later, bent her head as she adjusted the shoulder straps on Sylvie's bra.

"Wait here," Sima told Rachel, "and I'll bring you a few bras, so you can see what you like." She walked toward the stepladder, angled it under the wedding line — everything in white, and with extra embroidery — and slowly moved up the rungs. As she listened to Timna's laughter from behind the dressing-room curtain — "Okay, I promise I'll call their grandson if I'm ever in Chicago" — she was reminded of the excerpt from the book of proverbs that husbands recited to their wives each Friday evening, that Lev used to read to her, smiling self-consciously, in the early years of their marriage. "A good woman," it began, an ayshet chayal, and then the chronicle of thrift, modesty, cleanliness, a perfect code of behavior for the early-sixties housewife she had been, until one surprising line she'd never understood. Now, listening to Timna's laughter, that line rose suddenly to meet her on the stepladder: "Many women of Israel have been brave, but you have surpassed them all."

Sima stood on the stepladder, held on to the shelves, and tried to learn to let go.

■ ■ ■ ■

After the customers left — and Timna, too, nothing resolved, nothing more intimate than that one knowing glance between them all day — Sima stayed in the shop. She pulled a wood rolling-chair up close to the counter, bent her body over the green-lined pages of her accounting book. A half-hour passed, forty-five minutes; she could hear Lev shuffling upstairs, his uneven pacing reminding her of the vultures on those nature programs they watched some nights, circling the sky as they waited for death so they could descend on the remains. She thought: let him wait.

Before Timna left, she'd tried again to talk about what had happened, hoping both to explain her actions and to force Timna, finally, to confess. "Well," she'd begun, after Timna once again dismissed an apology, "If you want to know the truth of why I was so worried —" But Timna had interrupted, said only, "It's all over now," and quickly changed the subject: she and Nurit were planning a trip to Boston, and what did Sima recommend they see?

Sima had reluctantly answered, wondering, even as she described Newbury Street and the public gardens, what Timna meant by "all over." "I'll see you tomorrow then?" Sima asked as Timna pulled a multicolored wool cap over her head. "Of course," Timna answered, as if nothing had passed between them. Sima watched as Timna approached the door, buttoning a fake-fur coat as she walked; could it be she'd gotten thinner, Sima wondered, and, if so, when had that happened? "You're still feeling okay?" Sima asked, as Timna paused in the doorway to pull on purple gloves, "You seem healthier, somehow —"

Timna looked up at Sima, slowly shook her head. "Sima," she said, pushing the door open with her shoulder, "enough." She took the stairs two at a time — when had she last had such energy, Sima wondered — as she retreated, once again, into the night.

Sima watched her go; said nothing. "At least she's not angry," Connie pointed out when Sima called, quickly updated her on all that had happened — their argument, her failure to get Timna to reveal anything. Sima had agreed, said yes, thank goodness for that, though she suspected something perhaps worse than anger — sympathy maybe, or the leeway you give the crazy people in your life. When Connie began to talk about J-Date — "You have no idea,

Sima, the number of single Jewish men out there. And can you believe my own grandson showed me how to use it?" — Sima made an excuse to hang up.

She'd been in the basement a full hour when she heard Lev open the basement door, begin to slowly descend the stairs — pausing midway, she knew, for her to interrupt him, say don't come down, I was on my way up. "What is it?" Sima asked instead, massaging her temples when she knew he was looking.

Lev's white undershirt was stained with coffee from that morning; his navy slacks were faded along the thighs. "You eating dinner?" he asked.

Sima looked at him and then away, annoyed. "What, you want me to cook you something? You see I'm in the middle of this." She hadn't told him what had happened with Timna, dreading his I-told-you-so's, which, she'd have to admit, would be called for. For all her meddling she'd done nothing to help Timna, nor was she any closer to the truth of what had happened.

"There's nothing to eat."

"So? You want to go out and get something? You can pick us up falafel."

"Sima, it's pouring rain. I don't want to go out."

Sima recoiled at the whine in his voice. "You're like a big baby, always needing to be fed."

Lev didn't respond.

She sighed loudly. "Okay, if you help me a few minutes, then I'll come up after and cook something, okay?"

Lev nodded.

"Okay then. I need you to open that box over there," Sima motioned toward a small package by the door, "and check the contents against the packing slip. All right?"

Sima bent over the accounting book while Lev inspected the box. He pulled at the packing tape, and when he couldn't scratch it loose, stood up and walked slowly toward her, searching.

"What now?" Sima asked.

"Do you have scissors?"

"Lev, where do you think you'll find scissors, on the counter?"

Lev looked at her, didn't respond.

"No, by the sewing machine. Come on, use your head. You don't need me to tell you everything."

Lev walked over to the machine. He shuffled items around the table: a pad of paper, pieces of fabric, a few spools of thread. Not finding what he wanted, he turned to Sima, mouth open to ask a question, but seeming to think the better of it, lowered his head, opened a small drawer beneath the machine, and drew out the scissors from between rolling bottles of nail polish.

He returned to the first box and began cutting away the tape, pausing halfway to tear off the pink packing slip where it was set in plastic. After opening it, he carefully removed the top sheets of tissue paper, turned toward Sima, and waited a few moments for her to notice him. When she didn't he asked, "Sima, you want to keep this?"

Sima looked up, annoyed, but nodded her head yes, and Lev carefully folded the paper into a small square that he placed on the floor. Reaching in, he pulled out an extra-large navy blue cotton camisole.

"Ooh, hold that up for me."

Lev held it up against himself.

"Very nice. Don't you think that's nice?"

Lev looked down. "I guess so. Sure." He folded the camisole, placed it atop the tissue paper.

"Hold on, let me check it off the invoice." Sima put out her hand, and Lev brought her the pink packing slip. "Okay," she said, crossing the camisole off the item list, "what's next?"

Lev reached into the box. "Red night-gown."

"Sheer Sheath, Scarlet."

"Ummm . . . green cotton tank top."

"Hunter camisole. Right. Next."

"Blue. . . . What is this?" Lev held a powder-blue corset from which a pair of G-string underwear dangled by a thin, plastic cord.

"That's a bustier and underwear."

Lev turned it over in his hands. "Really?"

"Uh huh."

"How does it work?"

Sima looked at him slyly. "Stand up."

"Why?"

"Stand up."

Lev stood.

"Take off your shirt, then."

"Sima?"

"Come on, Lev. Timna does it."

"But Timna's a woman."

"Well, half the women I service have bodies not so different from yours. All of these items are plus sizes, and Timna can't try them for me, but you can."

"So can you."

"No, it wouldn't be right for me to do that — it should really be an employee, not the business owner."

"I'm not an employee."

"Well, it doesn't seem you have a job other than this one, so that makes you my employee."

Lev weighed the pale silk item in his hands, considering. Sima watched eagerly, slightly desperate. "Come on, Lev, it'll be fun," she said, "Then I'll cook dinner, I promise."

He hesitated.

"It'll just take a minute. Please?"

With his arms crossed he lifted his shirt over his head. His belly showed a slight half-moon above his belt, his own breasts pulled toward his stomach. Sima stepped behind him and opened the corset around his stomach, pulling it across his back with gripped hands.

"See? It doesn't fit me," Lev told her.

"It's supposed to be tight. Stay still, I'll get a safety pin." She moved quickly — even a little eager hop — to the sewing machine, rummaged through a drawer and then dashed back to secure both sides of the corset with a large pin.

The metal was cold against his skin. "This is horrible, Sima."

"You think? I think it'll look nice on you. Turn around."

Slowly, Lev turned around. The skin on his chest swelled above the top of the corset.

"Okay. How does it feel?"

"The wire is digging into my skin."

"Stop complaining. Go look in the mirror — see how it shapes you."

Lev walked to the dressing room, pulled aside the heavy curtain. Sima stood behind him, saw how the whiteness of his body surprised him: so many pale folds, so much exposed. Lev pushed a thin strand of gray hair away from his face and lifted his hand to smooth down the remaining hairs across his scalp, but glancing at the flesh of his armpit exposed — a deep recess shadowed gray — quickly brought his hand back down, pawed at the corset.

A scrim of sweat appeared on the fabric. "I can't undo it, Sima, help me."

Sima undid the pin. When she peeled off the corset, there were red lines on Lev's body.

Lev turned away from the mirror. "Okay, now can we have dinner?"

"Of course. But first we have the whole box to go through."

"Sima, are you out of your mind?"

"It's a small box, Lev." She held out a yellow kimono. "Here, try this. It's easier."

Lev waved it away. "Sima, I'm not playing dress-up! Enough!"

"But we've just begun."

"I said, enough. If you want Timna to be your little doll, fine. But I won't do it."

"This has nothing to do with dolls," Sima said, thinking how little he knew, how little control she had over Timna. "It's about business." She looked down at the kimono. "You know, you'd look awful in this."

Lev reached for his undershirt, pulled it on. "Thanks."

"Don't take offense — everyone looks awful in yellow. I can't imagine why Timna chose that color."

"Well, you can ask her tomorrow," Lev said, moving toward the staircase. "I'm going to get dinner, with or without you."

"Without me."

"Fine. Be that way."

Sima watched him turn away. "Thanks a lot," she said, wanting suddenly to stall him, "I ask for one simple favor, but as usual —"

Lev paused, tightening his grip on the banister. "As usual I disappoint you? I'm sorry if that's true, Sima, but I think this time you're asking too much."

"You don't trust me."

Lev turned around. "What are you talking about?"

"You should just assume, after all the time we've been together, that, if I ask you to do something, it's for a reason. But instead you always doubt me."

"Sima, how can you say I doubt you?" He stepped off the staircase, back toward her. "I've given you my life."

"Some life," Sima responded, whispering so he could hear.

"What?"

"Some fucking life." She knew she shouldn't say it, but once again felt she couldn't stop.

"What are you talking about?"

There was a pleading in his voice, desperation. She hardened against it. "I'm talking about you. I'm talking about what, over forty years at that school and not a single student keeps up with you, not a single coworker calls? All this time we've been married and it's all on me; I'm the one has to keep you fed, clothed, and then also provide the entertainment."

"You want entertainment? That's what you want?" Lev walked quickly toward the open box, reached in and removed a lace nightie. He pulled it over his head, tearing the arm slightly as he did so.

"You're tearing it!"

"So what? It's entertainment, right? It's always fun to laugh about me, right? Without me to make fun of, you wouldn't have any material for your friends anyway." The nightgown clung to Lev's body, lavender lace veiling his undershirt, gathering in a ring around the belt line of his pants.

"That's just the way women talk."

"Yeah? Well most women do more than talk."

"What's that supposed to mean?"

He paused. "Most women, Sima, most wives, love their husbands. Make them feel loved."

Sima looked at him, furious. "You're talking about sex. I don't have a goddamn uterus. Sex can't do anything for me —"

"It can't do anything, huh? And I can't do anything, either." Lev pulled off the nightgown, threw it back in the box. "Is that all you think about, who can do what for who? At least I don't spend all my time trying to control everyone else."

Sima stared at him. "Did Timna say something to you?"

"About what?"

"I called Shai," Sima said. "I called Shai to find out what was going on, so I could help, but then Timna got back together with Alon —"

"Alon in Israel, her old boyfriend?"

Sima nodded. "We had a talk, and I told her she was pushing him away from fear, that it took courage to stay —" Sima looked

367

at Lev. "It's a long story. She listened to me and called Alon, and they decided to give it another chance, but when I told her I'd spoken to Shai, of course she was furious —" Sima paused for Lev to ask, what did she say, the inevitable excitement of someone else's terrible story, but he just looked at her, waiting.

"She didn't come in yesterday at all. When she came in today, things were a little more like normal, but then you know what she said? She said I should stop interfering in her life and pay attention to my own." She looked at Lev. "Maybe it's true that I try to control too much. But believe me, it's not for me. It's for you, for Timna. I care so much about her, I try —"

"I know, I know." Lev shook his head slowly. "But what about your own life, Sima? What about me?"

Sima stared at him. "You want this?" she asked. She undressed quickly, dropping her green turtleneck sweater and gray wool pants beside her; she unfastened the thick, tan strap of her bra, lowered the belly-hugging underwear, kicking away the socks beside her. "This is all I have, is this what you want?"

The scar, white as bone, seemed to glow on her body, cut the round swell of her stomach in two, point a way between the heavy, brown-nippled breasts and the curl of her pubic hair, gray against the pale flesh of her thighs. Sima watched as Lev looked at her body: the thick of her ankles, the fold above her knees, the hair and the scar and the pull of her breasts and the veins, blue and still, waiting, on her neck. She stood before him, exposed, readied herself for his rejection — he'd turn away in disgust, she'd be left, for the second time, alone in the basement, abandoned.

Lev looked up, meeting her eyes. "Yes."

Sima was sixteen the summer she worked as a camp counsellor at Pinocchio Village Summer Day Camp, in charge of eleven nine-year-old girls. The girls made brightly colored construction-paper chains; sang Elvis Presley songs; practiced first, second, third position, their skinny legs pointed out at the knees; scrambled up and down the plastic slide that Sima, at their pleading, coated with water for coolness. Behind the fence was the rush of traffic, but on the rubber mats of the playground, fitted together like fingers intertwined, the girls sat in rows sipping milk from mini-cartons.

Afternoons Sima stewarded the girls across the street, single-file holding hands,

369

to the pool inside the boys' yeshiva. It was a new building, all brown tiles reflecting the glare from the lights above. The girls ran along the empty hallways, wearing their towels like capes and calling partners for underwater tea parties.

"You can't swim?" one of the lifeguards asked the first day, grinning. There were two of them, but he was the good-looking one, and it was obvious from the way he teased each girl — rustling hair, making up nick-names, introducing himself not as Stan but "The Stan" — that he knew it. Sima shook her head no, dangled her feet in the pool.

"Come on, you at least have to put on a suit."

"I didn't bring one." Her terrycloth shorts were damp from the wet concrete; she felt conscious of his eyes on her, reddened slightly. He was older than she was — eighteen, nineteen? His cheeks and neck were shaded with stubble.

"Uh-oh," he said, shaking his finger at her in mock imitation of Mrs. Lewis, the camp director. "Unprepared."

Sima practiced a pout. "Very funny." She concentrated on acting self-assured and sexy, like the women who lounged beside pools in movies: Grace Kelly, Katharine Hepburn.

"Next time," he told her, before turning his attention to her campers, their lips already purple with cold, to instruct them on the dead man's float.

"Let's try away from the pool edge, okay?"

Sima and Stan stood knee-deep in water, facing each other. He gave her a confident smile, told her she was ready. She nodded. He'd had her kick her legs while holding on to the pool wall for two afternoons already, concentrating on her while Bernie, the other lifeguard, took charge of the children with only a little protest.

Sima breathed in deep, half-lowered her body a few times, tried, unsuccessfully, to let go of the ground and float. She didn't trust that the water would support her, imagined it parting beneath her only to gather above her sinking body, a ceiling she would not be able to break through to breathe.

She lifted her legs a few times, reached up her arms to dive forward, but couldn't let herself go. "I give up," she told him, hoping her fear seemed flirtatious rather than pathetic. "I can't help it; it scares me."

Stan held his arms out below the water. "Okay, just lower yourself onto my arms. That's right. I've got you."

Sima lay lightly across his arms, bent her head into the water. Gone were the sounds of the children: the songs and splashes and high-pitched screams. She was weightless, and he was holding her; when he tipped her to him, moved her body against his own — her hips touching the wrinkled waist of his swim trunks, the soft hair of his belly — a heat coursed through her, and with that heat a fear deeper than water.

Sima opened her eyes beneath the blue, parted her legs, and, reaching forward with both arms, pushed herself free. By the time she realized she was swimming, she'd already escaped Stan's reach, and though she nearly stopped herself with the surprise of it, she forced herself to keep going instead: head above water, arms paddling furiously, legs kicking wild splashes up and down.

Stan chased.

Sima laugh-shrieked, swerving to stay free while Stan's fingers brushed her ankles, gripped her calves. He stopped her near the deep end, waited for her to catch her breath — she'd raised her elbows to the concrete edge, attempted a nonchalant pose though it made her arms ache — before gathering her to him, bringing her back into the water where, kicking for them both, he kissed her.

Some of the girls noticed and cried out,

but Sima didn't listen. His lips tasted like chlorine: clean and sharp. She kissed back.

Sima sent the girls up to the locker room without her, and stayed behind, as she'd taken to doing the last few weeks, to say goodbye to Stan. They made a production out of it, as her mother would have said: each kiss was supposed to be the last, but then one or the other would smile or stare or hold on a little too long until it was another kiss, and then another, and then just one more.

Stan wrapped his arms around Sima's waist. He pressed against her more closely than usual; she stepped back, unsure about such intimacy. She wanted him near, thought about him constantly, but when she was actually with him, found he scared her too. It had happened so quickly: the summer, Stan, their stand-up kisses in the hallway. Sometimes she still didn't quite believe it: an older boyfriend, with his own apartment — like something out of a movie, something she'd never dreamed could never be hers.

But, she thought, wrapping her arms around his neck, it was.

Stan stepped forward, keeping her close until her back knocked against the hallway wall. "Now I've got you," he whispered, his lips close to her ear. She laughed a little too loudly, and then louder still when he brought his hand to her collarbone, traced it slowly. He walked his fingers along her breastbone, pulled the neckline of her bathing suit away from her skin, and dipped his hand down her body.

Sima stood on the slick tile, conscious of the awkward pull of his hands, the uneven edge of his breath. She reached her arms around his back, thinking to tell him, as her nails caught lightly along his bare skin, that she had to go: the girls would be almost changed by now, they'd be waiting. "Stan," she began, speaking softly, but seeing him so close before her — his eyes closed, mouth open, face soft with wanting — leaned forward instead, brought her lips to his.

So this is love, she thought, as she moved her body against him, so this is what it feels like.

"Here we are," Stan said, holding open the door to his apartment. "Home sweet home."

Sima laughed nervously. Stan had been inviting her to spend the night at his apartment almost since they'd first kissed; it had become a joke between them: Stan asking, Sima saying no. She wasn't sure why she'd said yes the last time — just for something different, maybe, just to surprise him. It worked: he took her hand, squeezed it hard. "Friday night, then," he'd said, as she turned to join the girls, "no backing down now."

Sima nodded, the feel of his hand still warm on her wrist as she'd bounded up the staircase to the locker room, hurried the girls back to the day camp.

No backing down, she thought as he stood aside to let her enter, no turning back. She'd lied to her mother, told her she was spending the night with Connie. Her mother, as usual, was distracted, hadn't asked any questions. "Sima's such an easy child," Sima had once heard her tell a neighbor, "she never does anything, so I never have to worry."

Stan's apartment was small but clean: a bookcase in one corner of the main room, a radio on a small desk in another, a brown tweed couch in between with two wooden chairs facing. He shared it with a roommate who wasn't there when Sima arrived; "Out of town," Stan said vaguely, "for the weekend."

Sima nodded, though she knew he was lying: as if either of them knew anyone who went away weekends, as if that was something young people did.

She didn't mind the subterfuge, feeling it only added to the glamour of the moment: the bachelor apartment and the out-of-town roommate, even the most mundane items — two clowns dancing across the needle-point surface of a throw pillow, a cue stick leaning against the kitchen's slat-door — proof of an exalted life, one lived away from family, independent.

When he lay her down on the couch, her whole body shook. She'd borrowed a bra from Connie that Stan undid with one hand while the other reached for her foot, brought it up bent around his back. As he unbuttoned her blouse, she thought of her mother, imagined her discovering the truth, finding her with Stan. Sima brought her arms across her breasts, wanting to hide, but Stan kissed each wrist as he pushed them away, lowered his hand to unbutton her shorts. His weight was heavy and warm and safe above her; she closed her eyes as she pictured the two of them under water, free.

When the pain came, it tore inside, and she resisted for a moment pushing him away but instead wrapped her arms across his back, held on tight. Afterwards, when she'd wept and he'd kissed her and she'd told him she loved him and he'd repeated it back to her, she moved toward him again and this time, as she allowed herself to touch his body — her fingers circling a small mole below his bellybutton, brushing lightly down his sides to make him laugh — understood how to coax from him the ragged breaths, and then again, as he ran his hands down her back, how to yield to them herself.

It was only kissing that got them caught.

It was so unlike her not to hear the footsteps, Sima would later think, because all her life she'd been listening, concentrating on the movements of others as always so much more important than her own. Lou slamming the refrigerator shut, her mother yelling, "Don't slam!"; Max pouring juice and the drip-drip of some of it on to the floor; her mother switching off the radio, a hum to silence, calling "Dinner!"; her mother cursing as the dishcloth slipped, her hand touching the burning edge of the pot as she served the chicken: "Damn!"; the wet slap of meat on their plates, the smack of mouths closing around food; the scrape of chairs being pushed back as Max and Lou stood to leave, her father this time, "You didn't even have time to chew," and her mother, "Don't!", as too late the door slammed again; the fade of steps in the stairwell, the rolled-marble of her father cracking his knuckles, her mother's lowered voice, worse than raised: "Why do you have to do that, you know it drives me crazy"; Sima shuffling to the sink, her arms cradling dishes to lightly lower to the counter, careful not to crash, not to bang, because after all, it is better not to make too much sound.

In the weeks and months that followed, Sima would go over it again and again in her head — how could she not have heard Mrs. Lewis approach? How did she not hear the footsteps, the click-clack of heels rather than the soft suction of the children's plastic pool shoes?

The answer: for those few moments her body was so taken with Stan's that everything else disappeared, the only sensation his mouth, his hands. For those moments her mind was blank, empty but for the warmth of him.

She would never be that way again, her whole life.

"Well!"

When Sima heard Mrs. Lewis's cry, she pushed Stan away so violently that she banged her own head against the tile wall, turned to see Mrs. Lewis shaking her finger, "Shame on you, shame," as the pain swept across her skull and the chlorine burned her nostrils. Sima looked down, suddenly shocked by her own body: her stomach swelling under the damp navy swimsuit, her thighs wide and fleshy, goose-pimpled purple, her feet pale and veined, toes splayed on the mildew-spotted floor. From the corner of her eyes she saw Mrs. Lewis's finger condemning her, and she wished to slip under the tile as into the pool, to become once again both whole and weightless in the water's grasp.

"Get dressed, and come straight to my office!"

Sima, released from the place where the finger, shaking, had held her, took the stairs two at a time in her rush to escape.

She expected to hear him follow, chasing her again. She expected even then, despite the flip-flopping heat in her stomach, for him to grab her ankle, touch her leg, for the two of them to collapse together laughing, for him to kiss her fears away, plot the lies she'd tell her mother, for them to spend the rest of their now-empty summer days together, and then all their lives after that. She changed quickly, roughly drying her body with the towel, waiting for his tap on the locker room door, his apologetic kiss on the nose.

She checked herself in the mirror: dotted

on lipstick, pinched her cheeks pink, practiced a you-have-to-admit-it's-funny grin to hide the shame she felt circling inside.

There was no one outside the locker room, in the hallway, on the sidewalk. Maybe they're taking the girls up, Sima told herself as she crossed the street back to camp. She needed Stan more than the girls did, but she forced a smile to think of him holding their hands, promising whoever changed fastest a piggyback ride across the street.

She knocked on Mrs. Lewis's door, glancing through the hallway window to the yeshiva across the street — he still hadn't emerged, and why not — before heeding Mrs. Lewis's "Come in."

Mrs. Lewis sat behind a metal desk, a stack of envelopes on either side of her. As Sima entered, she brought an envelope from the pile on her left toward her lips, licked it closed, and placed it in the pile on the right. Sima watched the slow curl of her tongue, the wet path it left on the paper. "I don't need to tell you," Mrs. Lewis said, picking up the next envelope, "that you're fired," tongue arched, a thin line of saliva clinging to the paper, "Stan will stay, of course," closing the flap, snapping the saliva, "since we need lifeguards," placing the sealed envelope to her side, "I already spoke with him about it," picking up another from the pile, pointing the tip of her tongue along its edge, "and he has agreed."

Sima didn't reply, concentrated on breathing. She felt dizzy, nauseated — Mrs. Lewis's tongue uncurling against her neck, licking a moist trail along her throat.

"Are you surprised?" Mrs. Lewis asked, arching her eyebrows at Sima's silence. "But you must see," she said, an envelope in her hands, her tongue, pink, moving slowly against the glue, "his behavior is more understandable." She placed the envelope at her side, smiled at Sima. "It's no shock that he doesn't respect you, Sima. What's surprising is that you don't respect yourself."

An underwater echo filled Sima's ears; she heard the tick of the clock, the brush of Mrs. Lewis's nails against the cream-colored envelope, the buzz of the light overhead, trapped in its round metal cage. She found herself signing a form, accepting a check, lifting her hand in a timid goodbye that Mrs. Lewis did not acknowledge, all the time nodding her head as if to say, I understand, while the green colors of the room — pine-marbled tile; mint walls; olive leather chair — swirled around and over her, finally floating her out of the office, down the hallway, and past the plastic-mat courtyard.

Sima stood still, feeling the waves recede. Then she ran, lurching, two blocks, before leaning against an apartment building, vomiting onto the sidewalk.

When Sima didn't hear from Stan, she called, mouth pressed close to the receiver ready to whisper. When he did not answer, she took to walking down his block, hoping to bump into him. One afternoon Sima waited for Bernie outside the yeshiva, asked him, not caring how desperate she might seem, where Stan had gone. He told her he'd taken a position as a beach lifeguard somewhere in Queens. And then, blushing, he asked if she was free that Friday night.

She walked away, wishing she had the courage to slap him; leave him stinging on the street.

To Connie she only said, "He was getting boring anyway," and never told what happened between them.

Two years later she passed Stan on Coney Island Avenue, holding hands with a Polish girl. Sima put her head down to hurry past but knew anyway he would not recognize her; her body had changed since he knew it, the stretch marks curving over swelling skin, and though she'd taken to pounding her hips each evening, they had not gone away. She turned to see how the blond leaned lightly into him as they walked, and she dug her nails into her palm till it hurt — what you deserve, she told herself, all you deserve.

27

Even as she walked through the entrance to the bar, Sima thought, *I'm going too far, I should not be doing this.* Somewhere she was watching herself through her own fingers, humiliated yet unable to look away.

She'd followed Timna from the subway. They'd gotten off at Union Square again and walked the same streets, and Sima had worried it would end the same — Timna would disappear into the tenement, and how much used clothing would Sima buy before she gave up on trailing Timna? But instead Timna entered a bar, and Sima could see from the way she pulled open the door, stepped inside with her mouth already opening for hello, that she'd been there before.

Sima had hesitated, but only for a moment. She was wearing the green coat, and had tied the rose scarf around her hair like a kerchief. Timna wouldn't recognize her, or not right away at least. She counted to five and then ducked inside.

Inside it was crowded, dark, loud. Sima pressed against a back wall, breathed deeply while she surveyed the room. In the center two anorexic women moved languidly behind a long bar, seemingly unaware of the crush of young people who waved bills and flashed smiles as they pressed against the wood counter, desperate to be served. Sima looked for Timna, but couldn't see her. So many of them looked something like her — the same clothes, the same attitude — but none, Sima felt, had her beauty.

She forced herself away from the wall, watched as a young woman, her pierced belly button visible beneath a striped halter top, slid off her stool and walked to the back of the bar. Following, Sima passed through a narrow corridor that opened into a second room, just big enough for a pool table and a ring of bar stools around it.

Timna, leaning over the pool table, eased the cue stick through her fingers. Sima watched as she looked up at the man across the table — dark hair, a few Chinese letters tattooed around one arm — and grinned.

A gasp, a grunt, a sound Sima had never heard, wouldn't have recognized as coming from her, escaped; she brought her hand to her throat as Timna turned toward her.

Sima turned faster. Pushing her way through the crowd — a few bored glances following her retreat — she rushed out of the bar and across the street, thinking only: hide.

On the opposite corner was another bar. Sima slipped inside.

"What can I get for you?"

Sima was startled when the bartender addressed her. She hadn't realized she'd come so close, hadn't tried to catch his eye. But then the bar was practically empty: a young couple at one end, the woman slowly shredding her paper coaster; a man her age a few stools closer, the *New York Post* open on the counter beside him.

"Do you want a drink?" The bartender had greasy hair and sinewy arms; a black tattoo — a bird? a bat? — took up all the skin between his wrist and elbow.

Sima glanced at the shelves behind him, the colored-glass bottles arranged in straight lines. "A Bloody Mary," she told him, remembering a wedding a few years ago when she and Connie had drunk three, giggling each time they'd returned to the bar.

The bartender brought her drink; Sima stared at it, unsure. The coast is clear, Sima thought, remembering the phrase from childhood games of Kick the Can. She could leave, go home, and deny everything tomorrow morning. Of course it wasn't her, she'd tell Timna, why would she have been in a bar —

"New in town?"

It took a moment before she realized she was being spoken to. The man beside her set aside the newspaper, smiled at her. Sima thought to move away, but noticing what he wore — a button-down shirt and gray slacks, no visible tattoos — decided there was no reason to be rude.

"New in town? I was born here."

"Here, here?" He tapped the bar.

"At the bar? No. In Brooklyn."

The man laughed. "Fair enough." He introduced himself, told her his name was Patrick and that he was from Queens. "Pleased to meet you, Sima," he said, putting out his hand, and Sima, again not wanting to be rude, took it.

As she sipped her drink, Patrick told her about himself: how he'd been a house-painter but was now retired, swam in the mornings and took a few classes at Hunter in the afternoons — criminal law, history — sometimes came here in the evenings, just a place to unwind, meet new people.

He smiled when he said that, and Sima, ashamed, looked away. She considered leaving, but Patrick ordered another beer and she felt it'd be rude to leave before that arrived. While she waited, she sipped her cocktail, and he told her about his grandchildren, as if of course she'd be interested. "The youngest is only five so I don't expect I'll make it to his wedding," Patrick said, taking his pint from the bartender, "but the twins are fourteen already, so with them I have a chance —"

Sima smiled. Her customers made similar comments all the time. They wanted to live to see their grandchildren born, and then their grandchildren bar mitzvahed, and then their grandchildren married, and then the great-grandchildren. And it went like that, around and around, and some of them did and some of them didn't.

She wouldn't.

She sat beside Patrick and sipped her drink and, when she finished it, allowed him to buy her another. "It's on me, Sima," he said, and though she knew that it was the oldest trick in the book, she nodded demurely; it'd never been her book, after all. She faced him as he spoke, and she laughed, giving in to the warm fuzzy feel of the alcohol.

Patrick wasn't bad-looking, she noticed. Bald but for a ring of white hair along the bottom of his scalp and his belly a soft paunch, but he hadn't fallen apart as some men did: long hairs in their ears and nose, dandruff on their eyelashes, shaving cuts on rough cheeks as if suddenly they were teenagers again, unsure with the razor blade. His eyes were warm hazel; his shoulders still broad from years of labor. She nodded eagerly when he mentioned the neighborhood, how it had changed, and made him laugh when she told him about Liza, the homing device for used coats.

Still, some of herself she kept separate. In the separate part she pictured Lev on their bed and the empty space beside him that was hers, and even as she leaned over to look at pictures of Patrick's grandchildren — a tangle of kids on a front stoop, the oldest at the top with a baby on his lap — she was waiting to return to that spot.

But it was also all right, she told herself, to watch as his hands curled around his beer glass and think, vaguely, of what they would feel like on her body: cool and soft and knowing and sure. "Do you know what I mean?" Patrick was asking, and Sima nodded. She hadn't really been paying attention — something about his wife, cancer —

but she knew the question. How many women had asked the same of her, about their breasts and and bodies, about their children, husbands, parents.

"Do you?" Patrick asked. "That kind of loneliness, it's like a punch in the gut."

Sima nodded, but in her own mind she thought not like a punch but a stab, a knife where it's warm and dark and the cut of the steel takes your breath.

He was looking at her now, and in that separate part of herself she called, *Lev!* and he rolled over in their bed and she moved in to the warm space beside him.

"Should we go?" he asked her. "It's a little cold outside, but sometimes I like walking in the winter. You?"

She was so far from Lev and he would never find her. She left the bar.

Patrick walked quickly. In the bar he'd been attentive, but outside it seemed he'd forgotten her, or maybe he was just used to walking alone. Neither of them spoke. They turned down one street and then another, and Sima was sure they passed the very building where an uncle had lived decades ago; she started to tell Patrick but then stopped, thinking why would he care?

Their breath formed clouds before them. A young couple walked past and the girl smiled at them. No, Sima wanted to say, we're not what you think we are. But she let it pass.

"Here we are then," Patrick said, pressing his keys to click open a black car. "Sorry for the long walk, but parking around here is impossible —"

Again it took a moment before she understood: they'd been walking to his car all along.

"Where to?" Patrick asked.

Sima said no, she had to get home, she'd hail a cab. Patrick shook his head, said he couldn't allow it.

Sima swallowed. They were on a dark street not far from the highway. The street was empty, everything quiet but for the scuffles Sima could hear emanating from within a pile of black garbage bags. This is it, she thought: murder, rape, death. The blackness filled her.

"You're wondering if I'm the type of guy who stuffs women in my car trunk and dumps them in Staten Island, right?"

Sima looked at him. "No, it's just —"

"Sima, you're as pale as a sheet. I'm sorry, it's just when I walk — my wife and I used to walk a lot. I forget to talk, I guess."

She kept her eyes on the sidewalk, thought she'd never heard anything sadder.

"Come on, do I look like a cold-blooded killer? You know how it is — our generation, I have to see you home. But I'd rather give you a lift than cab fare. You know how much it'll cost from here to Boro Park?"

Sima laughed. "It cost me almost thirty the other day."

She got into his car.

The radio was set to a sports station, but Patrick moved the dial until he found some old jazz. He hummed along to the song — "Are there stars out tonight?" the singer asked — and Sima, relaxing, sank into the plush seats. "You know," Patrick told her, glancing over as they merged onto the Brooklyn-Queens Expressway, "If you wanted to come over —"

Sima looked at him. Smiling, he gave a small shrug — a gesture of hope. She shook her head, then began to laugh.

Patrick looked at her and grinned. He was happy, she saw, that he'd made her laugh; she didn't need to say it wasn't him she was laughing at. She thought of giving him Connie's number, but decided no, this one was her secret to keep. When he pulled up outside her house, she leaned over and gave him a kiss on the cheek. His car idled while she bounded up her steps, opened the front door. Turning back to him, she waved goodbye like a young girl before vanishing into the black house.

Connie updated Sima over omelettes at the Dairy Delicious. "Mr. Escort-shmescort," as Connie now called him, hadn't lasted. "A good man," Connie said; she felt they could have had a go at it, only she wasn't ready. That first date there'd been the thrill of discovery — "Life after death," Connie told her, and Sima understood: a boat lost on water and suddenly there's land — but the two dates that followed hadn't recaptured the initial excitement.

"No couch?" Sima asked, stabbing a mushroom.

"No nothing." Connie scooped up a square of omelette with a slice of buttered toast, took a bite. "It's just so much work," she said, two fingers pressed to her lips to hide her chewing. "You have to tell your stories, you have to learn his; my kids, his kids, grandchildren, friends, all to build — what?"

Sima sipped her coffee. "Maybe you're just not ready yet."

"That's for sure."

"And what about Art? Is he still leaving those messages?" Art had been calling constantly over the last few weeks. Connie rarely picked up — "We just end up crying when we speak," she'd told Sima — so, like millions of other penitents, Art spoke to the machine.

"Yup. E-mails too. It's 'I'm sorry, I'm sorry, I'm sorry' every which way, which is really all the same way, over and over. I'm telling you, it's so repetitive — I might have to take him back before I die of boredom."

"Oh?" Connie had never even joked about that before. Sima leaned forward, surprised at her own reaction: the quickening of hope, when she hadn't realized she'd been holding out for hope. "Nu?"

"Nu yourself."

"What's the debate?"

Connie sighed. Some moments, she told Sima, she found the whole situation absurd. "Almost fifty years," she said, "and I throw it away over some nothing? Who does that?" But other times the nothing was everything, the betrayal so painful because of the bedrock of their marriage. "I can forgive him," she said, her fingers interlaced around her coffee mug, "I've realized that. But we'll never be who we were again. And maybe that's the worst outcome. Maybe it's better to be alone than to be together, but —" she struggled for a word — "less than we were."

Sima looked at Connie. She thought about

Patrick, his car, the closeness of his body; a whole city of people like him and her, Lev and Connie and Art, all longing, all wishing for more than they had.

"I wish I knew what to tell you," Sima said.

Connie smiled wryly. "You, at a loss for advice? I must really be screwed."

"Am I that bad?"

"The worst. And also the best."

Sima leaned back again. "Okay then," she said. "Call him."

"Call him?"

"Meet somewhere. Coffee, whatever. I'm not saying take him back, but if you don't — it's just, do what feels right for you, not what feels necessary because you're afraid of not having what feels right."

Connie tipped her head to the side. "I think I followed that."

Sima took another sip of coffee. "I know you did."

Sima wiped down the counter while Timna handed Rita Grossman the altered bras, repeated the admonishment to never put them in the dryer.

"After what I paid for these," Rita said, "believe me, I won't."

Timna smiled, pulling on her coat before

Rita was even out the door.

"You have plans?" Sima asked, watching as Timna, bending over, ran her hands through her hair.

Timna nodded, flipping her head back up so that her hair settled in waves around her face. She drew a tube of lipstick from her purse, walked over to the dressing-room mirror. "A few of us are going to see a play in the Village. Nurit knows one of the actors."

Sima leaned forward over the counter, watched as Timna smoothed gloss over her lips, opened her eyes wide for mascara. "You look gorgeous," Dottie Katz had said when she stopped by that morning, and Sima had to admit it was true: Timna's skin was smooth and even, her body slim in black corduroys and a short navy cardigan. "What's your secret?" Dottie had asked, and Sima listened hard, hoping to hear, but Timna had just laughed it off.

She's back to her old self, Sima thought, as Timna closed the dressing-room curtain behind her. But that self, she had to accept, remained for her a mystery.

"Today's the first day that feels even a little like spring," Timna said, tossing a lipstick-blotted tissue into the garbage can by the door. "I can't wait to get out into it."

She opened the front door and took a deep breath; Sima breathed too, recognizing the damp green scent of early spring. "I didn't even realize how much I missed the sun."

Timna grinned as she waved goodbye, a child escaping into a new season.

Lev was sitting at the kitchen table when Sima entered the kitchen; the paper spread open before him. "How was work?" he asked, as she poured herself a glass of seltzer. "Anything new?"

Since their fight in the basement and the touch that came after, she'd felt shy of him, her husband of forty-six years. She responded to this fear in the only way she could. "What have you been doing all afternoon," she asked, "just sitting here reading the paper?"

Lev looked up, and Sima turned quickly away. She imagined Timna shaking her head, felt inside that disappointment. But Lev just shrugged. "So still no word from Timna, huh?" he asked.

Sima smiled, aware she'd been caught acting poorly but forgiven. "Nothing," she said, "and I've given up on throwing hints." She sat down at the table, both hands around her glass. "I'm telling you, Lev, maybe I was delusional all along. I should be committed to a mental institution, put in a straitjacket."

"They only use the straitjacket when you start foaming at the mouth."

Sima laughed. "I don't know," she said, circling the edge of her glass with one finger, "maybe sometimes no matter how much you love someone, there are things you aren't meant to know." She looked up at Lev, pressed her lips into a smile. "You still reading?"

Lev shook his head no.

"It's a beautiful day. Maybe we could go for a walk? Get a little sun?"

It was hard for them to keep pace with each other at first — it'd been so long since they walked somewhere together just to wander, rather than rushing from a car to a restaurant or with the groceries home. "Where are you going?" a neighbor asked, pausing to watch them go by. Sima shrugged, said something about the sun, spring, so that the neighbor glanced up and down at Lev, clearly evaluating whether he was ill and she hadn't yet heard.

They walked down quiet streets lined with square brick homes, past the occasional yeshiva — red or yellow tile buildings lined with dark bay windows, their wide concrete yards, empty squares behind a chain-link fence, silent in the late afternoon — and the old corner grocery store, its signs well-faded: Te-Amo Cigars, and Breyers, and Milk. Sima told him about Timna, about what Dottie had said that day, about how happy Timna looked, how beautiful. "It's not that I'm not glad for her," Sima said, "but I still feel, if only I'd been able to help —"

"But you did help. She's back with Alon, maybe because of you."

"Maybe you're right," Sima said, not admitting how much she hoped it was true, how she hoped her love mattered.

They walked quietly for a few blocks, Sima lost in thought about Timna — would Shai be at the play, she wondered, and would they speak about her? As they passed by a neighborhood daycare — plastic toys scattered on the steps outside, cartoon images on a worn paint sign beside the door — Lev cleared his throat. Sima looked at him, suddenly aware of the silence between them, afraid for what he might say.

"Sima," Lev began, "what you said before, about how sometimes maybe we're not meant to know everything, even about the people we care about most —"

Sima stepped more quickly, as if she could outwalk the conversation. Her stomach swarmed with worry. Not again, she thought, I can't do this again.

"Everything that happened, back then and now —"

She nodded, did not need to ask, when.

"The way I was cut out of it." Lev pulled at a dull green hedge, a few small leaves slowly circling toward the ground. "It's like, you took all the blame for what happened, but also all the sorrow. You didn't let me grieve along with you. You didn't believe I could."

Sima was angry. She stepped across one, two, three sidewalk squares before answering, thought of the old line: step on a crack; break my mother's back. "Lev," she said, "I never —" She turned to him, furious that he should push her when she already had so much on her mind, but seeing his head lowered as he waited for her response, as if readying himself for a blow, softened. "You're right," Sima said, "I did keep you out. But to say I didn't let you feel sorrow — that wasn't mine to take. How could that be mine to take?"

Lev reached out for another hedge, tearing a handful of tiny leaves loose.

"You turned away," Sima said, "to your work, your students. I used to watch the clock for hours. Remember, that stupid old clock we had with the orange and yellow marigolds around its face? I can see it so clearly, how I'd watch for you to come home. When you finally would, you'd be busy and tired and satisfied from a day of work and I'd just feel — how many days until the weekend, until we could both be unsatisfied?"

They crossed the street, turned a wide corner: an auto mechanic advertising spring tune-ups, cars parked at strange angles jutting into the street and a stack of snow tires arranged beside the front door.

"There wasn't room," Lev said. "There wasn't space for me to grieve. You were so pained, so tragic, and I just felt — you wouldn't have believed me, anyway, so what was the point?"

They stepped aside to allow a family to pass — three girls all in the same dress, velvet blue with a white sash across the waist, the mother wheeling a baby carriage as the father walked beside her, lean and pale in a dark suit. Sima looked around. The trees were beginning to bud, the square lawns deepening into green, and when had it happened, all this change around her? She tried to remember what it had been like with Lev back then, but all she could recall, it was true, was her own grief — and that only as a dark space inside, a misery she could not truly look back on without averting her eyes.

"Sima, do you see what I'm trying to say? I just want you to know, after all this time, that I hurt too. I wanted children too. You acted like I didn't care, like I never thought —"

"How come you're saying this now, Lev? Why didn't you say this earlier, at the time? Remember all those appointments, and you never came along. If you'd been there, just once for me, if you'd tried to understand —"

Lev stopped walking; turned to her, forcing her to halt. She brought a strand of hair behind her ear self-consciously; shifted her feet on the cold ground.

"It was a mistake, I know. I just didn't know how to, and then you didn't seem to want me there. So I let it go, because it was easier." He paused. "It's not an excuse, Sima, it's just for you to understand. Do you see how it was for me? Does that make sense?"

"We were both so young," she said, thinking how strange that it should take her so long to recognize such a simple truth.

"Like Timna."

"Like Timna."

Lev looked at her. "Is it too late then?"

Sima thought again of the old kitchen

clock — orange and yellow flowers round its white face, and when had she gotten rid of it, finally, why couldn't she remember some last image of it in a garbage can, the flowers half-obscured by coffee grounds, vegetable peelings? "Lev," Sima said, reaching for his hand, cold and soft and smaller than she thought it would be, "it's been too late for so long that I don't think time matters anymore."

■ ■ ■ ■

APRIL

■ ■ ■ ■

28

Sima snaked a rag along a cleared wood shelf while Timna mopped the floor, the spring cleaning timed to coincide with Passover preparations. "Guess who Connie's bringing to the seder," Sima asked, using her nail to loosen some gummed dirt in the corner.

"Who? Art?"

"No, not Art. Though — did I tell you? They met for coffee at the new Starbucks the other day."

"You think she'll take him back?"

Sima shrugged. "I honestly don't know. I don't think she knows. But — she is bringing a man to the seder."

"Who? Not the escort?"

"Nope." Sima looked over her shoulder to catch Timna's reaction. "It's Nate."

"Her son?" Timna raised her eyebrows. "I can't believe I'll finally meet him. After all I've heard."

"I know," Sima said, pleased she'd gotten a reaction. "Me too. I've hardly seen him since he moved away after college, but every time he sneezes I hear about it." She watched Timna swirl the dirty water against the floor, reminded herself she could always redo it later with Lev.

"Oh," Timna said, "speaking of surprises, I almost forgot to tell you." Sima heard a forced brightness in Timna's voice and turned immediately away, a thread of fear weaving down her spine. She looked at the rows and rows of shelves before her, the stacks of boxes on each shelf — none she could crawl into, no space where she might tuck in her legs, pull down a lid, hide.

"— I checked and L.A. was on sale too, so I went and bought the ticket: one way to Los Angeles, nonrefundable." Timna paused, but when Sima didn't respond, she kept talking. "It leaves at six A.M., on April twenty-third. Six A.M. — what time will I have to wake up for that?"

Sima ignored the question, gripped the shelf as she felt the plane take off across her body: slicing from her hip to her shoulder, cutting through her belly, her breast.

Timna was leaving her, the curtains closed, ball dropped, lights off — the brightest joy in all her days over. She laid her head against an empty space on the shelf before her and breathed in the damp smell of wet wood, transporting her back to childhood summers: jumping through the beaded strings of sprinkler water that fell against the frame of their Catskill bungalow while her mother sat smoking on the screen porch, laughing with other women over jokes Sima could never understand.

"Sima?"

"Mmmm?" Sima lifted her head, opened her eyes. "Just tired. Passover cleaning," Sima said, stretching her arms above her head, "is always so exhausting."

"Maybe you need a vacation, too."

Sima stepped slowly down the ladder. "Right, a vacation in the middle of spring." She placed the rag in the water, swirled it around in a soap-smoky trail. "Maybe you noticed," she said, gripping the rag in both hands, wringing it above the bowl, "I happen to own a store?"

"Exactly," Timna said. "You own it, so you can give yourself a vacation."

Sima looked at Timna. The rush of air left in the plane's wake disappeared through her body, swallowed by cells, carried away by rivers of veins. She felt a warmth rise in its place, concentrated to capture, for just one moment, its source: Timna — the gold of her. Sima took her in, marveling at how even in jeans and a black T-shirt, a pink silk kerchief knotted over her hair, Timna glowed. She basked a moment in that light before shifting the stepladder again, tackling the next set of shelves. "Maybe you're right," she said, swabbing the wood with water, "maybe it is time to go away."

Timna immediately suggested a cruise; green waters somewhere surrounded by white sand, palm trees. Sima nodded, pretended interest — Hawaii versus the Caribbean versus Mexico — didn't admit it wasn't the destination she was after, but the escape.

"Lev," Sima said as she came into the kitchen after work that afternoon, "Lev."

He looked up from the newspaper he'd been reading; she paused. She'd imagined, in the short flight of stairs to the kitchen, that she'd tell him Timna was leaving, that she'd cry, mourn her loss. She'd imagined, in the one-two-three-four-five-six-seven steps, sobbing out the news, and indeed the tears had gathered, her throat had softened with salt water. But as she opened the door, as she called his name, as she took in his calm gaze, the words fled her mouth, her eyes grew veils, her throat turned dry. He'd say, I told you so, I told you not to become so involved, and he'd be right. She swallowed the salt, turned it bitter.

"Yes?"

Sima stood in the doorway, touched her finger to the metal hook on the side of the accordion door — a pinprick, a press back to action. "I hope you're not just waiting for me to cook dinner," she said, "because I need to rest. I've been up and down the shelves all day cleaning, and then Timna mopped the floor with just the dirtiest water, so I'm going to need your help going over it later —"

Lev nodded, stood.

"I don't know what the story with that is, maybe they don't mop in Israel or something but —" she looked at Lev, who had begun to walk toward the sink. "Where are you going?"

"I thought I'd put on some water for tea."

"Oh." Sima stepped into the kitchen, sat down at the table. "So after dinner maybe you can help me with the mopping. One thing I won't miss about Timna is the way she cleans, I can tell you that much."

Lev filled the teapot with water, placed it on the stove.

"Anyway," Sima said, feigning distraction as she reached for the abandoned newspaper but raising her voice so he'd be sure to hear, "that's all over at any rate."

"What's all over?"

Sima, pleased, did not look up. "Timna."

"What do you mean?"

"She's over, that's what I mean."

"What — you're firing her because she can't mop?"

"No, I'm not firing her for anything. Lev, you really think I'd —"

"No, no. But then — what?"

"She's leaving, that's what. She bought a plane ticket to L.A.; she leaves in two weeks."

Lev didn't say anything. He opened a cabinet, took out two mugs, and put a tea bag and teaspoon in one. Sima folded the newspaper closed and clasped her hands above it, watching for Lev's reaction.

"Maybe we'll see her again? She might come visit New York."

Sima shrugged, impressed by the plea in his voice. "Maybe, but it won't be the same. Of course," she said, before he could, "I knew it was coming —"

"But something like this still always catches you a little by surprise."

Sima nodded, surprised and relieved he felt the same. She ran her hands along the table, her nails brushing the white Formica.

"We'll have her for Pesach," she told him, "She'll come to the second seder, and that's it."

Lev reached for the kettle, took it off the burner. "Well," he said softly, as he poured the steaming water into each mug, "you can't blame her, anyway. A trip like that."

Sima moved the paper aside as Lev approached, watching he didn't spill as he carefully set each cup on the table. "Who's talking about blame? She's young, she can do things like that."

Lev nodded. "And what will you do?"

"What do you mean, what will I do?"

"I mean, for a seamstress, for an assistant."

"Oh. Well, actually, I thought that maybe I'd reduce the shop hours for a little while." Sima kept her eyes on the dark surface of the tea. He could say no, dismiss her fledging plans — too much bother, too much money. "We could go on vacation now, not bother waiting until August."

Lev removed the tea bag from the second mug, placed it on a napkin. Sima watched the brown stain spread.

"Timna pointed out: I own my own shop, I can take vacation whenever I want. It's not like I need to worry about building up the business or something. If anything,"

Sima said, carefully building her argument, "I should reduce the hours. What do I want to work six days a week for, eight hours a day? We have your pension and my savings, it's not like we're desperate for the money —"

Lev nodded in agreement.

"So why sit around," she continued, "waiting until August to go somewhere unbearably hot for ten lousy days? I could close the shop for two, three weeks after Passover, and we could really take a vacation. Boston, Maine, Nova Scotia — there's a ferry, we could drive straight to Halifax."

"Halifax?"

"I've always wanted to go," Sima said. "Remember how we almost drove there on our honeymoon?"

"No."

"Anyway. It'd be a beautiful drive, and you've always loved the ocean."

"You think it'll be warm enough in April?"

"By the time we get there, it'll be May."

"I guess so."

Sima looked at him over the rim of her raised teacup. "Well," she asked, tensing for an argument — he'd say it was all about Timna, when one thing had nothing to do with the other — "what do you think?"

"I think it sounds like a good idea."

"Really?"

"Sure, why not?"

Sima nodded, sipped her tea. "Are you sure though?" she asked, because now that he'd agreed, she wasn't so convinced. "You don't think I'm just looking for an escape?" She paused, drummed her fingers against the side of her mug. "I mean, you don't think it's only because I got so caught up with Timna," she said, knowing as she spoke that they both knew it was true, but needing him to forgive her for it so she could forgive herself, too, "and so now that she's leaving me —"

"Why else do people travel if not for escape?"

"Yeah? I guess so. I guess maybe so."

29

Sima went again into the city. A few loose excuses in her mind — the farmer's market she still wanted to explore, the appetizing place she'd been told had stuck around, still sold herring the way Lev liked it — but mostly a desire to simply walk the streets once more, again experience that freedom.

She smiled coming up from the subway, imagined seeing her friends — Patrick from the bar, Liza from the used-clothing shop — laughing to recognize each other out on the street, Saturday morning, springtime. She walked through the Union Square Market, tasting and asking and for once not resisting her urge to buy: some cheese for Lev along with pink crackers in cellophane-ribbon wrapping; the beeswax candles and rose potpourri for herself, the scent of the dried flowers like the way it was supposed to smell after rain.

From the market she wandered east and

then south, following again Timna's footsteps and the echoes of the old people who'd once lived there. Hungry, she paused at a few restaurants to glance at the menus, but finally stopped at a small diner whose laminated menu was identical to so many others she'd known: the rice pudding and cottage cheese salad, the Greek and Italian specials and bagels with a schmear.

Her coffee had arrived but not yet her omelette when Timna entered the diner.

Sima saw her immediately.

She looked down, looked to the side — heart beating heavy as when she'd spied, thinking, *caught!* But then she felt Timna pause, see her, call her name with surprise but also warmth. She hadn't been following her, Sima reminded herself, she hadn't been following, yet here she was.

"What are you doing here?" Timna asked.

Sima, steadying, mentioned the market. Timna nodded, distracted by her ringing cell phone. Sliding into Sima's two-person booth, she answered her phone, glancing at her watch as she said something in Hebrew.

"Nurit's going to be late meeting me, so I'll sit with you a bit," she said, hanging up the phone. "So, the market? I wouldn't have thought that was your thing."

Sima showed her the purchases, disbelieving. Here she was opposite Timna — what she'd hoped for and feared all along. Timna lingered over the scent of the dried flowers, said it reminded her of a garden they'd gone to when she was a kid, wild roses beside the sea. When the waitress arrived with the omelette, Timna, complaining about Nurit's constant lateness, ordered a coffee. "Same check," Sima told the waitress, just a little proudly.

When the waitress had gone, Sima looked at Timna. She didn't want to end this easy chatter, but knew she had to say something, had to know where she stood. "You won't believe," she told Timna, "Lev and I are going to do it. A vacation — a road trip even. Up along the coast to Canada, Nova Scotia. We're leaving a week after you.

"Really? That's wonderful."

Sima nodded. "It's because of you. Seeing how you enjoy yourself — you've inspired us a little." She paused, cut a bite of her food. "Which is why I feel so bad, especially, about everything that's happened —"

Across the table Sima could see Timna gathering into herself, her body stiffening, a tighter smile on her face and her eyes cast down to the half-empty sugar packet she'd poured into her coffee.

Sima forced herself to continue. "I think

you know I acted out of concern for you, so I won't say more about that. No matter why I did it though, I was wrong. I'm sorry, and I was wrong, and I just wanted you to know that once and for all."

"I do know that."

"Well, I wanted you to know again."

There was a pause. Well, that's it, Sima thought. She'd done what she could, and if it wasn't enough — well, and how could it be enough? She'd ruined love. She always ruined love.

"Sima," Timna said, "it's okay. Really."

Sima looked at her skeptically.

"When I say it's okay I mean it's okay." She looked at Sima, smiled. "So, will you stop with all the melodrama now?"

Sima grinned. "Thank you," she whispered.

"And thank you for the coffee." Timna stood to go. "If Nurit isn't outside right now I'm never talking to her again." She grabbed her purse, looked at Sima. "Okay then? We never have to talk about all this again?"

Sima nodded. "I promise."

Timna took one last sip of coffee. "I'll hold you to that," she said, smiling.

After she left Sima sat, stunned. Such dumb good luck, she thought. And then: what she deserved, too.

30

Sima had cards with her new hours printed at the stationery store around the corner, tried to remember — angling the card tray before the cash register — to hand one to each customer. "I'm closing the shop for two weeks in May," Sima told them, "and when I come back, it'll be reduced hours, just noon to three." The women took the cards — a cartoon bra in one corner at Timna's suggestion, though Sima had put her foot down against the hot-pink print Timna preferred — said, "Good for you, easing your way into retirement," or "What, so many old businesses gone and now yours too?" Sima shook her head no, swore she'd die in the shop. And meant it: could not imagine her life without its safety.

Such a little shop, she thought: linoleum floor, polyester curtain, wooden shelves, metal racks. A hidden space, inconsequential, not even a pinprick on the borough map, but for her, standing behind the counter with light coming through the one window, a whole world. She couldn't envision closing the shop without also envisioning her own death; she saw the basement empty, thick with shadows and clogged with dust, and her own skeleton self forever sitting at the counter, awaiting customers who would never come. She remembered images from adventure books she'd read as a child — the pirate ship full of cobwebs, the beer stein from which the captain had drunk still clutched in his bony hand. Her life would be that abandoned.

And yet, she thought one evening as she watched car beams cut across the bedroom ceiling, perhaps all the years behind her were years of skeletons and cobwebs, and only since Timna's arrival had she experienced the return to full flesh. She'd made a business, a space for herself in the crowded city, walls she couldn't reach even with hands outstretched, a ceiling she could not jump to touch. Beside her store another home and then another and another, each just a few feet from the one that came before; blocks and blocks of houses and apartment buildings reaching through Brooklyn and Queens, crossing bridges to stretch into skyscrapers, so much brick and stone, so much brown and red, the bright painted metal of children's playgrounds and the green-brown of park grass curved around black tar. Somewhere the clouds, somewhere, just as far away, hills and streams, wildflowers alongside the highway. She'd made a physical space but had kept herself lonely, all the chatter of her days knocked limp, year after year, against the glass silence of evening.

How many others like her, she thought, how many others lonely within their walls? And then one day realizing that every room has a door, and opening it.

31

"Welcome," Sima said. Timna stood on the porch, a bottle of wine tucked under one arm.

"Welcome? After all this time I get a welcome?"

"You're a guest now, right? No longer an employee." Sima took the wine, linked her arm through Timna's as they walked into the living room. She kept her head turned toward Timna, admired the bright eyes that so easily narrowed to laughter, the soft lips that spread simply to a wide grin. Sima nodded but did not listen to a story Timna told — the walk over, a customer she'd run into. It was their last night together; she would allow herself to look as long as she wanted.

"So, what's the scoop du jour?" Connie asked, taking Timna's hands in her own, "when's the honeymoon?"

"It's not —"

"I know, I know. But, so, when do you

423

leave?" Connie reached for an olive from the coffee table.

"We leave Saturday."

"Two days, wow. And when will you be back?"

Timna lifted one shoulder slightly. "Don't know."

"Oh lord. To be off like you. Nate," she said, turning to her son hunched over the coffee table, spreading chopped liver on a matzoh cracker, "why don't you ever go anywhere?"

Nate paused midspread. He was skinny and a little sunken around the cheeks — "Too much laboratory light," Connie had said when she'd introduced him to Timna — and, seemingly shy of Timna, avoided looking at her. "I'm going to Paradise Island in a month, Ma," he said, raising an eyebrow as if to say: you know this.

"Paradise Island, Shmaradise Island. This girl really is going to paradise — Thailand, right?"

Timna nodded.

"They say youth is wasted on the young. Come on, Nate, start wasting!"

"Actually," Sima said, "we may do some traveling of our own."

Connie looked first to Timna, who shrugged, smiling, and then to Sima.

424

"What's this?"

Sima grinned. "I'm taking three weeks, and Lev and I are driving up the coast all the way to Nova Scotia. Then we're going to take a boat to Prince Edward Island, spend a few days there."

Connie put a hand on Nate's knee — exactly the touch she would have given Art if he were there, Sima noticed. "Sima Goldner. Why have you mentioned none of this to me? You just up and abandon your friends —"

"Three weeks only," Lev said.

"Without so much as an announcement."

"This isn't an announcement?"

"But how long have you known? You never mentioned —"

Sima shrugged, enjoying the chance to withhold detail, appear mysterious. "Two weeks? Once I knew this one was abandoning ship —" she lifted a bottle of wine, angling it slightly toward Timna before pouring Connie a glass, "I figured what the hell, why shouldn't Lev and I also have a little adventure?"

They toasted to Timna's journey, and then to Sima and Lev's, and then, because Connie brought it up, to Nate's receipt of a government grant, and then to each other.

Lev led the seder, and Sima watched proud and pleased as they followed the regimen: ate the parsley dipped in salt water, roasted egg, horseradish, chopped nuts and fruit; drank four glasses of wine; split the matzoh and, at her cousin Millie's urging closed their eyes while Nate hid a piece — though no one remembered to search for it after the actual meal. A dinner of symbols: desperate tears and deep bitterness, back-breaking labor and the rush of escape, but also fertility and rebirth, the round of the egg and the green of fresh herbs.

Sima studied the scene, hoping to hold it: the light cast from candles warming white circles on the tablecloth, the purple of wine streaking the sides of wineglasses, the gloss of plates cleaned of food (the casual crumple of cloth napkins abandoned beside them), and friends around a table, a holiday, spring, once again a sense of rebirth and new beginnings.

"Goodbye beautiful," Sima said, pulling away from the hug before she had the chance to hold on, "Be well." She stepped back into the shade of the porch, suddenly ready, after so much dread, for the moment to be over — she didn't want to cry in front of Timna, she needed to pull off an upbeat goodbye, a jaunty wave.

"Goodbye, Timna," Lev said, kissing her quickly on the cheek. "Keep in touch. Write to us, we'll write back."

"Just leave an address," Sima told her. "A hotel maybe, in the next city you'll be in?"

Timna nodded, said something about Los Angeles — Sima was barely listening, just counting down now until she could close a door behind her, collapse.

"Tell Alon we say hello," Lev said, managing the wave Sima hadn't — her own hands were clasped before her, slightly damp.

"Yes, tell him hello from us," Sima said, "and send some pictures, too."

Timna turned back once more, looked at Sima. Sima could feel the gaze in her belly, in her knees. "Thank you," Timna said, and the words coasted through the air between them and wrapped around Sima so that a warmth spread softly across her skin, and she had no words with which to say, bless you.

And then Timna was turning away, leaving them behind.

"Travel safe!" Lev called.

"Take care," Sima whispered as she watched the night enfold Timna. "Keep well, be well."

As soon as Timna was gone, Sima went

back into the house, leaving Lev on the porch. For once she ignored the dishes in the kitchen, piled up beside the sink, and instead unhooked the door to the basement and disappeared down the steps.

So this is what it's like, she thought as she sat behind the counter, this is that emptiness that the women talk about, the space left by children grown and gone. She looked toward Timna's chair, impossibly abandoned when she could imagine so clearly the shadow of Timna working there, the bras before her, the hum of the machine, Timna laughing, saying something offhand, unimportant — just some story that would make Sima smile, just some voice, speaking to her.

She laid her head on the counter, one arm below it for cushion and the other above, cradling. She was alone in the dark with an emptiness inside like she hadn't felt in years, decades: waking from dreams of babies to a quiet house, the weight of the child in her arms an ache she could not ease. That young woman had invited a ghost into her womb, locked its anger inside for warmth because she could not brave the longing. She thought of all the years she'd withheld herself only to come undone so late in life — a joke, hilarious. Like the line from childhood taunts: so funny I forgot to laugh.

Sima stroked her own hair, wishing she could stroke the hair of that young wife, wishing she could soothe, forgive, encourage the scared, sad woman she'd been, but all the years between them rendered the touch both impossible and unnecessary — she'd hardened early, and all the time gone since only gave gloss to the surface. She buried her head in her arms and whimpered, a child's cry of fear. It was too late to still the young woman who'd stepped off her porch that evening and too late to cry stop to the young woman she'd once been; joy escaped so quickly and disappeared in the dark of city streets, her legs couldn't take her fast enough to chase it, her eyes would not know where to look, her arms were too weak to reach out and hold it, swallow it back to a secret place deep inside.

The door opened above her. She could feel a warmth penetrating the dark before the saying of her name, some worry in the voice: "Sima?"

She looked up.

Someone was calling her name. After all the bitter years, after all she had done to betray, someone was calling her name. Sima looked up the green carpet of the staircase to the rectangle of light, her home, the shadow of Lev in the doorway.

"Sima?"

"Lev. Lev, I'm here." Sima stood. Walked toward him.

"In the dark?"

Sima stepped on the first stair. The second. The third. "I miss her," she told him, her hand gripping the banister. She looked at him, remembered again that he too had been young once, aching and longing for comfort. "I miss her."

"I know," Lev said, "I know."

At the top of the stairs he met her. His body was warm. So it was him too she'd been missing, and all along.

32

"Lev, do we have to stop here? It's freezing!"

Sima buttoned her cardigan before opening the car door, stepped out with her arms crossed against her chest for warmth. Lev had already stepped into the tall grass beside the road, his camera raised.

"Look at that view!"

"It's half-covered by fog," she said, though in truth she was glad to get the picture: the old fishing shack loomed silver-gray against the blue sea, half-swallowed by the tall grass — dots of purple, yellow, white wild flowers — that grew along its edges. "Did you get the island in the distance?" Sima asked, leaning against the car, "Is that in the picture too?"

Lev nodded yes, crossed back toward her. Sima opened the glove compartment and withdrew a map, unfolding it on the hood of the car. "It should be just another ninety miles back to Halifax," she told him, studying the highlighted route. "Want me to drive?"

Lev shook his head. "For now I'm okay," he said. "You?"

"I'm good," Sima told him, looking up. "I'm all right."

They followed the scenic drive along the ocean, though it was slower than the highway, pausing every now and then to say, "Look."

ACKNOWLEDGMENTS

Thank you to the organizations and institutions that have provided gifts of space, time, and money: Temple University's Master in English/Creative Writing Program, The Leeway Foundation, The Ragdale Foundation, the Toronto Arts Council, the Ontario Council for the Arts, the Money for Women/Barbara Deming Memorial Fund, and the Humber School for Writers Summer Workshop.

I began writing this novel during a one-on-one tutorial with Dr. Alan Singer at Temple University; I tried to channel his keen critical eye in the years that followed, and hope I did justice to his early encouragement. I also worked closely with the late Dr. William van Wert. His unwavering support has continued to sustain me, and I wish I could share this book with him.

Thank you to my many readers over the

many years: Valerie Reynolds, Ilana Kurshan, Juliet Latham, Betsy Frankenberger, and Rebecca Haimowitz. For advice and insight to fertility treatment in the 1960s, thank you to Dr. Aren Gottlieb in New York and Dr. Philip Hall in Winnipeg. Thanks also to my Victoria writing group: Julie Paul, Kari Jones, Laurie Elmquist, Hanako Masutani, and Alisa Gordaneer.

I am so grateful to my agent, Joy Tutela of David Black Literary Agency, who has been an exceptional editor and a tenacious advocate. Joy told me she never gave up on a novel, and meant it. My editor at The Overlook Press, Juliet Grames, is the kind of editor I had ceased believing existed: one unafraid to roll up her sleeves and get dirty in the revision process. Thanks to both of them, along with Francesca Sacasa and the rest of the Overlook team, for hard work on behalf of literary fiction.

Thank you to the wonderful families Stanger and Ross. The Stangers gave me Brooklyn and the bud of a story, and the Rosses gave me Nova Scotia, my very favorite place to write.

Jordan Stanger-Ross is simply the best reader I have encountered. How convenient, then, that he is also my husband. I thank him for smart criticism and stronger encouragement. I also thank him, along with our daughters Eva and Tillie, for joy.

ABOUT THE AUTHOR

Ilana Stanger-Ross was born and raised in Brooklyn. She holds an undergraduate degree from Barnard College and an MFA from Temple University. She is currently a student midwife on the University of British Columbia faculty of medicine. She has received several prizes for her fiction, including a Timothy Findley Fellowship, and her work has been published in Bellevue Literary Review, Lilith magazine, The Globe and Mail, and The Walrus magazine, among others.

The employees of Thorndike Press hope you have enjoyed this Large Print book. All our Thorndike, Wheeler, and Kennebec Large Print titles are designed for easy reading, and all our books are made to last. Other Thorndike Press Large Print books are available at your library, through selected bookstores, or directly from us.

For information about titles, please call:
(800) 223-1244

or visit our Web site at:
http://gale.cengage.com/thorndike

To share your comments, please write:
Publisher
Thorndike Press
295 Kennedy Memorial Drive
Waterville, ME 04901